THE REGAL

A Series of Worthy Young Ladies
Book Six

Kate Archer

Dragonblade Publishing, Inc. is an imprint of Kathryn Le Veque Novels, Inc.
P.O. Box 23
Moreno Valley, CA 92556
ceo@dragonbladepublishing.com

Produced in the United States of America

First Edition November 2022
Trade Paperback Edition

ARE YOU SIGNED UP FOR DRAGONBLADE'S BLOG?

You'll get the latest news and information on exclusive giveaways, exclusive excerpts, coming releases, sales, free books, cover reveals and more.

Check out our complete list of authors, too!

No spam, no junk. That's a promise!

Sign Up Here

www.dragonbladepublishing.com

Dearest Reader;

Thank you for your support of a small press. At Dragonblade Publishing, we strive to bring you the highest quality Historical Romance from some of the best authors in the business. Without your support, there is no 'us', so we sincerely hope you adore these stories and find some new favorite authors along the way.

Happy Reading!

CEO, Dragonblade Publishing

Additional Dragonblade books by Author Kate Archer

A Series of Worthy Young Ladies
The Meddler (Book 1)
The Sprinter (Book 2)
The Undaunted (Book 3)
The Champion (Book 4)
The Jilter (Book 5)
The Regal (Book 6)

The Dukes' Pact Series
The Viscount's Sinful Bargain (Book 1)
The Marquess' Daring Wager (Book 2)
The Lord's Desperate Pledge (Book 3)
The Baron's Dangerous Contract (Book 4)
The Peer's Roguish Word (Book 5)
The Earl's Iron Warrant (Book 6)

PROLOGUE

Hanover Square, 1814

IT WAS THE start of a new London season and the streets outside of the Duchess of Stanbury's elegant address were abuzz with vehicles going by in every direction. Carriages filled with people, and more carriages filled with their belongings, descended upon the town. Society was engaged in the great migration—the entertainments were set to begin.

The duchess, known to the wider world as Your Grace, known to her few equals as Duchess, and known to her closest friends as Theodosia, smoothed out her skirt. The brocade material was a rather wonderful selection Madame LeGrange had secured—a very dark blue with a repeated pattern of mustard-colored peacocks. Brocade was the noblest of silks and therefore it was her preferred fabric.

Those few ladies who had the privilege to call her Theodosia had been summoned to Hanover Square and were even now gathering in her drawing room. She had called a convening of *The Society of Sponsoring Ladies*.

Each year, one of the matrons of the society would escort a suitable young lady through a London season. "Suitable" had proven to be an acceptable background but not enough money. In this way, actual mamas were left behind and the ladies could experience all the joys of acting as a girl's mama, though they had not born daughters themselves.

There had been some bumps in the road, naturally. Though, when the duchess considered it privately, she thought the past few seasons had been more like dragging oneself up the Italian Alps only to plummet with sickening speed to one's final destination.

By some miracle and despite the efforts it had taken, all of the final destinations had been a church and the young ladies in their charge had been suitably married.

Now, however, the *real* moment of glory had arrived. She, the redoubtable Duchess of Stanbury, had finally found her girl.

Carlson discreetly opened the library door and closed it behind him. "Lady Featherstone and Lady Mendleton have both arrived, Your Grace." He cleared his throat, then said, "And Lady Easton keeps staring at the clock."

Theodosia hardly need be told that Lady Easton toe tapped. That lady was always on a schedule. Lady Mendleton though…

"Carlson," she said, "Lady Mendleton, she has not by chance…that is…she hasn't brought the VAB?"

"No, Your Grace," the butler said.

The duchess breathed a sigh of relief. Louisa had got in the habit last season of dragging her toddler granddaughter, otherwise known as the Very Advanced Baby, or the VAB for short, everywhere with her. *Bwandbaba*, as the little terror called her grandmother, had to be counseled to give up the habit. The duchess would not like to see any of her own porcelain broken, as so many unfortunates had.

"They are all gathered and waiting for me, then," the duchess said. "Lead me in, Carlson."

The duchess cruised majestically across the marble floor of the great hall as if she'd set sail for a foreign port.

Carlson minced ahead of her, a veritable dolphin running the waves of her brocade bow. He threw open the drawing room doors and announced, "The Duchess of Stanbury."

"Ladies," she said graciously, sailing forward to her favored chair and settling herself in.

"You've found someone, haven't you?" Lady Redfield said.

"Of course she has, Cecilia," Lady Heathway said. "Now tell us, Theodosia, who is she?"

The duchess poured the tea and said, "She is none other than Isabel Beaufort, daughter of the Earl of Somerdon. I've been told that family's line runs all the way back to the Plantagenets. Her blood could not be more rarified."

"What is the circumstance, though?" Lady Featherstone asked, completely missing the importance of the aforementioned rarified blood. "Why does not the earl bring her out himself?"

"Because he does not have two farthings to rub together. You know how these ancient families are—the money does sometimes run dry," she said.

The duchess hoped that was a sufficient answer. She'd really prefer the ladies not keep their attention on the girl's father. As far as she could gather, the earl did not have two farthings to rub together because he was a bit of an idiot. Being an idiot and being of rarified blood were not compatible, in her considered opinion.

"The Earl of Somerdon is my nephew's neighbor," Lady Easton said. "Bertridge says the man is mortgaged up to his eyes."

The duchess pressed her lips together. She'd realized that Lord Bertridge and Lord Somerdon lived in the same county, but not that they lived so close! What on earth would sensible Lord Bertridge have made out of Somerdon? The man's letters could have been better written by a small child—they were just a series of words, strung together haphazardly.

"So we can assume she's not got a dowry," Lady Redfield said.

"She has not," the duchess said. "However, I talked it over with the duke and we will provide something. In any case, the dowry is a minor detail. It is the girl herself who is the prize. Plantagenet blood, remember. *Rarified.* I intend that she marry at the highest echelons of society."

"Who do we think might be suitable for her?" Lady Mendleton asked.

Lady Featherstone smiled, appearing very pleased with herself. "Every other year and every other girl, we say it must be Lord Ryland. But now he is out of the running as he is my dear son-in-law."

Seeing some confusion on her friends' faces, Lady Featherstone said, "Not technically related, but I consider him so. Prudence is my cousin by marriage, somehow, and so you see…"

The duchess did not see at all, nor did she care. "I was thinking of Lord Lymington for Lady Isabel. He's to be a duke."

There were polite murmurs regarding that suggestion. At least, there were from most of the ladies.

Lady Heathway said, "But Lymington is a dolt. He tells the same story six times over and it's always about some horse or other."

The duchess was well aware of Lord Lymington's deficiencies. But he was, after all, to be a duke.

"His proclivities can be managed," she said firmly.

"When is she to come?" Lady Easton asked.

"I am to collect her in Hertfordshire," the duchess said. "I insisted upon going myself."

Really, she'd done no such thing, but it seemed the earl's carriage was in disrepair, and he would not be put to the expense of hiring one to send the girl to London. Nor did she have a suitable escort, as there appeared to be no lady's maid or other woman who might be employed for such a purpose.

"Very well," Lady Easton said. "I will accompany you, Theodosia. It will give me the opportunity to see how my nephew and Caroline get on."

The duchess had not asked for and did not want company. Based on her various letters exchanged with the earl, she was rather afraid of what she would find there. His last letter was so unintelligible that she and the duke had pored over it for more than an hour, and she was still not certain she'd untangled his meanings. She was hoping he'd written it while exceedingly drunk.

"I do not wish to impose upon the earl by bringing overnight guests unexpectedly," the duchess said.

Lady Easton suddenly laughed, which was not a thing she did often. "Goodness, you cannot stay at Somerdon House. Bertridge says the place is falling down around the earl's ears. We will stay overnight with my nephew, his drive is less than two miles from the earl's estate."

The duchess nodded. There was not much else she could do. If Clara were determined to get a look at the earl, she would find a way to do it. In any case, it sounded as if it *would* be better to avoid staying the night as the earl's guest.

"The earl's house, though—can it really be so bad?" Lady Mendleton asked.

"Oh yes," Lady Easton said. "Bertridge has told me you'd be very lucky to avoid being knocked out by a falling shingle from the roof as you stood at the front doors. My nephew has tried to counsel the earl on rectifying things, but he gets nowhere with it and has given up."

The duchess had not perceived that the situation was quite *that* deteriorated. It seemed the earl was not, as she had thought, a bit of an idiot. He was a complete idiot. Who allowed one's shingles to fling themselves from one's roof? Well-ordered shingles understood where they were meant to be.

She shook out her skirts like a bird settling its feathers. "Just as we have rescued other girls from unfortunate circumstances," she said, eyeing Lady Heathway specifically, "we will rescue Lady Isabel from her own situation. Forthwith."

CHAPTER ONE

LADY ISABEL BEAUFORD, daughter of the Earl of Somerdon, carried a bucket into her bedchamber and placed it under a drip from the ceiling. It had been raining all day and it seemed the roof had sprung a few more leaks.

That done, she changed for dinner.

She did not have a maid to help her, nor had she ever. She did not have a wide selection of dresses to choose from, nor had she ever. What she did have, though, was skill with a needle to keep what she did own in good order and an absolute refusal to succumb to her circumstances.

Nobody in the house, least of all her father, would care whether she changed for dinner. *She* cared, though.

She had scrimped and saved, mostly by way of an old aunt's yearly birthday present of a little money, to purchase a book on how things ought to be done. She was determined to do things how they ought to be done, as close as could be managed given her circumstances.

Isabel had been well aware from examples of other young ladies in the neighborhood that a woman should be educated and accomplished. She'd also understood it would be up to *her* to turn herself out as the lady daughter of an earl, as there was nobody else to do it.

She had never had a governess as those other girls did, and so she had used her father's library to teach herself. She listened to what the other girls studied and tried to find something similar amongst the earl's books. If they spoke of the Greeks, she read of them. If they mentioned Shakespeare, she read the plays.

Isabel had been fortunate in little, but at least the earl had not sold off the books as he had so many other things. He read next to nothing himself and had not the first idea that anybody else would pay him good money for them. The books had been her grandfather's and while her father had not added to them, he'd not taken them away either.

She had been thorough in her studies; she would not allow herself to be caught up short. She had been diligent in practicing her sewing with the help of Lord Bertridge's housekeeper. One of their close neighbors, Mrs. Roydon, had been kind enough to include Isabel in her daughter's pianoforte lessons and, while her own instrument had been forever out of tune, she practiced on it daily. Mrs. Campbell had included her in her girls' riding lessons and often lent her a horse for outings. The neighborhood had propped her up where her father could not.

Isabel was determined to do well in life, somehow. There was nothing her heart more longed for than to be settled in a marriage built on a substantial base. Her experience so far had been one of creditors and shortages, lack of candles for light, not enough wood for heat, and sometimes even a scarcity of food on the table. She never really knew what would happen next.

Her father did not worry about tomorrow, only what could be had today. He maintained a strange sanguine attitude that the future would work itself out. Something or someone was bound to turn up.

Now, the earl had gone so far as to mortgage the estate.

If there had been any advantage to her circumstances, it was that they had shaped her plans. She would not be one of those flighty women who leapt into a marriage without rational thought. She had made firm decisions about her future and would not be swayed from them.

Isabel did not wish for temporary security or the illusion of doing well, but for permanent and unassailable security. She wished for the sort of substantial base that could easily withstand a husband who gambled, or tenants who did not pay, or a fire burning down the house. In essence, a base that could stand solid and immovable, unperturbed by the cold winds of fate.

There were several components needed for that sort of security—plentiful money already in hand, a long-established title of suitable elevation, deep societal connections through marriages down the generations, and at least one estate of vast acreage.

He, whoever he was, would have a serious interest and unparalleled skill for managing his estate. The result would be no scrimping and no terror of the future.

She would, someday, live in comfort. She would be warm in winter. She would have new clothes each year. She would preside over a plentiful table and be carried about in a well-kept carriage. There would be no leaks in the roof.

Every door would be open to her and she would be able to afford to walk through them.

Her older sister had not done so. Margaret had married the first gentleman willing to take her on without a dowry. As poor Margaret had not had many choices in the neighborhood, she'd married a squire.

Her sister had initially set her cap on the Earl of Bertridge, their closest neighbor, but that had gone nowhere. Margaret was a capricious and giggling sort of personality, and the lord was reserved and serious. He had never seemed to know what she was talking about.

Now, Margaret would never starve, but the squire had been a decided settling.

Isabel had long vowed she would not settle. Her family's pedigree, if not their finances, was one of the best in England. She *refused* to settle, and she had prepared herself as best she could to be worthy of the idea.

She had even considered following in Margaret's footsteps and setting her cap on Lord Bertridge, though she found him unaccountably stiff. But then, he'd come home from Brighton married and so that idea came to an end. Initially, she'd almost wished she'd gone forward with it, as the new Lady Bertridge had somehow managed to loosen up the lord. Over time, she'd got to know Caroline, seen them together often, and it began to be more clear how the loosening up had come about. They were a well-suited pair—Lord Bertridge's off-putting seriousness had been softened and he had been much improved by his lighthearted wife.

As for who else in the neighborhood might be considered…there was nobody at present.

Now, she hurried down the stairs to the dining room. It was not prudent to be late. The offerings would not be generous, and her father would plow through it all were she to come in after the set time. She had gone to bed hungry on more than one occasion from just such a circumstance.

She passed by Rogers, their old and decrepit butler who had likely not been paid in a year. Isabel was certain he only stayed on because he did not have the money to leave. The footmen were long gone and Isabel only vaguely remembered having such servants in the house. There was no housekeeper, nor cook. A woman from the village brought in the meals and a lone stable hand took care of what was now their lone horse.

Over the years, even the tenants had left one by one. It had been impossible for them to stay on, as every time the earl was short of money, he raised their rents.

Isabel, herself, attempted to keep the house in some sort of order, sweeping corridors and dusting the drawing room, though she would never admit to it outside of the family. Her efforts did not result in much, the house was vast and she was only one person with a dust rag and broom.

She found her father already in his place at the head of the table. "What?" he said, pointing at her as she sat down. "A duchess, don't you know? Off with *her*. Arranged!"

Isabel did not have the first idea of what her father meant, nor did she often. It was as if whole thoughts and ideas occurred in his head but promptly blew apart and arrived in fractured pieces.

As Rogers limped in with the half of a cold chicken that would be their dinner, the earl slid a letter toward her plate.

She picked it up and unfolded it, very afraid it was from some creditor or other who was threatening something dreadful. The various people owed money had long lost whatever courtesy they might afford an earl.

There had been many such letters and the earl liked to hand them over as if she could make them stop coming.

Though, this time her father had mentioned a duchess and they had not yet been dunned by such an elevated personage. What had he got himself into?

My dear Lord Somerdon—

Though your last letter was not entirely clear, I will indulge myself in presuming that you are agreeable to the plan. Lady Isabel will be under my and the duke's protection, gaining entrance into all the finest houses in London.

I was able, through consulting with my duke, to under-stand one of the passages you wrote. He is certain you say you cannot be put to the expense of a wardrobe. Put that fear aside, my lord! It will be my honor to bring in my own modiste and outfit Lady Isabel as becomes an earl's daughter.

As well, the duke is sure that the last paragraph you wrote relates to your carriage being in disrepair. All difficulties are smoothed and I will come myself to collect Lady Isabel on the 9th of this month.

I look forward to seeing you then,
Theodosia Stanbury

"Father," Isabel said slowly, "what are these arrangements?"

The letter seemed to say that she would relocate to London for the social season and live with this duchess. The finest houses in London were to open their doors. There was a modiste and a wardrobe mentioned.

Could any of it be true? She must be certain before she allowed her hopes to bloom.

"Back, forth, back, forth," the earl said. He pointed to the letter. "The end."

The earl looked perfectly satisfied that he'd explained all. Isabel, having some experience teasing out her father's meanings, said, "Back and forth. There are other letters. Are they in your study?"

The earl nodded and then waved Rogers over with the half-chicken. Isabel leapt up. Her father could have the chicken. She must find those letters. She must know everything about what had been arranged.

MR. HARRY VANCE, only son of the 2nd Baron Leighton, surveyed the accounts with a satisfied eye. The estate was more and more profitable, thanks to his close management. His father, getting on in years, had taken a step back and handed him the reins. He had made sure the reins were in steady hands.

He managed things carefully for good reason. His family had somewhat recently joined the *ton* and it would be all too easy to slip out of it again. His grandfather had been a gunmaker who had done a particular service for the crown and been rewarded with a title and an estate.

Were Harry not careful and the estate was to run into financial difficulties, they might find themselves living as titled paupers. They did not have the network of rich and connected relatives that might bail a family out. Everything they did was up to them alone.

He did not have the luxury of going to Town and acting the foolish young gentleman—betting ruinously and then counting on somebody else to rescue him from his own idiocy. Nor did he imagine he would do so if he did have such a luxury, as it seemed very stupid to imperil one's estate by betting which color cat would pass by the bow windows of White's next.

As it was, the cash reserves had grown significantly, and he was well-cushioned. He had sought out advice from other gentlemen—some prudent and some not particularly. By far, Bertridge had provided the sagest counsel. People might find the fellow stiff on occasion, but he had been enormously helpful in showing him how to diversify to better protect his interests.

It was necessary that he protect his interests for his peace of mind—money built the walls of a fortress of security, and he intended his fortress to be very well fortified.

Someday, he would have a son. That son would experience his place in society as Harry did not. *He* was still too close in generations to trade. He was accepted by most, liked by nearly everybody, but peered down on by some. The likes of Lady Heathway and the Duchess of Stanbury could not be quite satisfied with his pedigree.

It would be different for the fourth-generation baron. That seemed to be, as far as he could gather, the magic length of time when a family's history was washed clean. His son would be better connected than he was, and then his grandson even more so. Eventually, his family would have a network of relatives through marriage that could be called upon if necessary.

Eventually, all thought of his family having come from trade would fade away.

He would be glad of it. Not because he was ashamed of his gunmaker grandfather. It was quite the opposite. That man had been hardworking, intelligent, and ambitious. His grandfather had been everything he admired in a man. No, he would be glad because it irked him whenever he felt the disdain for his grandfather's beginnings coming from another quarter.

He would be glad that his son would never feel it.

Harry smiled as he thought of the highhanded Duchess of Stanbury. She had been far more friendly to him last season than she'd ever been. Naturally, she had her reasons and they had nothing to do with his charm.

She was great friends with Viscountess Rembly and those two were forever intent on hunting down anybody who would consent to take the viscountess' daughter into supper at a ball. Miss Rightstone was a harridan of a female who'd been smacking her fan upon unsuspecting gentlemen through her fifth season. Still, he did not mind the occasional escorting, it was only a favor and as awful as she was, he did not like to think of a lady of any sort set adrift with no partner.

It had amused him to see what the duchess would try next. It seemed whenever she was particularly fearful that Miss Rightstone would be shunned, he was magically invited. She'd opened doors all over Town, somehow arranging that he would be invited when he usually would not have been. Then, she'd drag Miss Rightstone to his notice. If it were a ball, he was to take Miss Rightstone into supper. If it were a musical evening, he was to praise Miss Rightstone to the skies.

It was a testament to the duchess' supreme confidence in the idea that other mortals existed to serve her that she imagined he was a puppet dangling from her strings.

It was quite the opposite—he had kept *her* dangling on the line as if she were a fish. Sometimes he complied with her directions, sometimes he did not. It tickled him to recall the Tredwells' masque last season—he'd gone as a fox and dodged this way and that so he could never be caught. Miss Rightstone's Queen Elizabeth I and the duchess' Egyptian had looked for him all night.

Harry could only imagine what sort of gambits the duchess would roll out in the upcoming season as Miss Rightstone had left last season just as unmarried as she'd come into it. As for Miss Rightstone herself, he'd not indicated the slightest interest, as he had none. He would continue to squire her occasionally, as otherwise he was not certain who would.

He did not mind the duty too much because there was no lady so far that he *was* interested in. He hoped that circumstance would change, but so far it had not.

If he had one indulgence, it was that he would marry by preference, not by pounds and pence. He worked diligently to see that his funds needed no propping up with a dowry—he would give his time and effort to the estate, but he would not sell his heart to it.

While he was hoping to encounter *her*, the one that he looked for, the duchess would carry on with her schemes. He would do his part and squire Miss Rightstone when it was not too inconvenient. He hoped the lady would meet somebody suitable this season, as she was dangerously close to becoming a spinster.

In the very near future, he fully expected his arms to be once more bruised by the lady's surprisingly sturdy fan. He was set to go to London and open his house on the morrow, and Miss Rightstone was certain to already have that weapon raised and paused for a smack.

The season would unfold and he would walk through it as he always did—everlastingly cheerful, doing favors where he could, but quietly searching for *her*. He did not know who she was or what she looked like. He only knew that when he saw her, he would feel something.

The ladies he had danced and dined with through the seasons had all been most pleasant, excepting Miss Rightstone and one or two others. But even the most beautiful or kind or amusing had not stirred anything in him.

He was certain that when he saw *her*, he would know. When that happened, he would not hesitate in his pursuit. He would have his lady by his side.

If only he could find her.

As the duchess and Lady Easton barreled toward Hertfordshire, the rain came down in buckets. There was nothing to see out of the carriage windows but sheets of water blurring the countryside beyond.

"I do not understand what the weather is thinking of," the duchess said. "Carlson assured me that we would have only a mild cloudiness. A piffering cloud cover, he said."

"What is a piffering?"

"Oh, you know, just one of his technical terms he throws about."

The duchess was very proud of Carlson. It was not just anybody whose butler was a scholar. He had studied with the great Lord Ingraham who had records of the weather going back to the dark ages and he still regularly corresponded with that gentleman.

Lady Easton looked pointedly at the streams of water rolling down her window. "Not exactly piffering, is it?"

The duchess ignored the jab. Of course, Carlson was sometimes wrong. A pod of whales creating a disturbance in the North Sea, or a shooting star, or a sudden flight of crows, or an overrun of foxes, or even a foul wind coming from the poorer neighborhoods could all throw predictions off. He'd explained it many times.

The carriage careened around a turn. The duchess held on. She assumed Rumson was tiring of the weather, though he wore his oil skin. Carlson had informed him that he would have no need of that garb, but her coachman maintained a terrible disdain for her butler's advice. On a day like today that was perhaps fortunate.

"Do you suppose we'll end up having to pull Penelope aside like we did with Louisa?" Lady Easton asked.

The duchess sighed, as it had been on everybody's mind. Last season, they'd had to counsel Louisa to leave her grandbaby at home when making calls and to stop regaling near-strangers with the allegedly charming things the toddler said and did. Including outlining how advanced she was and that she called her grandmother *Bwandbaba.*

Now, Lady Heathway had been showing similar signs of that

particular madness. She had a grandniece a year old and at their last meeting she'd spent a good quarter hour explaining how alert the baby was.

"Another VAB," the duchess said. "First we had Louisa's Very Advanced Baby and now we have Penelope's Very Alert Baby," the duchess said drily.

Lady Easton nodded. "Are we to be expected to cheer over an account of how determinedly the baby reaches for things? Is that not what they do—just grab hold of everything in sight in an attempt to break it?"

"At least she does not have the baby in her possession," the duchess said. "She cannot bring it with her on calls like Louisa did, as the girl remains at Barlow Hall with her mother."

"For now," Lady Easton said ominously. "Though I fail to understand how Louisa and Penelope could have both lost their minds over babies. Those small creatures have no rationality, and they do things on their own schedule as if there are no other people in the household to consider."

"Louisa and Penelope have seemingly forgotten it is why we have nursemaids and governesses," the duchess said.

"This is Bertridge's lane to his estate," Lady Easton said, peering out the window and attempting to see through the rain on the glass. "Yes, I am certain of it. We just passed by that old oak that's been there forever."

They had arrived. The following morning, they would make their way to the earl's estate to collect Lady Isabel.

The duchess absentmindedly smoothed her brocade skirt. Her adventure as mama to a charming daughter was set to begin.

CHAPTER TWO

ISABEL HAD READ the duchess' letters over and over again. Though they were only comprised of paper and ink, she was very careful of them. The letters and the news contained in them were the most precious and valuable items she had ever been in receipt of.

There had been one other letter arrived since the duchess had written that she would come on the 9th and depart on the 10th. The lady informed the earl that she would go to Lord Bertridge overnight and then come to collect Isabel the following morning.

That had been an enormous relief. She had not known how they were to accommodate a duchess. Isabel had recoiled from visions of the duchess coming in too late for dinner and finding it gone. Or an evening trying to communicate with her father. Or Rogers dropping a tea tray in the hall. That had happened so often that Isabel had taken to going to the kitchens to carry it up herself and they were down to one very chipped old teapot. The silver sets had been long sold and the rest of the porcelain sets had been shattered in one mishap after the next.

She did not blame Rogers for it, the poor old fellow, but it had become apparent that he could not shoulder so many burdens on his own and Isabel had done what she could to alleviate some of it.

All of those calamities in the making had disappeared and she could relax while continuing to study the duchess' letters to try to better understand the lady.

The duchess, along with some friends, had founded *The Society of Sponsoring Ladies*. Each season, they would bring out a girl who had not the means to accomplish it on her own. The duchess wrote that the scheme had been wildly successful, and the *ton* was very admiring of their efforts. Now, it was time for the duchess herself to dip her toe in the sponsoring water.

Isabel realized rather quickly that the duchess had been drawn to *her*, as opposed to the hundred other ladies who must be in a similar situation, because of her family's history. The duchess used the word *noble* quite a lot in her missives. She mentioned the family's history and the links to the Plantagenets several times. She claimed there would be no gentleman out of reach for her.

There was even to be a dowry. The lack of a dowry had hung round her neck like a stone, though lack should weigh nothing. She did not know what the amount would be, nor did she care. If the duchess thought it sufficient, it must be.

All her father had said about it was, "Pounds. From *her*."

Isabel's dream was so close. She would go to London and there was a modiste who would be called in and she would attend balls and meet gentlemen. Somewhere, on some night, she would meet *the* gentleman, the one she would marry.

In her letters, the duchess had assured her father that she would carefully scrutinize any gentleman coming into Isabel's sphere and allow only the most elevated to proceed.

Isabel was determined to bring credit to this duchess-savior. It seemed she and Her Grace were very much similar in the ideas they had. Only the safest choices would be let through. As for herself, Isabel would be everything the duchess wished for and would not put a foot out of place.

She had spent the intervening days carefully going over her dresses and neatly stitching anything frayed. She'd practiced on the pianoforte though it remained out of tune. She'd fallen asleep each night with a book in her hand, determined to cram last minute bits of knowledge into her head. She'd reread her book on manners. She could not bear it if the duchess were disappointed in her.

Her sister Margaret was irate about the whole thing. She claimed it should have been her, had she not been married. Isabel sympathized, as she was no doubt right. But then, one could not guess what lay around corners and Margaret had not dared to turn the squire down for an opportunity that might never have arrived.

Someday, when she had her own pin money, she would send Margaret half of whatever it was to smooth her ruffled feathers and provide her the means to treat herself well. In later years, she would put as much effort into her sister's children being settled as she did for her own.

She had written Margaret a long letter that she would receive after Isabel had left for London, outlining those plans. She hoped it would turn her sister from irate to complacent and praying for her success. Margaret could be flighty and difficult, but she had a healthy respect for her own interests.

For that matter, Isabel realized she'd probably have to send her father some money too, else she did not know how he would carry on.

And then there was Rogers to think about. He could not carry out his duties too much longer and would need some sort of pension.

She supposed that, with all these different recipients the pin money would be divided between, she'd better marry someone on the generous side of things.

Isabel laid the duchess' letters back in the box she kept them in and prepared to go down to dinner. The windows to her bedchamber were open, the fresh breeze wafting in as if to drive away all the lean and scrimping years. The rain had stopped, the moon was rising bright, and the duchess was coming to collect her in the morning.

It was to be the last night of her life that she would have to run to dinner lest there be nothing left when she arrived.

Her new life was about to begin. Her one lucky chance had arrived, and she would hold onto it with both hands.

CHAPTER THREE

WHEN THE DUCHESS and Lady Easton had been shown into Lord Bertridge's drawing room the preceding evening, they had met a surprising sight. Lady Bertridge was decidedly pregnant.

Lady Easton had stared at Caroline's midsection until the lady finally said, "I see you have guessed—I am with child."

"Guessed? What is there to guess at? But," Lady Easton sputtered, "why was I not told? Richard, why did you not write?"

"We wished to be certain, that is Caroline thought…" Lord Bertridge trailed off.

"We wished to be certain I was past all early danger," Caroline said.

"How much more certain were you planning to get?" Lady Easton cried.

"Do not be cross, Lady Easton," Caroline said cheerfully. "You are here now, and we are delighted. You are the first to know our news."

"The first, well, if I am the very first, then I suppose that's at least a consolation," Lady Easton said, seeming cheered by the idea that she was the first to know, however late the news was in coming.

The duchess found this entirely amusing, as everybody in the neighborhood could not have failed to have noticed that Lady Bertridge was markedly with child.

"Yes, let us put this oversight behind us," Lady Easton said. "Now, everything must be done for this child! Richard, I have always known what your children will be—intelligent, comely, and proceeding carefully in life. They will be guided by ordered thinking, you understand."

The duchess sighed. Clara had seemed to throw over her disdain for Louisa's and Penelope's irrationality about babies and jumped on the wagon herself. What now? Were they to hear of the Very Ordered Baby? VAB, VAB, VOB—would the madness never end?

"I can have my things sent from Town easily enough," Lady Easton said, beginning to pace to assist her thinking. "My maid can bring what I require—she will know what I want. Goodness, there is so much to arrange, everything must be done just right. The house must be in order."

The duchess had pressed her lips together. The house must be in order for the very ordered baby. Naturally, the looks that had passed between Lord Bertridge and his wife over this idea were less than enthusiastic. She might even describe them as panicked. She supposed it would matter little what either one of them thought about it. Clara was moving in, and they'd better hope their clocks were all set correctly.

"Lady Easton, that is not at all necessary," Caroline said hurriedly. "At least not so soon. I am not due for another two months."

Lady Easton nodded. "Two months ought to be enough time to get this household in tiptop shape. If I work from dawn to dusk."

Lady Bertridge was gazing round her drawing room, no doubt wondering what on earth would take that much time to put in order.

"Aunt," Lord Bertridge said, "we would not take you away from the entertainments of the season, though we will forgo them ourselves."

"What are entertainments compared to this? I know my duty

to my family. One must do one's duty, regardless of the inconvenience."

"But certainly," Caroline said, "the ladies of the society must also have a claim upon you. I understood the duchess takes Lady Isabel to London this season. Surely she will require your good counsel."

"It will be a blow to the ladies, naturally," Lady Easton conceded.

The duchess, never one to miss a chance to entertain herself, waved her hands and said, "Nonsense, I will carry on well enough with the other ladies' assistance."

She silently cautioned herself not to roar with laughter as she watched the blood drain from Lord Bertridge's face. A very ordered house was coming his way.

"There, you see?" Lady Easton said. "It is settled. By the by, can that clock really be right?"

By the time she and Clara had been led up to their rooms to change for dinner, Lord and Lady Bertridge looked like two people on the verge of being struck down by a runaway carriage. It was a sort of dread, sprinkled with the sad acceptance of what was to come.

At dinner, they appeared quietly resigned. Though, the duchess was not certain Lady Easton had marked their changing attitudes. As far as she could tell, Clara presumed her relocation to the house was a matter of some delight.

The duchess had directed the conversation to the subject of Lady Isabel in a gambit to stop Clara from interrogating her hostess on the status of this or that thing in the household.

"She is a good sort of girl," Lord Bertridge said. "She seems intelligent and speaks with good sense, not at all like her sister who is now married. That one is rather discombobulated, while Lady Isabel appears very steady."

"She plays beautifully," Caroline said, no doubt having a better idea of what the duchess was interested in. "She is well-mannered and exceedingly lovely. Her looks are very elegant.

Her features are delicate, her hair is a wonderful auburn, and she has the complexion a redhead tends to have. She wears a bonnet with a very large brim and I have guessed she fears freckling."

"That sounds most intelligent," the duchess said gravely. "I would not prefer a freckled lady, though I will admit Miss Alcott seems to wear them with some aplomb."

The duchess was pleased to hear that her new charge was very elegant. She had assumed it, but it was pleasant to have it confirmed.

"I do not know what her father thinks of, or whether he thinks at all," Lord Bertridge said.

"I understand little of what he says," Caroline said. "But smiling and nodding seems to be sufficient."

"His estate, though," the lord said. "Why he does not do something with it, I cannot understand. He's got plenty of land and a good forest. With all of that, as far as I can tell, he's only managed a small patch for a vegetable garden. He's gone into a downward spiral—he does not have the means to employ people to do the work and will never have the means unless he employs people to do the work. Now he's mortgaged and I do not know where the situation will end up."

"Does he not have rents coming in?" Lady Easton asked.

"His last tenant left him years ago, finally tired of being mistreated. The earl looked upon his tenants as a personal bank. Whenever he needed funds, which was often, he tried raising the rents. At one point, a crowd of them threatened to burn his house down if he came round again."

"He sounds dreadful. Though, one wonders that he does not have some relative or other who might step in and bolster him until he was back on his feet again," the duchess said.

"I believe he has, and they have stepped in often. Even *I* have offered to lend him the funds to set the place right, but he's refused," Lord Bertridge said. "I do not like to see a neighbor, an earl, fall into such abject circumstances and I outlined an entire plan of farming, dairy, and forestry. No tenants, though. There would be no rational reason to revisit that fiasco."

"I do not know if it would be wise to lend such a person any money," Lady Easton said. "But on what basis does he refuse you?"

"It's hard to know exactly," Lord Bertridge said with a bemused smile. "He said something like: 'What? *Here*? Cows! Work, don't you know? Goodbye.'"

The duchess gripped her fork. Good grief. She must get Lady Isabel away from this lunatic with all haste. Further, it appeared as if he spoke just as he wrote. She would take Lady Bertridge's advice and simply nod and smile.

After dinner, the duchess and Lord Bertridge had played piquet, which the lord lost consistently as he was too busy admiring his pretty wife. That pretty wife glanced at her lord from time to time and smiled encouragingly, all the while listening to the series of requirements Lady Easton must see from the poor lady's servants. The ordered baby must land in an ordered house.

Now, a new day had dawned. The duchess had impatiently waited for breakfast to arrive to her room and for Lady Bertridge's maid to dress her. Once that was done, she'd made her departure without wasting another moment.

She'd left the house with Lord and Lady Bertridge rather forlornly waving her off, while Clara was too busy inside to bother with it. Last the duchess had seen her, Clara was interrogating the housekeeper and pointing out a cobweb she found behind a sideboard.

Lord Bertridge's house was about to go through an unlooked-for transformation.

As for Lord Somerdon's house, it had once been very grand. It still had the bones of a great house, large and staid, made of gray stone. However, roof shingles were scattered on the gravel and there were even some broken windows on the uppermost floor. A fountain in the center of the circular drive was covered in lichen and its basin filled with brackish water. The duchess presumed there had at one time been flower beds on either side, but they were now just a collection of overgrown weeds.

It was a crumbling mess.

The duchess had at least thought, since she was expected, that there would be somebody coming out to greet her.

As it was, she was forced to have her groom knock on the door and then waited for some minutes for somebody to come.

The somebody who came was a bent over and ancient fellow in a rather frayed suit of clothes. He had stared at her in an uncomprehending manner. Finally, she said, "I am the Duchess of Stanbury."

He'd nodded and said, "I am Rogers, the butler."

She had not the first idea why she was to know it.

Seeming to recall what a butler was supposed to do, he led her down the corridor in slow shuffling footsteps. The duchess was beginning to think it might take them a good half-hour to make it to the drawing room.

That was, until the old fellow sat himself down on a bench halfway there. He rubbed his knees and pointed down the hall. "That way."

The duchess looked down upon him in some surprise. "I am to continue on my own?" she asked.

"If you plan on getting there," the butler answered.

In such a manner, she proceeded to the doors that had been pointed out and let herself into the drawing room.

She found the earl and his daughter sitting complacently at a table. Lady Isabel leapt up and curtsied.

The earl rose and said, "Duchess. *Her.* Yes?"

"Yes, Lord Somerdon," the duchess said. "Excuse me for showing myself in, but your butler seemed rather under the weather."

"Rogers. Very old, don't you know. Very slow," the earl said nodding.

"Your Grace, my father thought it best that we remain in here to greet you, rather than going out to meet your carriage,"

Lady Isabel said pointedly.

The duchess assumed she was being told that so she would understand that her untoward mode of arrival had not been the girl's idea. She was glad of it, as it was a particularly bizarre idea, especially when one's butler could not make it down the corridor.

The earl waved his hands at his daughter's explanation as to why the duchess had been left to find them herself. "Me on the drive? *No.* Too eager, don't you know," he said, as if that made the slightest bit of sense.

"I see," the duchess said. Noting no tea service apparent, and heaven help them if they were to wait for poor Rogers to go get it, and feeling as if there was no rational conversation to be had with the earl, she said, "My dear Lady Isabel, are you packed? Shall we proceed to London forthwith?"

Lady Isabel nodded and looked exceedingly grateful that her departure would not be played out in any fashion.

"I have already brought my bags down," Lady Isabel said. "I can put them in the carriage myself as it might take Rogers…a bit of time."

Or until the end of time, the duchess thought. "Nonsense," she said. "My groom can see to it. Earl, your daughter is now under my protection. I will write from time to time to tell you how she gets on."

"Letters. *Short*, don't you know. A few," the earl said enigmatically.

"Come, Lady Isabel," the duchess said. "Kiss your father and we will be off."

Lady Isabel did as she was bid. The earl only said, "Very careful! *Rogues.* Goodbye."

With those interesting parting words, they left the earl and his crumbling butler to their own devices.

BALTHAZAR CARLSON HAD been the duchess' butler for some years. He had begun his rather storied career as the butler for a baronet. So many men of his ilk would have been satisfied with the position and consider themselves having reached the pinnacle of their careers.

Mr. Carlson shot higher, thank you very much. He was determined to serve in the most elevated houses—even the palace had not been considered out of reach.

But how to get there? How to distinguish himself?

He was short, so height would not help. He tended toward a paunch, so an imposing physique was out. He'd lost most of his hair and that had never been very good to begin. Looks would not serve him.

It must be his mind and manner that would inspire awe.

His manner was well-polished and needed no further refining and so he set to work on his mind. He must become knowledgeable; he must be an expert on…something.

It had taken some little time to home in on what he ought to be an expert in. He had briefly toyed with flora, but then who really cared about plants, and they had a gardener for such things. He'd considered Greek history, but could that be worked into everyday conversation on a daily basis? He'd thought about herbal tonics and cures, but that was traditionally woman's work.

What did every Englishman really care about?

As he searched and wondered, a personage named Lord Ingraham had visited the baronet's estate one summer and had spoken at length on predicting the weather.

That was what every Englishman cared about. What had the weather done, what was it doing now, and what would it do next? It was an endlessly fascinating topic and one that everybody wished to converse about.

It had been true that Lord Ingraham had not been often correct in his predictions during his stay, but the gentleman explained he was using the formulas for Cornwall and clearly the formulas for Bedfordshire differed.

That had made perfect sense and Carlson was highly intrigued. To predict the weather! That would really be something. Was there another butler in England who could predict the weather? He thought not. What value it would bring. What esteem and renown it would garner.

During Lord Ingraham's stay, Carlson did everything he could to ingratiate himself with the fellow. He sent books to his room that he thought would be of interest. He made sure his coffee was just how he liked it. He poured extra-generous glasses of port. Most especially, when he could find an opportune moment, he asked the lord questions about predicting weather.

He had been cautious about approaching the gentleman, as there were some who would take it as a liberty—a step too far. Not so Lord Ingraham. He'd been congenial in answering those questions at length. Carlson was fascinated to discover that weather prediction had been an interest of Lord Ingraham's family for generations and that he had notes on the weather in Cornwall going back to the dark ages. Some of them were even recorded on animal skins!

The end of it was, they'd agreed to correspond on the subject. And so, his training in weather prediction had begun.

Those were thrilling days. Each time he opened a letter, he discovered some new information he'd not ever imagined possible. A flight of crows could disturb the atmosphere and bring in a dense fog. A pod of whales migrating literally shook the sea floor, which in turn sent up waves, disrupting the clouds and setting off a lashing rain. An overrun of foxes in a neighborhood rustled the earth to such a degree as to cause undue heat in summer. Lord Ingraham was unlocking the very secrets of nature!

When the baronet died, Carlson made his exit from that house. The man's son was an idiot who would no doubt run the estate into the ground. It was time to jump off what was sure to be a sinking ship and take a step up in the world as a butler who could predict weather.

He'd only answered advertisements for positions that hinted at being in service to the highest elevated families. He had been intrigued to read of a *noble household* and had applied forthwith. It had not been the palace or even a prince, but it *had* been the duchess. That was suitably elevated in his opinion. When that lady had been informed that he was studying weather prediction, she'd hired him on the spot.

The duchess was so enthusiastic about the idea that she'd gone so far as to write to Lord Ingraham, requesting that her butler be allowed to come to him for three months in the summer and study the art.

What a summer *that* had been.

As it turned out, there were no records going back hundreds of years. There was one single notebook spanning five years and filled with rather pedestrian observations—*rained today* or *didn't rain today* or the oft repeated *rained again.*

There was no consistent theory of anything. One minute, crows would bring in a dense fog, the next they would bring in tornadic gusts. The pods of whales, who were originally supposed to bring in a lashing rain, might sometimes be charged with causing gusts of wind from the slapping of their tails.

Further, there was no formula for Cornwall weather—his predictions were just as wrong there as they'd been in Bedfordshire.

Lord Ingraham talked about the weather all day long, often pacing back and forth in front of him and delivering a lecture, but it was all so muddled and contrary.

It had not been many days before Carlson had realized that Lord Ingraham did not know any more about the weather than the next person looking out a window.

He could not tell the duchess that, though. She'd already bragged to her friends about his expertise and his continuing studies. So, he stayed on for those three months, his eyes rolling to the back of his head most days. With great relief, he returned to her service pretending he'd unlocked many secrets.

He'd been pretending and trying to develop his own theories ever since.

The preceding day, he'd watched the storm clouds roll in after the duchess had departed to collect Lady Isabel. He'd watched them gather and the rain pour down after he'd assured her of a piffering cloud cover. She would return today with her charge, and thankfully it was not storming this particular day.

He only hoped that she remembered that a pod of whales might be doing something in the North Sea to throw all predictions off.

He was not a God! He could not be blamed for what the whales were doing!

CHAPTER FOUR

ISABEL COULD NOT have got out of her father's house fast enough. The poor duchess had experienced a very bizarre welcome to it, though Isabel had done her best to hint that it had not been her idea to leave things up to Rogers.

The duchess did not seem much the worse for wear, though. She had been happily chattering along ever since the carriage had trotted down the drive.

"I went so far as to make a guess at your size and then overestimate it, as it is no great matter to take a dress in," the duchess said. "I thought I must, as we are to have a dinner on the morrow."

"That was very kind, Your Grace," Isabel said. A dress had already been made! There was to be a dinner so soon!

"You'd better call me Duchess," she said, "we will be much together, and I do not wish to be your graced and ma'amed to death."

"Yes, Duchess," Isabel said.

"Now, as to that dinner, I have been rather pushed into it. Viscountess Rembly is a very old friend, we've known each other since we were girls. Well, she has a daughter, Miss Rightstone."

At the mention of Miss Rightstone, the duchess frowned and quietly sighed.

"Miss Rightstone has not had the luck of an engagement and it is now getting rather late as this will be her sixth season."

Isabel was surprised to hear it. She'd no idea a lady could keep coming back season after season. It rather filled her with dread, too. What if she did not make a match this season? Would the duchess even bring her back for another?

"Her mother and I are attempting to engineer a match between Miss Rightstone and a Mr. Harry Vance. He is to be a baron, which is all well and good, however, his grandfather was in trade. He is very recent, you see."

Isabel did see. Recent was not steady or substantial.

"We think it will not be a love match, at least not on his side, but serviceable all the same. Her dowry is large and her family is old. Exactly what a gentleman recently arrived will require. I think he will see that fact this season. Or *face* that fact, as the case may be."

"So the dinner is to give them an opportunity to meet?" Isabel asked.

"Precisely," the duchess said. "Goodness, I did send out the invitations last minute. I do hope he's accepted and I shall be very put out if he has not."

Isabel thought Mr. Vance would do well to accept. She would not personally wish to put out the duchess.

"As for your own prospects, Lady Isabel, we will aim far higher of course."

"My primary requirement, if I am indulged to have one," Isabel said daringly, "is a gentleman who can provide a suitable household with no danger of it ever becoming less so. I would like to have a firm foundation and unassailable position."

The duchess nodded vigorously. "Very well said, entirely wise, my girl. So many other young ladies would have had stars in their eyes and said their primary requirement was love. You have seen for yourself what can happen when one stands on shaky ground, and you are right to think of security first. Love can come later."

"Yes," Isabel said, feeling very encouraged, "that is just what I thought."

"Fear nothing, I will guide you," the duchess said with supreme confidence. "Plantagenet blood has the right to marry at the highest strata of society. With that idea, I have also invited Lord Percy Lymington to dinner. He is to be a duke, his estates are vast, and that family could burn money for heat and not feel the pinch."

Isabel's heart leapt at the description. That was precisely what she looked for. A well-funded duke was unassailable. His duchess would be unassailable. Further, she'd never heard of a duke who struggled for money and this one certainly did not. She would be very interested in being introduced to this Lord Lymington. Would it not be something if he were pleasant too? And perhaps handsome?

The duchess went on to describe the dress that a certain Madame LeGrange would arrive to fit and take in on the morrow. It was a pale green chiffon with dyed lace edging and it sounded divine. She'd never owned a chiffon dress—the material was too dear in cost, too easy to tear, and too difficult to mend.

"I considered a brocade," the duchess said, "but Madame LeGrange assures me that a young person cannot carry off that noble fabric."

Isabel was rather glad that brocade had been ruled out. While it might suit the duchess, she could not imagine it on herself. She might well look like a pair of walking and talking curtains.

Chiffon would do very nicely.

MR. HARRY VANCE stared down at two items of paper that had arrived to his house on Bedford Square.

"Interesting," he said.

One was an invitation from the Duchess of Stanbury for a dinner, no doubt to ensure Miss Rightstone had somebody to partner who would not complain too loudly about it. The other was a letter from Bertridge explaining that the very same duchess had brought Lady Isabel Beaufort to London to launch her as a project of *The Society of Sponsoring Ladies*.

Bertridge, careful and considerate gentleman that he was, had written to him and a few select others to alert them to Lady Isabel's arrival and request that they look after her when they saw the opportunity. Specifically, to steer her clear of any man who might not be quite the gentleman.

According to Bertridge, the girl was penniless, but exceedingly pretty, intelligent, and well-mannered, with a very fine background.

Well, if Bertridge thought she was well-mannered, Harry could at least assure himself that Lady Isabel would not wield her fan as a weapon. His bruises from Miss Rightstone's proclivities in that direction had taken some time to fade after last season.

He had no particular wish to be captured at table beside Miss Rightstone so soon. On the other hand, he was curious to see this lady that Bertridge had taken the time to write about. As well, it amused him that the duchess had gone so far as to invite him into her house. Were things to go on as they had last season, he would be invited everywhere.

"I think I will write the duchess and accept her very kind offer," he said to Smith. "I'll wear one of the coats that just came in. She is a duchess after all."

His valet nodded as he wrote out his acceptance of the Duchess of Stanbury's kind invitation.

He suspected this dinner would be very entertaining.

WHAT A DAY it had been already, Isabel thought. She watched the sun set over the roofs of Hanover Square from her bedchamber window, a cup of tea kindly sent up by the duchess just now warming her hands.

Madame LeGrange had come in the morning to do a final fitting on the chiffon dress. It had not needed much work, just a little tuck here and there and a hemming. It was positively glorious. The lady had then sketched out a few new dresses. Now that she had Isabel's measurements she was able to give the duchess various delivery dates on what else had been already ordered.

It seemed she was to have quite the wardrobe—day dresses, morning dresses, walking dresses, ballgowns, tea gowns, a riding habit, spencers, reticules, parasols, cloaks, shawls, gloves, shoes, bonnets, and even underclothes and nightdresses had been ordered.

She had been introduced to the Duke of Stanbury and had found him exceedingly genial. He was welcoming, did not put on airs, and seemed very fond of the duchess. Isabel could only be grateful for his generosity of both purse and spirit.

Then, the duchess' particular friends, the ladies of the society, had come for tea. She'd heard how Lady Easton had gone to stay with her nephew, Isabel's own neighbor, Lord Bertridge. It seemed the lady had just discovered that Lady Bertridge was with child, though of course the neighborhood had been long apprised of it.

Isabel had been informed by Lady Featherstone that the brooch she wore and the walking stick propped beside her had both been won at a mystery ball, whatever that was, two seasons running. She'd also been given a cipher and she promised Isabel that she'd send her a letter in code.

Isabel had thanked her for the courtesy but was not entirely clear how she was meant to unravel the code. All she knew was that it was to contain something interesting about Lord Ryland and Lady Prudence's adventure of last season.

Lady Mendleton had told some stories about her granddaughter, who it seemed was walking and talking far advanced for her age.

The duchess had eventually cut her off with a muttered, "All right, *Bwandbaba*, that is sufficient."

Lady Heathway took that opportunity to claim her grand-niece was exceedingly alert and grabbed for things with gusto. She had quite the grip, apparently.

"Another VAB," the duchess whispered to Isabel.

Isabel did not know what a VAB was, but she got the distinct idea that the duchess did not like them.

Lady Redfield spoke of a distant cousin of some sort, Lady Arabella, who had married the duchess' son, Lord Blackwood. While the other ladies spoke of children, it seemed Lady Arabella was the proud owner of a menagerie. She'd recently written of a very recalcitrant stoat with an injured paw she was just now treating, and she had yet another hedgehog living in the drawing room and was beginning to think the species was suited to that location.

This led the duchess to explain what sort of close relationship she had with Lord Blackwood. It seemed there was never a son more dedicated to his mother's happiness. They understood each other's minds even when they had not spoken in some time.

While these conversations were sometimes odd, they had not been personally embarrassing. That was not quite true when they moved on to who might be suitable for her to marry.

Lord Lymington was discussed at length and, while she could not be certain, it seemed his love of horses somehow ran against him. She could not understand why, she would be delighted to have the use of a well-stocked stable.

All in all, Isabel thought the ladies might be a bit eccentric. As she had not encountered very many elevated London ladies, she could not be absolutely certain. More importantly, though, they were kind and seemed very invested in her future.

Of course, her neighbors at home had all been kind and helped her where they could. But this was the first time she had been surrounded by people who were all so intent on her and her success. It felt very encouraging and fortifying, as if she had been encircled by a warm blanket on a cold day.

After the ladies had departed, a series of maids arrived to be interviewed by the duchess. Isabel was to get her own maid! She had not even thought of such a thing, as she'd never had one.

A woman named Betsy had been selected. She was middle-aged and the duchess found her experienced and eminently sensible. The duchess said a less experienced maid would not do, as the last thing a young lady needed was a flighty maid to put bad ideas into her head.

Lady Easton had apparently learned that lesson the hard way, as it appeared that the new Lady Bertridge had once had such a maid. Isabel was amused to hear that it had been Bemmy, who she was well acquainted with. Bemmy and her husband ran Lord Bertridge's cheesemaking operation. Yes, she could see very well how a person such as Bemmy might lead one into all sorts of trouble.

Betsy was of an entirely different ilk and had the further recommendation of being able to start immediately. She was to arrive any moment to help her dress.

For Isabel, it was all rather thrilling. She was living the life she had so often dreamed of.

There was a quick knock on the door and Betsy herself came striding in. "Lady Isabel, are you ready to be dressed?" the maid asked.

She was a comfortably plump woman with an air of confidence about her. She was very like some of the matrons of her own neighborhood, who seemed inured to ever having their feathers ruffled.

"I am," Isabel said. She hesitated for a moment, and then decided she must plough on. "Betsy," she said, "you will no doubt find this unusual, but I have never had a maid."

She waited for the look of shock on the maid's features, but none came. Betsy only nodded. "Ah, some of these families do get themselves into a bind here and there. Don't you worry 'bout a thing. All that's required is allow me to do the work. You do your job and I'll do mine and we'll get on just fine."

Isabel smiled. There was something very comforting about Betsy and she was very glad she'd not tried to act her way through her first time being dressed by a maid.

Over the next hour, Betsy put her clothes in order, then she put Isabel in her dress, all the while chattering on about this or that. It seemed Mr. Carlson thought himself a great predictor of the weather and had forecasted a fine night. Betsy found that amusing. She was a farmer's daughter and said anybody with eyes could see the flat clouds with a gray tone that portended rain.

Finally, Betsy sat her at the looking glass and did her hair.

What a marvelous thing she'd done with her hair! It far exceeded anything Isabel could accomplish on her own. Though it had taken some time to achieve, it appeared soft and unstudied.

"There now," Betsy said cheerfully. "You are ready to go down and dazzle the gentlemen with your beauty. They'll all have arrived by now, as the duchess asked me to hold you back for a bit so you might make an entrance."

"Dazzle? Betsy, I hardly think—"

"Now, don't be modest with *me*," Betsy said. "I'm the one who put you together and I take pride in my work. Off with you, now. I'll be here to undress you at the end of it."

Betsy very much sounded like a mother affectionately scolding a daughter. Isabel found she did not mind it at all.

⟫⟫⟫✳⟪⟪⟪

HARRY HAD ARRIVED to the duchess' very grand house in good time. It was the first time he'd been admitted into her residence, and he was very interested in what he would find there. He had ideas around how he would live himself in the future, and if his finances went on as well as they had, no London address would be out of reach.

The duchess' butler had seemed rather surprised and dismayed to find him coming in with a wet umbrella. He'd said, "It's *still* raining?" in tones of disbelief and outrage. Harry guessed the poor man thought the weather some sort of affront to the duchess.

The duchess herself was in full brocade regalia, with Miss Rightstone by her side. Harry quietly sighed as he surveyed the rest of the room.

It seemed it was to be a small party for dinner and he recognized everybody just now milling round the drawing room. Lymington was there and he could not imagine why, as he was certain the duchess found him tedious. Lady Redfield was laughing at something Lord Jeffries just said to her. Lord and Lady Heathway, Lord and Lady Featherstone, and Miss Rightstone's parents, Lord and Lady Rembly, were in attendance. But where was this Lady Isabel that Bertridge had taken the trouble to write to him about?

The duchess had Miss Rightstone by the arm as they made their way over to him.

"Mr. Vance, how good of you to come," the duchess said.

"It is my pleasure, Your Grace," he said.

Miss Rightstone smacked his arm with her fan and said, "Well, were you pining all summer Mr. Vance?"

The duchess had the good grace to blanch over this fishing expedition.

"I naturally thought of *all* my friends in Town, Miss Rightstone," he said noncommittally.

"Oh I see," she said coquettishly, "I'm to be lumped in with *all* your friends."

Harry did not dare answer that particular salvo as there were only two ways to go. He must say that she was not lumped in, singling her out and giving her something to hold onto, which he certainly would never do. Or, he must tell her the truth—once his bruises had faded, he had not given her another thought.

Through the open doors of the drawing room, he saw a lady descend the stairs. She was of average height, but that was all that was average about her.

She had glorious auburn hair, glinting red and gold in the candlelight. Her features were very delicate and well-proportioned. Her eyes were bright and her rather perfect nose overlooked amply generous lips. It was as if a painter had stepped back from his canvas and thought, 'Now, what would be perfection?'

Her head was held high and she wore a floaty, dreamy dress. She looked like a young queen descending to her subjects.

She was marvelous.

The duchess followed his eyes and said, "Ah, there is Lady Isabel." She left him with Miss Rightstone to greet the lady and lead her into the room.

Miss Rightstone followed his eyes too. He was smacked again, rather harder than the first time, though she said nothing to accompany the assault.

ISABEL HAD SEEN Lord Lymington from the stairs. He was virile-looking and athletic, and he wore a very well-cut coat, as of course a lofty lord would. He had dusky blond hair, the sort that would lighten in the summer sun and darken again over the winter as if it changed its mood to suit the season.

His jawline was strong, his eyes, she thought blue though she was at a distance. His complexion was tanned, as men found themselves when they spent most of their time on horseback rather than hiding inside a carriage.

Their eyes met. Lord Lymington saw her. And he smiled at her.

She had no idea the eldest son of a duke could ever be so handsome. How was it possible that such a man remained unmarried? He was an Adonis come to life.

"Lady Isabel," the duchess said, meeting her at the bottom of the stairs, "I knew I could depend upon Madame LeGrange and her exquisite taste—that dress suits you very well."

"It is the most beautiful dress I have ever worn," Isabel said with simple honesty.

"Come, I will introduce you to everybody."

They made their way into the drawing room and Isabel fairly quaked. She was not usually nervous about meeting new people, but Lord Lymington… He was stirringly handsome and he just might, if she were not an absolute fool, be her future.

Lord Lymington stepped forward. Oddly, the duchess had Isabel's arm and it almost felt as if the lady attempted to steer her away from him.

"You must be Lady Isabel Beauford," the lord said. "Your neighbor, Lord Bertridge, wrote me that you would come and charged me with looking out for you when I could."

"Did he," the duchess muttered.

"Did he?" the lady next to him said, sounding strangely petulant.

"That was very kind of Lord Bertridge," Isabel said. "And of course, any assistance you would offer would be greatly appreciated, Lord Lymington."

Isabel was not quite certain what she'd said wrong, but it had been something. There was consternation on both the lord's and the duchess' face, while the lady standing nearby covered her mouth and snorted.

Had it been presumptive to thank him before he'd actually done anything?

"My dear," the duchess said hurriedly, "this is not Lord Lymington. This is Mr. Vance."

Isabel's heart dropped. He was not Lord Lymington. Why was he not Lord Lymington? Why had she assumed he was? Most of all, why must this beautiful man be Mr. Vance? Unsuitable, new to the *ton*, Mr. Vance?

"Excuse me, I am sorry, Mr. Vance. I do not know why I assumed…"

Mr. Vance had recovered himself quickly and said cheerfully,

"On no account should you trouble yourself over the mistake. I find I do not experience it unpleasant to be taken as the eldest son of a duke, rather than the lowly eldest son of a recently arrived barony."

"Indeed," the duchess said, looking not as cheerful as Mr. Vance. "Lady Isabel, this is Miss Rightstone."

Isabel curtsied, as did the lady, though it seemed a rather shallow effort.

The duchess led her away and her embarrassment should have lessened after Mr. Vance's genial brushing off of the mistake, but it seemed every minute that went by only compounded the feeling. Especially when she considered that Miss Rightstone was all too likely to repeat the story.

It had been very stupid to assume she knew who a person was before being told. His looks, his manliness, his…something, had clouded her mind and that was very stupid indeed.

The duchess brought her to one grouping of people after the next. She had of course already been introduced to the ladies of the society, though their lords, excepting the duke, were unknown to her until now. They were all pleasant gentlemen.

Then, there was Lord Jeffries, who appeared to be a particular friend of Lady Redfield's. She met Viscount and Viscountess Rembly, Miss Rightstone's parents. He was courteous enough, but there was some sort of unpleasant undercurrent to the viscountess.

Isabel thought the lady must be on edge regarding having a daughter coming for a sixth season. She could not remember her own mother, but she had seen other mothers in her own neighborhood get almost fretful in considering their daughter's future.

The last gentleman she met was, much to her surprise, the real Lord Lymington. He was a hulking sort of individual with a doughy face and a bit of a paunch. He would have been the last gentleman she would have singled out as a future duke. Of course, she did not know any young gentlemen destined for a dukedom, so it had only been her preconceived notions.

After her curtsy, Lord Lymington said, "I was just telling Lord Featherstone about a horse that keeps throwing a shoe. I really think he's doing it on purpose. Horses, you know."

"Goodness," Isabel said, as she could not think what else to say.

"Did I say his name is MacBeth?"

"No, Lord Lymington, I do not believe you did," Isabel said.

"Right," Lord Lymington said, "so MacBeth keeps throwing his shoes. I really think he knows what he's doing."

"I see," Isabel said, though she did not see at all. Though, she thought she *did* begin to see what the ladies had been debating about when they'd discussed Lord Lymington's unfortunate interest in horses.

Carlson appeared at the doors to the drawing room and nodded to the duchess.

"We will go through," the duchess said to the room. She turned to Lord Lymington. "My lord, do be so kind as to take in Lady Isabel."

The lord nodded and put out his arm. "Lady Isabel, did I say that MacBeth is descended from the Byerley Turk?"

"You did not," Isabel said.

"I sometimes wonder if the Turk threw *his* shoes. MacBeth throws his shoes and I think it's on purpose."

"Yes, you mentioned that."

"Did I? Horses…"

CHAPTER FIVE

HARRY WAS, AS expected, seated next to Miss Rightstone. The delightful Lady Heathway was on his other side. At least, he supposed Lady Heathway could be delightful when she felt like it. Most of the time, he found her rather acerbic.

He hardly needed to note Lady Isabel seated across the table and next to Lord Lymington to understand the evening's point.

He had been brought in to entertain Miss Rightstone and Lymington had been thought suitable for Lady Isabel. The rest were just filling chairs.

Well, perhaps not all of them. Lady Redfield was a widow and Lord Jeffries was a widower and they seemed to hit it off very well.

What an introduction to Lady Isabel he'd had! She had assumed he was Lymington. She'd assumed he was the eldest son of a duke. The look of disappointment when she discovered he was not had been unmistakable. He had since overheard the duchess tell Lord Featherstone of Lady Isabel's rarified Plantagenet blood.

Harry presumed she shot rather high in the marriage mart. To be introduced as a marquess, eldest son of a duke, was to be greeted with all smiles. To be nothing of the sort, only a Mr., engendered disenchantment.

He ought to laugh it off and turn his mind away from the lady. And yet, he could not quite do so. She was magnetic and he was having a very hard time controlling his staring. Left to his own devices, he would look at her all night long.

He was beginning to wonder if Lady Isabel might be *her*. The one he'd looked for. He could not know it in any logical way; he did not know the lady's temperament or her views on things. He might very well be mistaken. But what he did know is that he'd been struck the moment he'd seen her. He did not want to stop looking at her.

He had never been struck before, not by any other lady during any other season. He had almost begun to wonder what was wrong with him. How was it when so many gentlemen were bowled over by this or that lady arriving to Town, all he felt was a disinterested shrug. He had begun to fear he never would be bowled over.

Now he had been. He'd been struck hard.

It had not occurred to him that *she*, the one he looked for, might be entirely uninterested in him. He had somehow assumed that there would be a mutual attraction.

He must find out if it was really her, the one he looked for. He must get to know her and see what feelings developed. As for her obvious disinclination to stoop to his rather unexalted level…well, he'd cross that bridge when he came to it.

At the moment, he would like to get up and throw Lymington from his chair and take it for himself.

Instead, he had turned to Lady Heathway and prepared himself to row hard across a conversational lake neither of them was interested in traversing.

"Lady Heathway," he said cheerfully, "Gresham writes me that he has been blessed with a daughter. He says you are very much involved and have been a comfort to Lady Gresham."

Gresham had written him no such thing, but there were times when society's wheels needed to be greased.

As if he had greased a lock with a magical key, mention of the recently arrived baby had transformed Lady Heathway's features. She actually smiled.

"I do not mind telling you, Mr. Vance, that grandniece of mine is extraordinarily alert!"

"Interesting," Harry said. "I have read that a particularly alert baby denotes high intelligence."

And *that* was all he had to say about the baby. Lady Heathway took the oars from there and he spent a far more pleasant quarter hour than he had expected, listening to the lady rattle on about the unusually alert, and now highly intelligent, baby.

As all good things must end, it was eventually time to turn to Miss Rightstone and she steered the conversation rather differently. He was left to listen to the lady's catalogue of all of her dislikes while dropping heavy hints that they were the sorts of things a future husband must know. Apparently, the lady had an aversion to pickled vegetables.

She then went on to list things she *did* like, and he was forced to hear her opinions on a wide variety of biscuits.

Harry thought that if the footmen would bring round the wine more often, he'd like to get pickled himself. He might throw a few of Miss Rightstone's favored biscuits at Lymington's head while he was at it.

Though, he perfectly well knew why the footmen did not bring the wine round often. It was Miss Rightstone who would get pickled, as she had done on more than one occasion last season.

ISABEL WORKED TO keep her countenance cheerful. The dinner had been a long one and the ladies' retreat into the drawing room had not been that much more comfortable than being at table.

Lord Lymington had droned on and on at dinner. Was the story of that horse named MacBeth never to come to an end? She now knew he was a chestnut, had thrown a shoe six times in as many months, what he had cost, when he'd been bought, from who he'd been bought, and how many hands high he stood.

On top of all that, the lord had not asked her a single question! Where were his manners? Did he not wonder where she was from? Or how she knew the duchess? Or even what she thought of London so far?

General conversation was so easy to make—why did not he make it?

It had been tedious in the extreme. For all that, though, she could not dismiss that he would be a duke. No, she really could not. She had vowed to put her future in an unassailable position. She would not be so foolish as to dismiss Lord Lymington simply because he liked to talk about his horses. Unmarried gentlemen who would inherit a dukedom would not exactly be falling from trees.

In any case, did not Lord Bertridge used to talk too much about his cheesemaking operation? She had been at a dinner once when he had gone into excruciating detail about the difficulties inherent in producing a superior blue. Lady Bertridge seemed to have cured him of that habit.

Certainly, a deficiency of that sort could easily enough be either tolerated or rectified. She hoped.

She'd found it difficult, over dinner, to stop herself from glancing at Mr. Vance. He really was so handsome. She'd been embarrassed to be caught at it twice as it seemed he was rather regularly looking at *her*.

There was some sort of attraction between them. She felt it, like iron and lodestone coming too close.

He was not in an unassailable position, though. It was a shame, but he was not.

Finally, the ladies had withdrawn. The duchess had said she was certain her duke would not keep the gentlemen behind long, and when they came in they would have cards and music.

But then, Isabel had found herself in a corner of the room being practically lectured by Lady Rembly.

The viscountess, having an unswerving and almost unnerving

interest in her daughter's prospects, had thrown off any subtlety she'd ever possessed.

Though the lady smiled and almost seemed to be making polite conversation, she was not.

"The duchess has told me of your family's storied history," she said. "I cannot imagine that you would settle for someone low, for instance a mere baron. A *new* baron, at that. Well, no matter, I believe Mr. Vance is quite set on my daughter. He all but asked last season. You know how young gentlemen are about these things and of course he is very new to it all. *Very* new."

Her tone had suddenly darkened as she said, "Still, it *is* in the offing."

Isabel had recoiled and got the distinct feeling that the viscountess had noticed her looking at Mr. Vance. Had it been that obvious?

But who could avoid looking at that man?

She was relieved when the gentlemen came in and the duchess called from the far side of the room. "Lady Isabel, do play something for us."

HARRY HAD FOUND the port after dinner exceedingly dull. The only bright spot was whenever Lymington attempted to add to or modify his story about some horse who threw shoes, the duke cut him off.

How could the duchess imagine that someone like Lady Isabel ought to pair off with Lymington? That fellow would only stay married if he wed a lady who had need of an ear trumpet that she continually misplaced. She might see his lips moving but remain blissfully unaware that he was still talking about MacBeth and that horse's thrown shoes.

Was Lymington's position enough to outweigh his vast deficiencies?

Harry would like to think not, but he knew he would probably not be right.

Still, a lady like that to throw herself away on such a fellow! It could not be right.

Finally, the duke had risen and they made their way to the drawing room.

Miss Rightstone was at the tea tray with a plate of biscuits. He now knew but did not care that her favorite was almond.

Lady Isabel had just been directed to the pianoforte by the duchess. He made his way there under the glares of Miss Rightstone and her mama.

"Lady Isabel," he said, as she sat down on the bench, "might you allow me to turn your pages?"

"Yes, of course, Mr. Vance," she said, failing to meet his eye.

He did not take her acquiescence as any ringing endorsement, as it would have been hard for a lady to refuse such a request. But he would take it all the same.

She had chosen a gentle sonata. As she played, she said softly, "What a magnificent instrument."

"Do you have one like it at home?" Harry asked, certain that she did or she could not play so well.

He felt, by her expression, that he had in some way embarrassed her.

She'd paused when considering the question. Then she'd said, "Nothing even approaching what this is. My own is very old and always out of tune."

He laughed. "What neighborhood is this that does not have a tuning man somewhere about the place?" he asked.

Again, it seemed he'd somehow gone astray, though he could not imagine how.

After a full minute of silence, he was on the verge of apologizing though he did not know for what.

Lady Isabel finally broke the silence. "I come from Hertfordshire, nearby Watford. But perhaps I ought to be direct, Mr. Vance, as I do not believe my circumstances will remain unknown. My father's estate is in a very bad way and there has not been the opportunity to accommodate any luxuries."

How stupid of him. She was from Bertridge's neighborhood in Hertfordshire, the man had said so. Bertridge had also said the lady was penniless. Harry had just not thought that had meant *actually* penniless. He'd imagined her dowry was on the small side.

Her pianoforte had not been tuned because her father could not even afford that small fee.

"Please allow me to apologize, Lady Isabel," he said, turning the page. "I never meant to land on an uncomfortable subject, nor make you feel forced to explain anything about your circumstances."

"It's quite all right, Mr. Vance. I would just as soon not pretend to be something that I am not."

"I think what you *are* is rather wonderful," Harry said.

Lady Isabel did not answer that comment, nor had he expected her to. Instead, she put all her attention on where her hands were traveling across the keys.

He marveled at his own daring. It was the first moment he'd gone so far as to hint to a lady his admiration. He'd been scrupulous about never doing so, never crossing that line, lest he get himself into a situation that would be difficult to extricate himself from.

"I imagine the duchess will take great care with you this season," he said.

"I imagine you are right," Lady Isabel said, smiling. "The duchess has been kind enough to understand me and will guide me in the direction I wish to go."

It was an enigmatic answer and Harry felt there was far more behind it. "What direction is that?" he asked casually, hoping she would answer but not certain that she would.

"Because of my father's circumstances, I have understood what poverty means. I wish to have a position and never go near poverty again. I wish for an *unassailable* position."

There it was. Her declaration.

"Such as a dukedom, I imagine," he said, attempting to keep the sulk from his tone.

"If that is where my future leads me," she said firmly.

Dash it. *That* was why she might consider Lymington. She had not just a garden variety interest in becoming a duchess. She had a drive created by circumstances that he suspected had been harrowing. She would not speak so plainly were it not the case.

"Perhaps, though," he said slowly, "it might not be fair to the gentleman, were you only to marry for an unassailable position."

"It would be very fair, as I would never deceive anybody regarding my feelings."

That was bold. He'd not considered that a lady determined on securing a lofty title might just come out and say so. Unfortunately, that *was* rather fair. And Lymington might just be stupid enough to be led into it.

"Mr. Vance," the duchess called, "do come and partner with Miss Rightstone for piquet. Lord Lymington tells me it is not his game, and so he can turn the pages for Lady Isabel."

Blast. He'd far rather stay where he was and speak more to Lady Isabel.

Even worse, Miss Rightstone's game of piquet was downright painful. If he lost a trick, her fan would strike, if he won a trick, her fan would strike harder.

He was to leave the duchess' house a battered man.

Still, after all these many seasons, he might just have met *her*.

BETSY HAD KINDLY brought Isabel a tea tray in the morning. Though she had always gone down to breakfast all her life, at least whatever breakfast could be scared up, the duchess thought that would not be convenient in her house. She did not go down herself and the duke generally only had coffee before retreating to his library.

This breakfast was very unlike what she had been used to. There were fried eggs, bacon, a sausage, toasted bread, butter, strawberry jam, and a pot of tea. It was glorious.

As she worked her way through the plate, she considered the evening before.

She knew she could not change one iota of reality for wishing, though how she wished she could! How she wished her initial assumption that Mr. Vance had in fact been Lord Lymington had been true.

Isabel had never been a particularly indulgent person, she considered herself to have a disciplined mind. But Mr. Vance was proving a challenge.

It had been so hard not to look at him last evening. When he'd come to turn her pages at the pianoforte, it had been so difficult to ignore how close his broad-shouldered person was to her. He told her he thought she was wonderful and her heart had skipped a beat. She had an overwhelming urge to touch his hand, to see if it were warm. She'd done no such thing, but she could not help thinking about it.

It was hard not to picture him in her mind now.

If she were to go by her feelings alone, she would have spent all her time with Mr. Vance and Lord Lymington could ride off on his horse who threw shoes with nary a backward glance.

That, though, she could not do. If she indulged her feelings and inclinations now, she might find sometime in future that she deeply regretted it. After all, Mr. Vance's grandfather had not been a gentleman until he was made one by the crown. It was doubtful his estate was large, he was too recent to have any deep connections in society, and he did not have powerful relatives. He had no net. If things were to go wrong, there would be nobody to catch him.

Her father, as poorly as he managed things, had been bailed out several times by relatives and likely would be again. Even their neighbor, Lord Bertridge, had offered to lend her father money and help him execute a plan to restore the estate. That was the advantage of being an earl from an old family with blood relatives far and wide. That was what Mr. Vance did not have.

Isabel would not mind becoming a baroness under the right circumstances, but she *would* mind becoming a baroness standing on unsteady ground.

She wished for solidity. For surety. For a very large and sturdy net. She had all but said so to Mr. Vance last night at the pianoforte.

She must find a way to like Mr. Vance less and like Lord Lymington more.

Suddenly, she laid her toast down and said, "Oh dear, I am a goose."

Betsy, who had been organizing a pile of gloves, said, "What have you done, Lady Isabel? I'll fix it, whatever it is."

"Oh no, Betsy, I am afraid you cannot fix this. I have spent the past half hour thinking about the unsuitability of a certain gentleman and how I ought to drive him off."

"That doesn't sound very goose-like to me," Betsy said.

"Yes, well, I am afraid it is. The gentleman I was considering driving *away* has not made particular intentions known that he planned on driving *in* other than a pretty compliment he's probably handed out many times. It is all too likely he does not have the faintest of interests."

"I do not see why he wouldn't," Betsy said.

"He is very handsome and seems exceedingly genial. I suspect he is very popular in London."

"Well, if he is unsuitable, best cement that in your mind now. Then you'll be ready to drive him out if he attempts to drive in."

Betsy was right. She must only make a firm decision and follow it without thinking about it all the time. Without thinking about *him* all the time.

She must make that decision today, as she was certain to see him again this evening. Viscountess Rembly was hosting a ball and the duchess had promised they would go.

As it was likely that the ball was to be another opportunity to throw Miss Rightstone and Mr. Vance together, he would of course attend.

Isabel wondered what he thought of the proposed match. She had not noted any signs of affection coming from Mr. Vance in Miss Rightstone's direction. In fact, she got the sense that he was put off by the lady, despite the viscountess heavily hinting that an engagement was in the works.

But perhaps he was of a practical mind, as she was herself. The duchess had said the Miss Rightstone's history and dowry were precisely what a new-to-society baron would require and that he would certainly see that.

Perhaps he *had* seen that.

The idea irked her, though doing the sensible thing was exactly what she planned for herself.

She did not fail to see the irony of it.

CHAPTER SIX

HARRY WAS AT once looking forward to the Remblys' ball and dreading it. He had, at first, declined the invitation. The lady and her mama might chase him round the town, but he would not do anything to actually express a particular interest.

He did not wish to be presented to Miss Rightstone on a silver platter, in her own house, and had determined that this would be one of the times he would confound the duchess by declining to comply with her wishes. After all, Miss Rightstone was unlikely to need him there. It was her own family's ball, her card would fill, and somebody would act the gallant and take her into supper.

That had been his decision. However, the duchess, so little liking to be crossed, had found the temerity to turn up to his house regarding it.

At first, he could not fathom what she did there as there seemed to be no point to the visit. She'd spent a deal of time outlining her shopping plans for the morrow.

Lady Isabel was to choose several new bonnets befitting a Plantagenet. Harry certainly hoped not, as he thought a Plantagenet headpiece, stiff and reaching for the sky, would not suit the lady at all.

Then the duchess spoke of a proposed visit to Rundell and Bridge to receive a long-awaited tiara that she and Mr. Rundell had designed between them. Apparently, this headpiece was to be of gold and contain some of the best emerald stones in England. It would perhaps have the unfortunate effect of reminding Lady Featherstone that her emerald brooch was, after all, just a brooch. But that could not be helped.

Harry was well aware of Lady Featherstone's brooch, as was everybody in Town. She took great pride in it, having won it at one of Ryland's mystery suppers. He mused that this group of lady friends were more like spies for enemy nations—never revealing themselves entirely, always presenting with a smile, but working to get the better of one another. Except for poor Lady Redfield, of course, who could not get the better of a flea.

After a thorough description of the gold setting of the tiara, the duchess had dramatically reached her hand toward the table, and then seeing nothing there had pulled it back again. He thought, if he were not mistaken, that she had pretended to reach for a teacup and then acted as if she'd been taken by surprise to recall that none had yet been offered.

Harry suppressed a sigh and rang the bell to order a tea tray. He was beginning to wonder when the lady planned on leaving. Perhaps he should set a dinner place for her as well?

Tea finally turned up while the duchess enumerated the emerald stones, their weights, cuts, and clarities, that would be set in her astounding new tiara.

After the door was closed and the tea was poured, the lady did an about face from shopping and droned on and on about the duties of participating in society. This tedious lecture culminated in how put out Lady Rembly was to discover that he had declined her invitation.

Now they were getting to the real reason for the visit. He let her ramble but did not reply.

She then out and out said that they all had hopes that he would marry Miss Rightstone.

His look of incredulity must have been apparent, as she then hurried to lay out all the reasons why it would benefit him.

Then *he* informed *her* that he had no need of the lady's dowry, did not need that much of a leg up in society, and had done her the favor of sometimes taking Miss Rightstone into supper because he did not think she'd have any takers otherwise.

Lady Rembly, if she wished to marry off her daughter, ought to take her in hand and for the love of heaven get that fan away from her.

The duchess had appeared stunned to hear it. At least, he supposed that was what it was. She'd risen, then staggered, then sat back down.

Harry presumed this was the end of his being invited to places at her urging.

"But surely, you have paid Miss Rightstone some attention."

"No more than any other lady," Harry said. "Last season I took her into supper three times out of the fifteen balls where I encountered her, and all at your request. I am perfectly amenable to doing a favor where I can, but a wedding is really a step too far to ask."

"Mr. Vance," she said, hardly above a whisper, "I have encouraged Lady Rembly. I was certain you would see the sense… why do you not see the sense?"

"The sense?" Harry asked. "What sense could there possibly be in chaining oneself to a lady who is often drunk, and even sober is of vile temperament? Miss Rightstone will not marry until she encounters a gentleman entirely *lacking* in sense."

"But—"

"There is no 'but' or 'however' or 'though,'" Harry said firmly.

The duchess stared hard at her teacup and Harry was all but certain she was looking for a way out of the mess she had created through her own highhandedness.

"Now listen," she said, "Lady Rembly cannot take in this news all at once. In one blow, as it were. She is a rather nervous creature, particularly on this subject. It must dawn on her slowly while I try to…dig up somebody else. Do come to the ball and take Miss Rightstone into supper."

Harry had been on the verge of saying no when another idea came to him. "I'll do as you ask, if you do not mind me taking a dance with Lady Isabel."

"Lady Isabel?" the duchess said with a small laugh. "I'll leave that up to her. I should warn you though, she has very high aspirations. A barony, a *new* barony, well, it will not do at all. She's said so quite decisively."

"Yes, she's told me all about it," Harry said.

"Has she?" the duchess said, nodding approvingly. "Excellent. Again, I leave her choice of dance partners up to her. She is nothing if not filled with good sense. You will come, though?"

"Very well."

He did not know precisely what he would say to Miss Rightstone, but if the duchess and her mother had been putting ideas in her head that must be corrected.

Miss Rightstone had made vague references about things like what a husband should know about her. But that did not signify, she did that with every gentleman she could corner.

For a while, she'd been on the hunt for Ryland with the same sort of nonsense. Two years ago, she'd handed Blackwood a list of things she liked that he could study at his leisure. She'd even tried it out on Bertridge, enumerating what she would require from a husband, though that had only been one time. The look of consternation on Bertridge's face would have been enough to penetrate even Miss Rightstone's less than perceptive mind.

Further, was it not his duty to rescue Lady Isabel from a life wasted with Lymington? Even though she did not appear to wish to be rescued?

He rather thought it was.

In the meantime, the duchess had very helpfully outlined her plans for the following day. While he could not fathom where she was to go looking for a Plantagenet-worthy bonnet, he knew perfectly well where Rundell and Bridge and her fabulous tiara were located.

Perhaps he would take his horse out on the morrow, in the

vicinity of 32 Ludgate Hill.

CARLSON HAD FOR some days now felt a sense of impending doom. He knew the cause perfectly well, as it had happened to him more than a few times over the years.

The duchess was at risk of experiencing a disappointment.

His mistress had her mind firmly made up that Lady Isabel and Lord Lymington were to be a match. A brilliant match, secured by her own hand.

And yet, Carlson could not avoid what he'd seen at the dinner.

First, Lady Isabel had taken Mr. Vance as Lord Lymington. Then, the looks between those two people at table. If Mr. Vance was not staring at Lady Isabel, then Lady Isabel was sneaking glances at Mr. Vance.

It was perhaps not ideal that the chosen partners for those two people were less than compelling. Why could not Lord Lymington look a little less rumpled and why could he not talk of anything but horses? Why could not Miss Rightstone just stop talking, period? The lady was comely, but once she spoke, well, it was rather unfortunate.

It was also unfortunate how many times she gave the footmen meaningful looks, no doubt wishing her wine glass to be refilled.

What *was* fortunate, he supposed, was that he'd already directed his footmen to ignore her hints. This was not the first time he'd served Miss Rightstone at dinner and on no account should Mr. Vance witness just how off the track she could go. Not on his watch, at least.

He really felt that Lady Isabel had no interest in Lord Lymington and Mr. Vance had no interest in Miss Rightstone.

Why could not they all cooperate with his duchess? Did they

not understand how little she favored being crossed? Did they not know that the lady's elevated place in the world prevented her from perceiving that she was in peril of a disappointment?

He was very afraid this circumstance would be similar to when the duchess had not become Queen Charlotte's Mistress of the Robes, though she had fully expected to. Rather, she had lost out to the Marchioness of Bath.

What awful times those had been. The circumstance had only been got over when the duchess realized it was she, herself, who had the most refined sense of what nobility really was and began pronouncing things noble or ignoble. The Marchioness of Bath being the first to be named lacking in all noble qualities.

What was to be the way out of *this* terrible circumstance, though?

HARRY HAD BEEN slowly walking in the vicinity of 32 Ludgate Hill for hours. His reason for being in this neighborhood, if he were asked for one, was there being a tailor at number 38. There *was* a tailor there, just not his own.

He'd made some guesses on what time of day the duchess would choose to retrieve her jaw-dropping and no doubt noble emerald tiara. It would not be very early—a lady like that no doubt slept in and breakfasted leisurely. It would not be too late, as the Remblys' ball was this evening and he assumed a lady had much preparation in dress and probably liked to rest ahead of time too.

He'd chosen the early afternoon.

Of course, that still encompassed more than a few hours. He'd arrived just after one and now it was closing in on three.

He'd paid a shopkeeper's boy to take his horse, water it, and find some shade. There was no point in them both expiring in the heat.

Harry began to wonder if all he'd come away with for his efforts was an intimate understanding of this part of Ludgate Hill. He'd been watching a young lad for quite some time who he was certain was up to no good. He did not seem to work anywhere, and his clothes were near in tatters. He mainly leaned against shop windows until he was chased away from them.

He was bound to make off with something before the day was through. Though, if it were a loaf of bread or some other foodstuff, Harry fully intended on turning a blind eye.

Harry had just come out of a bookseller's little shop. He'd bought a book on geography to account for his lingering there. Suddenly and much to his relief, as it was getting unbearably hot, he saw the duchess' carriage come to a stop in front of Rundell and Bridge.

Her diabolical footmen had the carriage doors open and the duchess and Lady Isabel were out and into Rundell's before he could manage to casually encounter them.

No matter. They were here now, and he would be nearby when they ventured out again.

He thought it would be wise to be lurking near the back end of the lady's carriage. Else, the coachman would surely perceive what he was doing. Depending on how familiar his relationship with the duchess was, he might well tell her of it.

Of course, it had been the duchess herself who'd told him where she would go this day. She would understand what he'd done easily enough, but best that she could not prove it with reports of him lounging about outside.

The boy who had been doing a lot of lurking himself, though not in pursuit of a lady, leaned against the far column of Rundell's.

"Off with you, now," Harry said quietly.

The boy shrugged and took himself to the column on the opposite side of the door into the shop.

Harry had hoped the ladies would not be in there too long, as they were only meant to receive an item already ordered, but he'd been standing round for almost a half-hour.

He stole a glance through the shop windows from time to time. It was always the same view—the duchess admiring herself in a glass, resplendent in her new tiara.

Harry could help but laugh at the sight. The tiara was positively ponderous. It was as if the duchess had said, "Mr. Rundell, I do not care how heavy it is, I do not care if I can barely hold my head up. I wish for all the gold and emeralds in the world to be perched upon my head."

As for poor Lady Isabel, she was left to do an endless amount of smiling and nodding. The footman standing in attendance did his own nodding and Harry assumed the duchess' entire household revolved round showing approval for the duchess' every word and action.

Now, though, the moment had come. He'd just spied Mr. Rundell take the tiara from the duchess' hands and place it in its velvet-covered box.

Harry straightened up and waited for his moment.

He peeked in again and saw the footman step forward to take the box, but the duchess waved him off. *She* took the box from Mr. Rundell and held it as if it contained the crown jewels which, he supposed, she thought it did.

The footman, seeing he was not to carry the box, raced to the door. It swung open, and the duchess sailed out of it.

"Ah! Your Grace!" Harry said, striding toward them as if he'd been just coincidentally passing by.

"Mr. Vance," she said coldly.

"Lady Isabel," he said. "Charming to encounter you at such a chance moment."

The duchess stared at him, no doubt wishing to communicate that she was not at all fooled.

At that moment, the boy, who had all along seemed rather desultory in his wanderings, leapt away from the column that had propped him up. He was between the duchess and her carriage in a slice of a second, grabbed her velvet box, and made off with it.

The duchess screamed. Lady Isabel gasped.

The footmen looked terrorized, and the coachman clambered down from his box.

Blast.

He'd have to get that ridiculous tiara back.

Harry set off after the boy, his legs pumping as fast as he could make them go. The coachman had begun the chase too, but the man was portly and would not last long at it.

He must just keep the boy in sight. A lad like that might be able to run fast, but not for long. He would be too underfed for too many years to have any real stamina.

The boy made turns this way and that, down small side streets. Not once did he make the mistake of taking a dead end. It was clear he knew the layout of the town well enough. Harry had an idea of where he was headed. Regardless of the many turns, they kept going roughly in the same direction. They were going west.

The fellow was headed to the vicinity of the Seven Dials. He'd plan to go right into the Rats' Castle and disappear into its warren of dark streets and refuse-strewn lanes. There, a gentleman had better think twice before entering if he planned on leaving again.

The boy was running out of his wind though. He was slowing and Harry was gaining.

Harry got close enough and grabbed the back of tattered his coat. They fell in a heap, rolling on the cobblestones, and were soon surrounded by curious onlookers.

EVERYTHING HAD HAPPENED so fast that it had taken Isabel some moments to even comprehend it. One minute, they'd been in the shop, the next they'd encountered Mr. Vance and her stupid heart had leapt. Not a moment later, a street urchin was making off with the duchess' new tiara.

Isabel watched in some admiration as Mr. Vance did not hesitate to set off after the thief. Rumson had gone too, but he'd exhausted himself very quickly. Mr. Vance had kept going until both he and the boy turned a corner and were seen no more.

The duchess had been every emotion that was not happy—frightened, angry, faint with the shock, insulted, and grief-stricken. It had taken some convincing to get her into the carriage and leave the scene.

Isabel had assured her that Mr. Vance would do everything possible to retrieve her tiara. There was nothing helpful they could do by standing about. Mr. Rundell had promised the duchess that he would remain on the scene, and he was certain the boy would be caught and hanged.

The duchess had seemed to take comfort in the idea of a hanging.

Then Rumson had further urged the lady, noting that she'd got very pale and it could not be good for her health. The duke would not like to see her in such a state.

Finally, she was resigned to the loss of her lovely emeralds, as she had no faith whatsoever in Mr. Vance, and consented to go home.

Isabel had poured her a large glass of sherry when they'd reached the safety of the duchess' drawing room and that did seem to help the lady regain her composure.

"I am sure I do not understand what is happening to this town," the duchess said. "To be robbed. I, a duchess, in broad daylight. Well, it would not have happened if Mr. Vance had not paused us on the street."

"You cannot blame the gentleman, though," Isabel said. "It might have been any acquaintance you had encountered on the street."

The duchess did not look convinced, and Isabel had the feeling she was determined to blame somebody for this disaster.

"Just think," Isabel said, "you know ever so many people.

Everybody wishes to be acknowledged by you when you are seen out and about."

In a mollified tone, the duchess said, "That is true, I suppose. Is there anyone of any significance who does not know me? Of course not."

"And then, just consider," Isabel pressed on, "of all those people who clamor for your notice, how many of them could have chased after the boy with such speed?"

"I could have done so myself, were I not in a state of shock," the duchess said.

Isabel did not doubt that. The lady was rather athletic. Instead, she said, "There is still a chance you may get the tiara back. We must be hopeful."

The duchess sniffed. "If I do, it will be no thanks to Mr. Vance."

Isabel did not know what to make of that statement. If the tiara was somehow recovered, it would be entirely thanks to Mr. Vance.

❯❯❯❯◅◅◅◅

HARRY HAD TACKLED the boy to the ground and wrestled the jewel case from his hands. As he'd hauled him up, it was no surprise at all that a crowd began to gather. There was nothing the citizenry of London liked more than a collaring of a thief.

Harry looked down at the boy, who looked up at him with round terrified eyes. He had a right to be terrified. If he were not hanged, the best he could hope for was a commutation. His life was, effectively, over.

"I'll go for the magistrate," a round-bellied tradesman said authoritatively.

Harry looked him over. The fellow's middle was fairly bursting out of his waistcoat. He had very obviously never gone hungry, as the lad he'd just chased down most certainly had.

"I will take him," Harry said.

"You'll need some men with you," the fat tradesman said, "lest he slip out of your grip. These young thieves are crafty."

Harry drew himself up and counted on his air of a gentleman to manage the situation. "Thank you for your courtesy, but I require no assistance whatsoever. Stand aside."

The crowd, not knowing he was only to be a lowly baron, rather than a duke, did step aside. Harry pulled the boy along as fast as he could, leaving the concerned citizens behind.

"This is what you will do," he said to the young scoundrel. "While I retrieve my horse, you will make your way to 28 Bedford Square."

The boy looked up at him slyly and said, "I am to take *myself* to the magistrate?"

"That is my address," Harry said sternly. "Ask for Smith. Tell him Mr. Vance sent you and tell him to throw you in a tub. You had better do as you are told. This is your one chance in life. You will not get another."

Harry let go of the waif. Seeing he was free, the boy looked exceedingly surprised. He tipped his cap and set off jogging. He was going in the right direction, but Harry had no idea if he would actually turn up or not.

Nor did he know what to do with the boy if he did.

For now, though, the duchess must have her unwieldy emerald and gold tiara.

CHAPTER SEVEN

ISABEL HAD BEEN seated at the sofa next to the window, wishing that she would see the duchess' tiara miraculously arrive to the house. She prayed that Mr. Vance had somehow managed to get it back. It seemed almost impossible. How could a man catch a fleet-footed and desperate young thief? Still, she must hope.

As for the duchess, her opinions had wandered all over the world. There were moments when the tiara was lost forever. Then by turns, perhaps it would somehow come back, no thanks to Mr. Vance. Then occasionally wondering how her duke would take it if she were to order another one made. And once even decrying the lack of it to make her point to Lady Featherstone.

What that point was supposed to be, Isabel was not at all clear on. That it had something to do with Lady Featherstone's emerald brooch was clear enough. But what was the message? That the duchess had more emeralds?

She heard the clatter of hoofbeats come to a stop in front of the duchess' house.

Isabel leapt up and pulled the curtains aside.

There he was. Mr. Vance. And he carried the jewel box.

"He's got it!" she cried. "Duchess, Mr. Vance has got your tiara!"

The duchess hurried to the window to confirm the idea.

They both watched Mr. Vance dismount and hand the reins to a footman.

He had such energy! He'd just chased a thief for…how long? It might have been a half mile, or even more. And yet, he looked as if he'd done nothing at all.

Mr. Vance tucked the box under his arm and bounded up the steps. He disappeared from view.

The duchess hurried back to her place. "Do sit down, Isabel. We should not appear eager or as if we have been waiting for the gentleman to appear."

Isabel did as she was told, though she nearly burst with laughter. Of course they had been waiting and of course they were eager. How could they have been anything else?

The poor duchess. She was so fortunate to get her tiara back. But now, she would have to thank Mr. Vance, which was bound to be a trial.

Isabel hoped the lady would not choke on the words that must be spoken.

The drawing room doors opened and Carlson came in with the box. There was no Mr. Vance coming in, though.

Isabel leaned back to glance out the window. He was out of the house and mounting his horse again.

He had not come in. Rather, he trotted away looking very cheerful.

Isabel felt a pang that he had not come in.

"Your Grace," Carlson said, walking in with the box as if he were delivering the Holy Grail, "Mr. Vance has just returned your tiara. He wishes me to say that the thief was caught and that he does not impose upon you personally because he is certain you have been through an upsetting ordeal and would not wish for visitors at this delicate time."

He was so thoughtful and kind, Isabel thought.

Then, she had another idea. Mr. Vance seemed to be a very astute individual. He would have guessed that the duchess would have a terrible time thanking him for the return of her tiara and he had very kindly relieved her of the duty. At least for now. Though, really, the duchess would have to thank him sometime.

It was very generous.

"Well," the duchess said, her tone far more sanguine than Isabel had thought it might be, "I imagine he cannot face me just now. After all, if he had not stopped us…"

Goodness. Perhaps the duchess would not bother to thank him at all.

Isabel would, though. It had been a rather heroic thing he did.

Though, it did pain her when she thought of Lord Lymington in similar circumstances. She was very afraid the duchess' tiara would have certainly been lost forever.

⟫⟫⟫⟪⟪⟪

HARRY HAD EXPERIENCED a rather fuller day than he had anticipated. He had only wished to arrange a chance encounter with Lady Isabel, but had ended up rescuing the duchess' tiara, and the thief who took it to boot.

The boy had, by some miracle, turned up at the house as he had been told to do. Smith had not been enthused to see him, but did scrub him down as he had been directed.

Or, somebody scrubbed him down. Likely one of the junior footmen had been assigned the chore.

Clothes had been got from one of the grooms and Smith had promised the provider of said clothes that the master would buy him a new set.

By the time he had arrived home after returning the duchess' tiara, the boy, now known as Ben, had been cleaned up from what he was. He'd also been fed, and Smith said he ate like a heathen and put away enough for two full-grown men.

Harry had conducted an interview with the little fellow, who appeared grave and silent when he was escorted into the library. He demanded to hear an accounting of how the boy ended up robbing people on the street and what on earth he thought he was going to do with a duchess' tiara.

Ben had been living with only his father, his mother long-dead. His father had left for work one morning and never came back. After a day went by, Ben had looked in their one set of drawers and found it empty. His father had gone somewhere, leaving him behind, and it did not look as if he was ever coming back. It would only be days before the landlord would come knocking, looking to be paid, and then he'd be off to the workhouse.

Hunger driving him forward, Ben began to steal loaves of bread, apples from carts, and anything else he could get his hands on.

"I understand stealing food," Harry said, "everybody has to eat. But what would you do with a tiara? What flash house could find the funds to pay for it, even if they had the nerve to touch such a high-profile item? How could they resell it? You stole jewelry from a duchess."

Ben had sighed and said, "How should I know she was a duchess? Anyhow, there was a man nearby the Seven Dials what was showing me how to steal watches and whatnot and then he'd feed me, and I could sleep on the floor with the other lads."

Harry nodded. There were places like that too many to count. Though, he could not imagine that whoever this man was, he'd sent the boy out and said, "Grab something expensive from a rich-looking lady."

"But then I had an idea," Ben went on. "Instead of going on like that, stealing small things day after day, I would just steal one big thing. See? I got less chance of getting caught if I do it less. Then I saw that lady struttin' round the shop with that crown on her head and I thought, I could get two pounds for it. *Two* pounds, mind—I wouldn't take less. That'd keep me for a while. Then, I'd go steal another big thing."

"Two pounds?" Harry asked.

"Not a farthing less," Ben said proudly. "I was prepared to haggle viciously."

"That piece you stole likely cost seven or eight *hundred*

pounds."

Ben was rather staggered by that information, never having considered such a sum in his life. Finally, he said, "What ya hint at, I reckon, is that I went a little *too* big."

"Rather," Harry said drily.

"Live and learn," Ben said, shaking his head.

Harry thought him an odd little creature, but what could one expect from a nine-year-old who had nobody to manage him? He determined to put Ben in the stables as a new hand. If there were anybody who could keep him walking in straight lines, it was Jakes. His coachman was a barrel-chested beast of a man with a voice that could carry to China. He did not brook nonsense.

Harry's last words to Ben were, "If you dare steal from *me*, I will be inclined to beat you senseless. I will not have to though, as Jakes would have already done it."

Ben had nodded gravely and said, "So that's the lay of the land."

"Yes, that's the lay of the land. If you are smart, you will work hard and work your way up. You could end up a coachman yourself in some years' time. *If* you work at it."

"I ain't afraid of work," Ben said, his tone carrying a hint of defiance. "It ain't easy stealing, you know. That is hard work, I don't mind sayin' it."

"I'll take your word for it."

Now, having dispensed with Ben's future, Harry had finally gone up to dress for the Remblys' ball.

"Whatever you judge as the best of my new dress coats, I'll wear that," Harry said to his valet.

"The dark blue ordered from Mr. Weston has come in. Miss Rightstone will be in transports," Smith said drily.

"If she would transport herself back to the countryside, that would be very convenient. Though not likely."

"But why are you going? Do not tell me that confounded duchess has pushed you into it."

"She has, but not for the reasons she thinks," Harry said with a smile. "The duchess has possession of something I want."

Smith frowned. "Do be sure you do not accidentally wed Miss Rightstone in the midst of playing confound-the-duchess chess. Your staff would decamp en masse before serving such a harridan. We all saw how she spoke to Mr. Gregory that day when she and her mama called here last season."

Harry nodded. He had been in some disbelief himself. Gregory was an experienced and dignified sort of butler and Miss Rightstone had spoken to him as if he were a young and unseasoned footman. In front of the actual young footmen he employed.

It had been a testament to her lack of manners and lack of care for other people.

To soothe his butler, and himself, Gregory had been given strict instructions that if those two people darkened his door again, he was not at home. Further, the butler had been directed that he might employ his loftiest and most condescending tone while he relayed that disappointing news.

"Yesterday," Harry said, "the duchess informed me that she had decided I ought to marry Miss Rightstone. *I* informed the duchess that her decision is lunacy having nothing to do with me and she'd best look in another direction."

"Does she believe you, though? Does she even care what your opinion is, as it does not align with her own?"

"She may not give a farthing for my thoughts, but she has been informed of them and may ignore them at her peril."

"I see. Dare I inquire what the duchess has that you want, as it is not Miss Rightstone?" Smith asked.

He smiled to himself. Smith *always* dared to inquire and Harry had his reasons for not minding it much. Neither his grandfather nor his father had bothered with society. His father rarely came to Town and only to do business.

Harry had decided to change their mode of going on. He wished his future sons and daughters to be able to walk down every path in life. However, he'd not been at all acquainted with the habits of the *ton* outside the few families of his neighborhood. Smith had been, though, and he'd had the good luck to hire him.

His valet had guided him through that first season, dodging all sorts of mistakes he might have made and ensuring his clothes were appropriate for every occasion. Smith subscribed to the Brummel mode—unstudied and subtle, but very fine fabric that was very precisely cut.

He and Smith had never really had a master and servant relationship. It had begun as tutor and student and was now rather more like friends.

"Her name is Lady Isabel Beaufort, she has no intention of having anything to do with a lowly and newly-acquired barony, and I am struck by her."

"Struck? You? I see the plot thickens," Smith said. "Yes, Mr. Weston's blue coat will do very well."

THE DUCHESS CHATTERED away as the carriage trotted down the darkened streets in the direction of Lady Rembly's ball. Her tiara was firmly on her head and she seemed to think no more of its temporary disappearance.

It really was something to behold. It was not precisely to Isabel's taste, as she would have preferred a silver or platinum setting, and perhaps a much more delicate composition. Isabel was not quite sure of its weight, but it looked exceedingly heavy. She hoped the duchess did not get a headache from it.

Isabel glanced down at her dress, which she far more adored. She could hardly keep her eyes from it. Madame LeGrange had brought over three more gowns that afternoon and Isabel had chosen a divine midnight blue silk. The material was the very best and the cut was refined—it was not ruined with overdecoration. It was the sort of dress she had conjured in her imagination during those days of endlessly mending her very worn muslins.

"Now, my dear," the duchess said, "have you formed an opinion on Lord Lymington?"

"An opinion?" Isabel said, taken off guard by the question.

"Oh, I know you do not know him well enough at this point to absolutely decide, but what do you think? He is to be a duke, after all. You could begin your adult life as a marchioness and end as a duchess. Old family, high rank, secure as England itself."

"That, of course, is precisely what I would wish," Isabel said slowly.

Sensing her hesitation, the duchess said, "I realize he talks about horses far too much, but those sorts of things can be managed satisfactorily."

"Can they?" Isabel asked. She had assured herself the night before that it must be so. But then she'd also pondered how one would manage it. She'd never been able to affect her father's habits one iota.

"I'll tell you a secret," the duchess said confidentially. "There were a few things that needed correcting when I wed the duke. Most unfortunately, he had an unnatural taste for Indian spices and his cook made things to his taste. My mouth was on fire for a month before I remedied that problem."

"And now he no longer favors those spices?" Isabel asked.

"Oh no, he likes them just as much as ever. However, he mostly just seasons his own plate these days so the rest of us do not go up in flames. Goodness, the man even puts pepper sauce on his eggs in the morning."

"How did you accomplish the change?" Isabel asked.

"Straightforward," the duchess said, "that's always the way to go. I said—'Duke, you are coming close to watching my hair go up in a blaze with all these curries.' He understood me perfectly and Cook was promptly informed of the new arrangements."

Isabel was surprised that the duke's habits were modified with so little fuss.

"You might have noticed Carlson bringing the duke a tray with an array of porcelain containers. I really do not know what exactly is in them other than they are dreadful. If it's some particular dish he wants, Cook makes it separately. It was worked out satisfactorily for both of us."

What if Lord Lymington could be taught to make better conversation? She would still be left with his looks, which she was not attracted to at all. But how much did that matter, really? Looks faded. Security did not. As well, a pleasant conversational-ist might make up for a whole host of other deficiencies.

"Do you think I should be so forward, though?" Isabel asked. "It would be bold to correct the lord on any matter when we are so recently acquainted."

"I do not say you come at it without thought. Do some gentle fishing and then if he seems amenable, tell him of your require-ments." The duchess sighed. "Goodness knows, *somebody* is due to tell Lord Lymington that nobody cares about his horses!"

"Perhaps I will mention it," Isabel said, "if the right oppor-tunity presents itself."

"Yes, do, my dear." The duchess heaved a heavy sigh. "That is, I am afraid, the least of the problems presented to me today."

"Does something else trouble you, Duchess?" Isabel asked warily, hoping it was not anything regarding the tiara and how it must be Mr. Vance's fault.

"It is not something, it is *someone*. Mr. Vance."

Oh dear. The duchess had thoroughly convinced herself that Mr. Vance was responsible for her stolen tiara, though he was the only reason she'd got it back.

"Mr. Vance has positively refused to see that a marriage to Miss Rightstone would be to advantage. Yesterday, he looked me straight in the eye and said he was happy to do me favors when asked, but a wedding was entirely too far."

Isabel did not say anything. Her thoughts were far too busy to speak. It was nothing to do with the tiara. She was angry at him for failing to see the sense of wedding Miss Rightstone.

"He even had the nerve to decline the invitation to Lady Rembly's ball."

Isabel felt her spirits drop just the littlest bit to hear it.

"Naturally, I went to his house and demanded he come and take Miss Rightstone into supper."

Isabel had no notion she'd made such a visit. Or that a duchess could interfere with a gentleman's decisions on where he preferred to go. "So he comes after all?"

"Oh yes, he comes, though he had the temerity to demand that he be allowed to request a dance from *you!* Well, I said he could ask but it was entirely your decision. I also told him, in no uncertain terms, that you were destined for something far greater than newcomer Mr. Vance!"

"Oh, duchess, you did not in such terms…"

"No, not in those terms precisely, but he understood me all the same. He said you had already told him."

"I did not exactly tell him *that*," Isabel said, "but I did make clear my priority was stability."

"Never fear, Lady Isabel, he understood your meaning. And I hope he does not delude himself that I did not understand how he came to be in front of Rundell and Bridge yesterday. I mentioned I would go there. That stunt was entirely engineered and there goes my tiara."

Isabel was not certain whether she was pleased or alarmed to know that Mr. Vance had not been outside the jewelers by happenstance.

The carriage had come to a stop and a footman opened the door. Isabel felt a flutter inside of her. She was very sorry to find that flutter was not caused by Lord Lymington, as it should be.

But could it be? If she tried? And perhaps remade his conversation?

Certainly, it was at least possible. She must believe it was possible.

CARLSON SAT AT the head of the servants' table with his ale, ignoring the babble around him, which was as usual comprised of speculation and unfounded gossip. It had been a night of light work as the duchess and Lady Isabel had gone to a ball and the duke was off to his club. Though it had been light work, his thoughts weighed heavy upon him.

When the duchess had departed, the sky had been clear and the stars were out. That circumstance was rather different from the one he'd described to the duchess when she'd asked for a weather prediction earlier in the day.

He'd predicted a *vertical spout*, the sort of rain that comes straight down and is not blown about by wind. After all, it was England and one ought to have a pretty good chance of being right if one predicted rain.

The confounded weather! It had defied him again.

Prior to the duchess setting off in the carriage, Carlson had been forced to explain that the change of weather had likely been caused by overpopulated streams and rivers that fed into the ocean. The masses of fish pushed the currents in the wrong direction, which changed the wind direction. The rain that should have been coming down in London was now battering the North Sea.

If only fishermen would try harder to keep the stocks under control, these things would not happen! He could not be blamed for the failures of fishermen!

He'd called this particular error a rare *reverse windage*.

Somehow, the duchess had seemed perfectly satisfied with the explanation. Though, he'd detected the smallest smile from Lady Isabel.

How long could he go on like this, the predictor of weather who was almost always wrong?

Further, it seemed that Betsy, Lady Isabel's new maid, had a certain knack for predicting the weather just by looking out a window. How was she doing it?

"I'm telling you," Fleur said to Mrs. Pennington, "the duchess has it all arranged. Miss Rightstone is to marry Mr. Vance and Lady Isabel is to marry Lord Lymington."

"That may very well be," Mrs. Pennington said with a sniff, "I only say that Mr. Vance and Lady Isabel would make a dashing couple."

"Nobody can deny it," Jeremy said. "Vance is a specimen of a man and Lymington is a lump."

"The lumpiest," Brian concurred.

"Lumpity-dump-dump," the housekeeper said nodding.

"But he is to be a duke," Fleur said. "A *duke*, you realize."

"I realize it, but he's still a lump," Jeremy said, his features settling into obstinacy.

Carlson was certain he ought to step in and stop the conversation at once. It was not at all suitable for the footmen, or the housekeeper for that matter, to speak so disparagingly about a gentleman who would attain the highest rank.

Lymington really *was* a lump, though.

CHAPTER EIGHT

Harry had duly arrived to the Remblys' and, as promised, put himself down for Miss Rightstone's supper. Now that he understood that the duchess had encouraged Miss Rightstone and her mother to think of him as a future husband, he was determined to make himself clear to the lady.

It still amazed him that she had taken the thing so far. What he'd thought he had been doing was stepping in as a convenient partner for a lady who had a lack of them. Now, he'd found out they'd been preparing to catapult him into a church and rope him to Miss Rightstone forevermore.

It would never be. Miss Rightstone certainly was not *her*. Lady Isabel might be, though.

Had he not been so interested in Lady Isabel, he would surely have followed Carlson into the duchess' drawing room and enjoyed her forced thanks for returning her tiara. She would hate to do it and, as she so infrequently did a thing she did not like, it probably would have been entertaining.

Harry had not done that, though. But only out of consideration for Lady Isabel. Not the duchess.

Now, he had relocated himself away from Miss Rightstone in all haste and currently hung round near the coatroom, waiting for Lady Isabel to arrive. He had learned long ago that if one wished to be the first on a lady's card, one ought to be nearby where she would collect her card. A more unseasoned gentleman might hover round the front doors, but then what? Awkwardly follow the lady to the cloakroom like a footman wishing to relieve her of her coat?

"Vance," a powerful voice said.

He turned to find Lord Ryland and his lady. "Ryland. Lady Ryland," he said. They were a fine-looking couple and Harry rather got hope from their union. Ryland had avoided marriage for quite a few seasons, just as he had. Then, it seemed he'd met the one he'd looked for all along and things had moved speedily after that. The same could happen for him, could it not?

"Mr. Vance," Lady Ryland said, as her lord handed over her coat to a footman and collected her card. "I do hope you plan on attending my husband's mystery ball this year."

Lord Ryland had returned to them and handed his lady her card.

"I was surprised to receive the invitation," Harry said, "as I thought you did not favor attempting to solve a murder, Lady Ryland. The town was abuzz last season with the idea that last year's activities were changed to riddles to please you."

"That is correct," Lord Ryland said.

"I do not favor thinking about a murder at all," his lady said laughing. "But my lord has been so kind as to remove all mention of violence and mayhem from my notice for three hundred and sixty-four days of the year that I find myself agreeable to hearing of it on one day of the year. That mystery evening does make him happy and so I am happy too."

Ryland smiled indulgently at his wife.

"Of course I will come, then," Harry said.

"It is to be a complicated case," Lord Ryland said.

"It is *always* a complicated case, at least to me," Harry said. "Though, I suppose Lady Featherstone will prevail one way or the other."

Lady Ryland smiled and said, "I do hope it for her, as she enjoys it more than anybody, I think."

"Ryland," Harry said, "will you perhaps do me a favor in the seating? Will you sit Lady Isabel Beauford at my table? She is here with the Duchess of Stanbury this season."

Lord Ryland nodded.

"Did I hear my name spoken?" a distinctive voice said behind him. It was the duchess, and her tone did not sound amused.

Harry turned to find the duchess in question behind him, along with Lady Isabel, who looked positively smashing in a dark blue silk.

The duchess stared hard at him and he wondered if she thought he'd been talking of the theft of the tiara. He had no intention of spreading the tale, but then she did not know him so well as to know his boundaries.

However, he had no intention of revealing what he *had* been talking about either.

"I was just extolling the superiorities of your recent dinner, Your Grace," Harry said, hoping Ryland and his marchioness would not give him away.

The duchess nodded, seeming appeased by the notion. "My cook does know what he is about," she said.

The duchess introduced Lady Isabel to Lord and Lady Ryland with all the grandeur of a foreign diplomat presenting a princess at court. Harry had a feeling that might be for his benefit, a reminder that Lady Isabel was out of his range.

Lady Ryland said, "Lady Isabel, I will call on you, if I may. It seems rather a tradition amongst those of us the society has been kind enough to take in hand. Lady Langley, Lady Gresham, Lady Bertridge, Lady Blackwood, and myself write to each other often and see each other when we can. We are quite the club, and you must join in."

Lady Isabel nodded and said, "I would be delighted to see you, and it is most kind to think of including me."

She was all grace, Harry thought. She did not have that giggling or shy mien that so many ladies did when arriving to London for the first time. There was a maturity about her that prevented her from being ruffled.

"If I may, I will retrieve your card, Lady Isabel," Harry said. This chitchat was pleasant enough, but it was not getting him any closer to his real aim.

She nodded, though the duchess frowned at him. He was perfectly happy to pretend he had not noticed the duchess frowning.

Harry went to the counter where a footman was handing them out, retrieved the lady's card, and was back to the group in under a minute. Their conversation had moved on to Ryland's ball and Harry prayed that Ryland would have enough sense not to mention his recent request. The duchess would not find favor in his maneuvering to have Lady Isabel at his table.

He held Lady Isabel's card up and said, "May I?"

"Yes, of course, Mr. Vance," she said.

As he could not take supper, though how he would have wished to take supper, he put himself down for the first. The duchess could frown and fuss with her monstrous tiara all she liked about it.

ISABEL HAD BEEN so determined to like Mr. Vance less and like Lord Lymington more. Why did it seem near impossible to do?

The moment she'd seen him her breath had nearly caught. Good grief, he almost took her breath away.

How could he not have, though? He was attired so elegantly in his dress clothes, his coat outlining his broad frame and his neckcloth tied in a subtle and unstudied manner. His face was so handsome—those eyes, the shade of blue found at the deepest part of a clear lake.

And then, what seemed to be *inside* the clothes. He was powerfully built, as she could very well see from the width of his sleeves.

Isabel felt flushed and she could not decide if it were his striking person, or embarrassment that the duchess was so cool with him and apparently not intending on thanking him for the return of her tiara.

She admitted to herself that he, his presence, was the cause. He'd been chivalrous in setting off after the duchess' tiara and she thought that just now he might have been waiting for her nearby where she would collect her card. She could not know it, of course, but she felt it. He had, after all, waited for a lull in the conversation and then offered to retrieve her card for her. Then, she also knew that he would put his name down on it, as he'd bargained with the duchess to do so.

He was very much the man of action.

Mr. Vance had taken the first, and then bowed and moved on under the duchess' glare.

Isabel reminded herself of her plans. Her well thought-out and considered plans. He was a fine man, of course. But her future was at stake and she could not throw it away over what was certainly only a girlish infatuation.

Had she not once imagined herself desperately in love with Miss Cremerdon's older brother? Had she not made a cake of herself a dozen times in his presence—adoring his dark looks and brooding manner? She had been just fourteen and his gloomy mien had seemed the height of romance.

Of course, she eventually fell out of whatever nonsensical feelings she'd had as she got to be better acquainted with him. She had been won over by his looks and his air of mystery, but he turned out to be only a sullen and morose sixteen-year-old.

Mr. Vance was likely just the same, though there was nothing of the sullen and morose in him. She had only been bowled over by his looks and she must un-bowl herself this instant.

She'd nearly convinced herself of it when she'd been approached by Lord Lymington. He always seemed to look rumpled, even when well-dressed. He launched into some story about a horse until the duchess cut him off.

"Lady Isabel's supper is still free, Lord Lymington, but do not dally as it will not long remain so," she'd said.

Lymington had taken the hint. Or, the order, as it more sounded. He'd attempted to return to his story, but the duchess cut him off again by saying, "Save that delightful tale for supper, my lord."

The duchess had then taken her arm and guided her firmly away from the gentleman.

He really did not compare well to Mr. Vance. But then, somebody else might. Lord Lymington would not be the only eligible gentleman in town. Perhaps she would meet a man not quite as elevated as a duke's eldest son, but more attractive while remaining a sound choice.

Her card had been filled and all the gentlemen on it seemed genial. But they did not measure up to Mr. Vance. Surely somebody would, though? Surely?

Now, Mr. Vance had come to collect her. The moment had come, she would touch him.

He led her with confidence and experience. She could feel the strength of his forearm as she laid her hand on it. It was as hard as a stone. Of course it was. And Lord Lymington, if his looks were anything to go by, would have forearms of jelly.

"I find I must do the duty of thanking you for retrieving the duchess' tiara, as she has not had the opportunity to do so herself," Isabel said, hoping that would go some way toward excusing the lady's very deliberate oversight.

Mr. Vance smiled and said, "Very well composed, Lady Isabel. Though I am not particularly fooled. The duchess would find being in debt to me on any matter an impossible idea."

"Is that why you did not come into the drawing room to deliver it yourself?" she asked.

"Not quite," Mr. Vance said. "It was not that I was opposed to putting the duchess in an uncomfortable position. I would have been amused by it, as I think she is so rarely made uncomfortable. But I thought I'd rather not force you to sit through such an awkward play."

Isabel was exceedingly flattered, though determined not to show it. "Well, I am glad the thief was caught and others will be saved from having their belongings ripped from their grasp in broad daylight."

"Everyone will be safe enough from the little villain," Mr. Vance said, "but I did not turn him over to the magistrate."

"You did not?" Isabel asked.

"He was hungry and abandoned. He'd been stealing bread and such to keep himself alive. It then occurred to him that if he stole something bigger, he would not have to be out stealing every day. He imagined he could get at least two pounds for the *crown*, as he called it. He informed me that he would insist on two pounds and not a farthing less."

"Oh, goodness," Isabel said, laughing.

"In any case," Mr. Vance said, "I implore you not to tell the duchess, but I have taken the lad into my stables so he is no longer forced to wildly misjudge the value of items he might sell for bread. If she knew, she would likely send the magistrate to my door and the fellow would have no chance at all."

"That was very kind of you to do," Isabel said. "Of course, I will say nothing of it. Though, I hope he does not end up stealing from you."

"I think not. A boy like that knows very well when a chance has fallen in his lap. He will not throw it away. As well, my coachman will guide him as a father. A rather stern father. Ben, that is his name, will turn out quite all right."

It was so generously done! The boy had caused no end of trouble and she assumed Mr. Vance had been quite vexed by the time he'd caught up with him.

"I think you must know," he said, "that I bargained with the duchess to be allowed on your card. Though, had she refused I would have asked you anyway."

Isabel had not expected him to be so direct. She did not know what to say.

"I've been thinking about our conversation at the duchess'

dinner," he went on. "I imagine you seek stability as a response to the instability you have experienced thus far."

"Yes," she said, quietly. "That is so."

"Though," he said, "a lofty title will not protect you from that. Had it, you would not have experienced instability to begin."

"Any family may experience instability," Isabel said slowly, "from any number of causes. But regaining that stability often requires other family members, both close and distant, to step in and assist."

"And that wide web of connected relatives is what I do not have."

"I suspect not, though of course I cannot know it certain, Mr. Vance."

"Well, I do not mind admitting that I do not. My father married a local lady in our neighborhood. My mother was every bit a lady and very well respected, but she did not extend our reach in any particular way."

Isabel nodded. She had been sure that was the case. His family had no net.

"But I must say," he went on, "that I do not have the need for that sort of help."

"Perhaps not now, but in future…"

"Not ever," Mr. Vance said resolutely. "With good management, my estate will continue to provide and I intend on managing it well."

"It is precarious though," Isabel said, "to depend upon one man's efforts. What if you were to die? What would happen to your family then? Would the estate go to a trusted and reliable younger brother?"

Mr. Vance looked uncomfortable and did not answer. Isabel thought it was not the idea of his dying that perturbed him. There was no younger brother who might be counted on to do his duty and properly look after an older brother's widow. The estate was entailed and would go to some unknown and unpredictable person, she was certain of it. His widow would have nothing but her jointure and there was no more distant relation who might take the lady in.

It felt like the final nail in the coffin of her not very sensible inclinations. Mr. Vance's prospects were not just a little at risk for instability. He was a potential disaster. She must dismiss him from her mind. Even if she were to talk herself into going forward with someone in his circumstances, she knew herself well enough. She could not live with the day-to-day terror of the sword of ruin and poverty hanging over her head.

"For one thing, Lady Isabel, I have not the least intention of dying!"

"Nobody ever does," she'd said softly.

Mr. Vance, seeming to sense the conversation could not find any good direction to proceed in, changed the subject and they talked of more commonplace things for the rest of the dance.

Isabel was glad of it, though sorry for it too. She might have to dismiss him from her mind, but as she was dancing with him now, there was no reason she could not enjoy it. And she did enjoy it. He could be very amusing when he wished, and he asked her a lot of questions that led to merry conversation. She suspected there would come a time when the memory of this moment would be something she might pull out to examine on a lonely and rainy afternoon.

She parted from him regretfully, but with purpose in mind. Isabel paid close attention to her next partners, looking for that spark. That something.

She did not find it.

Before she knew it, she was being led into the dining room on Lord Lymington's arm.

Her dance with that gentleman had been got through. Lord Lymington was not terrible at the activity, but he was a rather lumbering creature. And, as she had suspected, his arm did not have the feel of stone.

Though, she admitted her imagination had gone rather far in

expecting jelly. It was simply more cushioned than Mr. Vance's had been.

"Ho, there, Ryland," Lord Lymington said as Lord Ryland led his lady into supper.

Isabel had been surprised to see that Lord Ryland had danced with his wife and now took her into supper. She had understood from her book on manners that it was not the done thing. But then, Lord Ryland also hosted a mystery ball about a murder each season, so she supposed he did not much care what the done thing might be.

"Lymington, how do you do?" Lord Ryland said. "May I present Lady Ryland, you would have known her last season as Lady Prudence Landry."

Lord Lymington bowed. "Of course I remember Lady Ryland. Charmed. I say, Ryland, did I tell you about my horse that throws shoes? His—"

"His name is MacBeth, he's descended from the Byerley Turk, he is a chestnut, he's thrown shoes six times in as many months, he cost eighty pounds, you bought him last year from Lord Gerald, and he is sixteen hands? That MacBeth? Yes, you have mentioned him."

Isabel suppressed a giggle that was part amusement and part embarrassment for Lord Lymington. Lord Ryland's response had taken her entirely by surprise.

Lady Ryland kept a serious expression, somehow, and only said, "That horse sounds like quite the handful."

Lord Lymington nodded eagerly at the comment and seemed poised to elaborate on what was already a long set of facts about the equine, but Lord Ryland smiled, nodded, and moved off with his bride.

They entered the dining room and found two open places, while a footman came round with a delightful hock. It was precisely what she would have chosen had she been hostess. Its fruity acidity would cut the richness of the white soup.

She might not know so much about wines had it not been for

the kindness of Lord Bertridge. He maintained an extensive wine cellar and regularly sent bottles to her father with a written note about its variety, qualities, and pairings. She had saved the notes and pieced together more from a book she'd found in the library, determined that she should not be caught up short on any subject.

As for her father's own wine cellar, that had been empty for over a decade.

She was just about to compliment the host's choice of wine when Lord Lymington said, "What Ryland *doesn't* know about MacBeth is that just two days ago he threw off *two* shoes. On the same day."

This really had to stop. Isabel did not know if this were the right time or whether or not Lord Lymington would be offended, but the duchess was right—somebody had to speak to the lord about his lack of conversation.

"I do not even know how he did it. MacBeth, I mean."

"Lord Lymington," she said firmly, "do you think Lord Ryland would be dejected upon understanding that he'd not heard about the two shoes?"

The lord's face screwed up, which Isabel prayed was a signal that he was thinking. "I am not sure," he said. "Though, I could always ask him."

"I bid you do no such thing."

"No?"

"No. Though, I will ask you a few questions, if you do not mind it."

"About MacBeth?"

"Certainly not. What do you read?"

"Well, I get a few periodicals I read over breakfast."

"Are they all about horses?"

Lord Lymington nodded.

"And what do you think about all day long? Politics? Music? Gaming? Estate management? Anything like that?"

Lord Lymington slowly shook his head. "No, nothing like

that." He suddenly brightened and said, "I suppose I think about horses, mainly."

"Clearly. Now, I do not wish to be unkind, but you must understand that other people do not care for your horses with the same…fervor that you do. For example, I like to sew. Would you be very engaged if I were to only talk about my sewing and my missed stitches and the thread I prefer?"

"Talk about sewing? Why?"

"Exactly. Do you see, Lord Lymington? You must broaden your conversation, it cannot all be about your horses. As well, if you *are* to tell a story, you ought to tell it just one time and not start over because you forgot a detail. If you've forgotten something, you just must live with it."

This seemed to be a lot of information for Lord Lymington. His eyebrows had been approaching each other and now they met at the top of his nose.

In a softer manner, she said, "I will help you if you wish it, as I think that underneath all of that horse talk, you are a very genial gentleman."

"Excellent, yes," Lord Lymington said, his brows retreating to their respective sides. "My mother has said something similar. She says I ought to marry soon but I'll never talk anybody into it at the rate I'm going."

Isabel felt a pang for Lord Lymington. "What does your father say about it?" she asked, rather afraid of what *he* might have said.

"Oh, we don't talk about it. We only talk about our stable," the lord said cheerfully.

Isabel suppressed a sigh. Of course they did. "I challenge you, Lord Lymington, to forgo mentioning horses for this entire supper."

If Isabel was at all competent at reading expressions, this suggestion had fallen hard upon the lord. He looked as if she'd just asked him to stab himself. He also looked as if he did not know where to start.

"For instance," Isabel said, "I find this wine delightful. I believe it to be German."

Lord Lymington desperately looked at his wine glass and grabbed it, taking a gulp. "I think you are right," he said with an air of triumph.

She looked at him encouragingly. He stared this way and that and then cried, "Oh wait, I know—what do you think of the weather?"

Isabel smiled. It was a start, anyway.

CHAPTER NINE

HARRY LIKENED LADY Rembly's ball to one of darkness and light. He had danced with Lady Isabel and it had been everything he thought it would be. She was so gloriously beautiful and graceful, and her manner was everything elegant.

He could have led her round the floor all evening.

He'd thought he would plough right in with his campaign to overturn the lady's notions of marrying high. It was security she really sought, not a title, and so he had attempted to make a case for that.

Though, it was clear enough that the lady had spent vast amounts of time thinking about security and all the ways it might go wrong. He had not given a thought to the idea that the estate was entailed, as he would surely have a son.

But, as the lady had so directly pointed out, what would happen to a wife if he were to die before a son arrived?

He had not said what would happen, but it was rather worse than she might imagine. The estate would go to his cousin Martin. The fellow was a farmer, he was coarse, and he was uneducated. He was all those things not for lack of opportunity, but for preference. Harry's father, the current baron, had offered to educate him but he'd paid no attention to his studies. He'd been offered some financial support so he might live as a gentleman, but he was not interested in that either.

What Martin liked to do was some desultory work on his

small farm that never produced very much, and then trundle down to the local tavern, get hideously drunk, usually start a fight, stagger home late at night, get up with a black eye, and start all over again.

Martin would destroy the estate one way or the other in a few short years. He certainly would not take any special care of his cousin's widow. His father had urged him to marry to avoid that disaster, but Harry had insisted he would hold out for *her*. He could not bear the idea of making a compromise and then taking this new wife to Town one season and encountering *her*. Of knowing he'd made a disastrous mistake in not waiting.

Harry had told Lady Isabel he did not have any plans on dying. Truth be told, he did not dare die until he had a son.

Her words had given him pause. Would it really be right to put Lady Isabel into such a situation? Even if the chances of him dying before a son arrived were remote, it *could* happen. Worse, once she became acquainted with his circumstances more closely, once she got a look at Martin, she'd have to live with the idea every day until sons were produced and had passed out of the usual childhood dangers.

But then, the thought of throwing over the idea of pursuing Lady Isabel struck him hard. The thought of giving her up, though he did not actually have her, struck Harry very hard indeed.

No. He simply would refuse to die under any circumstances and then all would be well.

Dancing with Miss Rightstone was the usual project to be got through, full of demands, fan hits, near insults, and strange innuendos.

Now he escorted her into the dining room. He could feel both Lady Rembly's and the duchess' eyes upon him. This could not continue to go on. He must be direct with Miss Rightstone. The duchess had meddled a step too far.

The lady accepted a glass of wine from a footman and promptly drained it. Harry had seen her do this before and was fairly certain she'd dispatch four or five more before the evening was out.

That she had a ghastly drinking problem might be one of her lesser challenges, though.

"Mr. Vance?" she said, holding up her empty glass.

He sighed and motioned to a footman. As the footman was employed by the lady's family, the young man did not seem too surprised at the rapidity of the request.

"Now, as I was saying earlier," Miss Rightstone said, "I simply can't abide an over-reserved and haughty manner. It grates on me, Mr. Vance. Positively grates."

"I see," Harry answered noncommittally. He had no idea who had got on Miss Rightstone's nerves this time, but she was generally irritated by two classes of people. One, those females who might be perceived as more attractive, and two, those gentlemen who did not give her what she considered her due.

"I mean really," she said, draining her glass, "who does she think she is? Does she think she is better than me because she is an earl's daughter? My mama says she is poor as a church mouse. And then of course, the hair. A very bold sort of color, far too red. And she dares look superior because…well I really do not know why. It grates, Mr. Vance. Positively grates."

As this diatribe went forward, it became clear that Miss Rightstone was directing her vitriol at Lady Isabel. The audacity of the lady! Lady Isabel was far superior to Miss Rightstone. She was far superior to every lady.

"I will get you another glass of wine, Miss Rightstone," he said in a grim tone. "I suspect you are going to need it."

Miss Rightstone, who paid so little attention to anybody else's changing tones and demeanors, only said, "Yes, do."

After the footman had filled her glass for a third time, Harry said, "Miss Rightstone, I have recently been informed by the duchess that she has encouraged you in the idea that there may be a match between us. I—"

"Oh yes, she has been very determined about it," Miss

Rightstone said, cutting him off. "But I warn you, Mr. Vance, I have not absolutely decided."

"There is nothing to decide," Harry said firmly. "The duchess has experienced a flight of fancy and attempted to make it fact."

"Nonsense," Miss Rightstone said, draining her glass and snapping her fingers for the footman to bring more wine. "My mama says the very same thing about it."

"Because she has been told it by the duchess," Harry said. "I am sorry that the duchess has inconvenienced you in such a manner, but the lady has never bothered to consult *me*. There is no match. We would not suit at all."

Miss Rightstone's features darkened dangerously. Harry had once seen her throw a wine glass at the head of a gentleman who took another lady into supper rather than her. Fortunately, it had missed the gentleman and hit the wall behind him. The viscountess had put it about that the stem of the glass had soap remaining on it and had slipped out of her daughter's hand. If that were so, it had been quite the energetic and hurling slip. He began to fear that a similar hurling might occur now.

"How dare you?" Miss Rightstone said. "You are a lowly…what? You'll only become a baron and your grandfather was in trade. Who do you think you are to be too good for a viscount's daughter? As it happens, I would never have lowered myself to accept you."

"We have a meeting of the minds, then," Harry said. "I happen to know that the duchess is busy finding someone more suitable for you than a lowly baron."

Miss Rightstone's ever changing moods took another turn. "Who? Who does she think?"

"I am not certain she knows yet."

In a guttural tone, she said, "He'd better be a marquess at least!"

"No doubt."

The next hour was spent trying to slow Miss Rightstone's drinking while she spoke of how it was sure to be a marquess, how Ryland would have been ideal had he not gone off and married some irritating lady, how Lymington might do if he would only shut up about his horses, how her looks were the superior of the season, and how grating this or that lady was.

When she rose after it was finally over, she would have fallen to the floor had Harry not caught her arm and held her up.

Later, the duchess cornered him and said, "Did you say something to her? Does she know of your unaccountable recalcitrance?"

"I did and she does," Harry said cheerfully. "My advice is, take the fan away, tell her to stop criticizing other ladies, and make the footmen cut off her wine."

He bowed and left the duchess to consider those pieces of advice.

ISABEL'S RIDING HABIT had been delivered. It was so lovely, a very dark green with marvelous pewter buttons. Her old habit had been a birthday gift from a generous neighbor and had been worn for many years, it had more patches and mending than anything else and did not fit her very well anymore. This was fresh and new and perfectly cut. It was wonderful.

She and the duchess had slept in very late this day and were to go riding in the park in the late afternoon. To her surprise, the duchess would take a horse too. In Isabel's own neighborhood, the matrons preferred the comforts of a carriage. But then, she supposed the duchess was no ordinary matron.

It was still too early to go, and Isabel sat in the drawing room with a book from the duchess' surprising collection. It was a gothic novel about a poor young woman named Annabelle who was trapped in a castle by a man who might be a murderer or a savior. Isabel was at a loss as to why Annabelle went there in the first place and why she had not taken the rather numerous opportunities to escape. She was afraid that she would have little sympathy for the lady if she met a bad end, which certainly could not be the author's intent.

Isabel closed the book and reflected on her own far more sensible goings-on. She felt she must be satisfied by the events occurring at the Remblys' ball. She had once and for all put any thought of Mr. Vance to rest—he was far too dangerous a choice. As for Lord Lymington, could he be made into something? Perhaps so. He certainly was willing and that must be seen as encouraging.

Her commonsense mind was in no doubt as to how matters stood. Her heart, though, was taking its time catching up. Her heart beat faster for Mr. Vance and there was nothing she could do about it. However, she was confident that her heart would see sense in its own time. She was no Annabelle, walking into danger without a lick of sense.

The duchess came into the drawing room and said, "There you are. Well, I've slept half the day away. Last evening was exhausting."

Isabel did not know why it should have been, as the duchess had spent most of the night in the card room.

"How did you get on with Lord Lymington?" the duchess asked.

"I spoke to him about his lack of conversation and he made an effort to converse on subjects other than his horses," Isabel said. "He was very willing to try, anyway."

"That is promising," the duchess said. "I cannot say anything about Miss Rightstone's prospects are going so well. Mr. Vance, on top of losing me my tiara, saw fit to inform Miss Rightstone that there was to be no match."

Isabel was rather fascinated by how the duchess' mind worked. Despite Mr. Vance having rescued her tiara, he was now firmly the cause of its disappearance.

She was determined not to think about the idea that he'd made clear he was not interested in Miss Rightstone. Who he preferred or did not prefer had nothing to do with her.

"He is infuriating," the duchess went on, "why did he not have the courtesy to give me time to dig up somebody else and gently steer Miss Rightstone and her mother in another direction?"

"*Can* you find somebody else?" Isabel asked. If the lady was indeed in her sixth season, it would seem that she must know everybody by now.

The duchess frowned. "That is indeed the problem. I am not a sorceress, after all. Oh, how I would like to strike out at Mr. Vance. How I would like to send letters flying out of the house and ordering everyone I know to cut him. I do not believe he is the slightest afraid of me and I do not like it."

"Can you do that? Make everybody cut him?" Isabel asked, thinking the idea rather awful.

"I could, but I will not. I must not draw any attention to Miss Rightstone's plight. If only the girl would…well, if she would only stop being so…her. She is comely and a viscount's daughter, coming with a sizable dowry. That ought to do it, if she would only…put her fan down and be quiet. Well, I do not know how we are to get her married."

Miss Rightstone's plight sounded more terrifying by the day. She could not allow such a thing to happen to her.

Of course, such a thing would never happen to her. The duchess would not bring her back season after season. If she did not make something of herself this season, she would likely find herself back in her father's house.

Carlson entered the drawing room with a tea tray. "Carlson," the duchess said, "what will we have for weather in the park?"

The butler laid down the tray, surreptitiously glancing out the window. "I believe, Your Grace, you shall have what is known as a *puffing easterly*. A mild temperature and gentle breeze."

"Excellent, that will be just the thing," the duchess said, appearing very sanguine over her butler's predictions.

"Naturally, Your Grace," Carlson hurriedly put in, "we must

just hope that the pods of dolphins off the coast of Brighton do not become too energetic, thereby creating a disturbance."

The duchess nodded knowingly. She said to Isabel, "The average person has no idea how much trouble the dolphins can stir up."

Isabel dabbed her napkin against her lips to stop herself from laughing. Could dolphins affect the weather? It did not seem likely.

She did not know much about predicting the weather herself, other than watching clouds gather and assuming it would rain. However, Betsy had told her that Carlson attempting to foresee future conditions was like a man stumbling round in the pitch dark with his hands waving in front of him.

"Carlson, have the horses brought round in an hour. That will allow us to finish our tea and change to our habits."

"Yes, Your Grace."

HARRY WAS STILL abed at three and had a tray sent up with a large pot of coffee. As Smith bustled round the room, brushing off a coat here and gathering things to be laundered there, Harry said, "I managed to unburden myself and burden myself, all in one night."

"Dare I inquire into the actual facts?" Smith asked.

"I spoke very directly to Miss Rightstone. She is under no further illusion that she will one day wake beside me."

Smith shivered. "What a notion. It would be akin to waking up next to Medusa each morning, you'd die all over again."

Harry laughed despite himself. Smith was a wry creature.

"So," Smith went on, "that would be the unburdening. What was the burdening?"

"I made an attempt to address Lady Isabel's fears regarding the stability of my prospects, but I am certain I only managed to increase her concerns. She has thought deeply on the subject and she asked me what would happen to my wife if I died before producing an heir."

"Oh dear. You did not tell her about Martin?"

"No, but she is clever and certainly divined that the estate is entailed. She's likely also made the guess that the fellow waiting in the wings cannot be looked upon with any confidence."

"I fear you will get nowhere with a lady whose priorities lay in that direction. Is there nobody else? No lady just arrived that you have not encountered before who might be made of sterner stuff?"

"Lady Isabel is made of *stern stuff*, as you call it. She has not told me all of her circumstances, but as she can guess at mine, I can guess well enough about her own. At home, she has a pianoforte that has never been tuned. A household that cannot absorb a small fee like that is precarious indeed. I suspect there were days when there was not enough food on the table, never mind other necessities."

"Ah, and so the lady is determined she will not find her future in a similar situation."

"Exactly. Though, I do think she likes me. I do not think I'm being vain about that. I really do sense it in her."

"What shall you do next?"

"I am not certain. Though, I have arranged with Ryland to have Lady Isabel seated at my table at his mystery supper. His tables seat four and I dare not attempt to take her supper as the duchess is no admirer of mine at the moment. However, I can at least be in close proximity. What I will do with the proximity, I do not know."

"You will likely not think of anything while lollygagging in your bed. Get up and get on your horse. A ride through the park will clear your head. You're sure to think of something."

Harry nodded. Really, he could roll over and go back to sleep if it were not for thinking of Lady Isabel. He'd only got to sleep after the ball by drinking a very large glass of brandy.

His head did need clearing. He could hardly think straight, which would not be helpful in coming up with an idea.

THE DUCHESS AND Isabel left Hanover Square with two grooms on horseback behind them. Isabel was rather taken aback by the lady's prowess on a horse. The duchess was in firm control of her massive horse and weaved round carriages and graciously nodded to acquaintances as they made their way through Mayfair. Both horses were spirited and did more than a few sidesteps to show their enthusiasm.

"We will make our way to Rotten Row," the duchess said. "As soon as Cleopatra sees greenery, she will wish to be at a gallop. You do gallop, Lady Isabel?"

"Oh, yes, indeed," she said. She could not claim vast experience with her own stable of horses, but that had perhaps proved an advantage. Various families with daughters from her neighborhood had always been happy to lend her a horse so that she might ride out.

She'd become experienced with handling a variety of strengths, speeds, and temperaments. Including Violetta, the Bensons' rather notorious mare who seemed to find humor in flinging ladies to the ground. Violetta had needed stern handling and Isabel had handled her.

"Excellent," the duchess said. "We will tire out Cleo and Guinevere and they will settle. Ah, here is the gate."

They made their way to the Row and the horses, knowing full well where they were going, sidestepped and pranced and urged their riders to allow them to go faster.

"Let us be off!" the duchess cried, giving her horse its head. Isabel quickly followed suit.

Isabel tugged on her hat to assure herself that it was secure—the duchess had insisted on having made a particular style that was well-lined with cork that would cushion a fall. She urged her horse forward, though that creature required very little urging.

The speed of it was rather marvelous, far faster than could be done in her own neighborhood of gentle hills and trees to be wound around.

They passed two gentlemen who had stopped to talk, and Isabel did not know who they were, but they seemed very surprised to see the duchess in the midst of a mad dash. Isabel supposed they tipped their hats, but she did not dare look behind her to find out. Guinevere required all of her attention.

There were more gentlemen ahead, some having moved their horses onto the grass as they engaged in conversation, and some riding. Though, none of them were riding as fast as she and the duchess. They would easily overtake them.

Isabel lightly touched Guinevere with her crop. As she had thought, this particular horse did not require any firm prodding. The mare stretched her neck and surged forward.

They weaved around the gentlemen and the duchess shouted, "Good day to you, Lord Lymington."

The lord at first appeared surprised, then he urged his mount forward, racing along with them. Though Lord Lymington was a rather lumbering individual, he did not seem so on a horse. He rode a sixteen-hand chestnut who must surely be the oft mentioned MacBeth, and it seemed as if atop a horse was the lord's natural habitat. No wonder he liked to talk about his horses so much.

The horses began to get winded and the duchess brought Cleopatra to a canter, then a trot, then down to a walk. Isabel followed suit, as did Lord Lymington.

"Ladies," Lord Lymington said with real enthusiasm, "what a terrific ride! Duchess, Lady Isabel, I had no idea you were both such skilled horsewomen."

"If I do a thing, Lord Lymington," the duchess said, "I determine to do it creditably." She glanced down at his horse's hooves and said, "Your horse has seemed to have kept all his shoes, so it is a fine day for everybody."

"Yes, well, we'll see what happens about that," Lord Lymington said. "Did I tell you that only last week…wait, no. I know what I'll ask, what do you think about the weather?"

Isabel smiled. He'd stopped himself going into another horse story. One could not fault Lord Lymington with lack of effort.

The duchess said, "My butler is an expert on the weather, my lord. He says it is to be a puffing easterly all day. That is, unless the dolphins are too energetic and throw the whole thing off. Most people have no idea how dolphins can affect the weather."

"Gad, do they really?" Lord Lymington said.

"Oh yes, if they are too lively, they create a disturbance."

"I had no idea," the lord said. "That seems like a smashing topic of conversation. You know, because Lady Isabel told me to stop talking about horses."

"I fully back the suggestion to pull the reins on the subject of horses, Lord Lymington," the duchess said gravely. "Though, one must have a very deep knowledge of predicting weather to speak creditably on it."

Seeing the lord's downcast expression, the duchess followed up with, "But if you are truly interested, you might interview my butler on the subject. Carlson would be delighted to share his expertise."

Isabel's eyes widened. Where on earth was this going? She only wished for Lord Lymington to learn how to speak about commonplaces. Not predicting the weather like Carlson with his dolphins and who knew what else. Betsy said he'd even mentioned that crows could bring in fog—what a notion!

"I would consider it a great favor, Duchess," Lord Lymington said.

"Your eyes are about to be opened regarding mother nature, Lord Lymington. Your eyes will be opened *wide*."

As Isabel considered this looming disaster in the making, a lone gentleman walked his horse toward them. And not just any gentleman. It was Mr. Vance.

CHAPTER TEN

I SABEL WATCHED HARRY Vance take his horse from a walk to a trot when he spotted them. He was disarmingly handsome astride. Of course he would be.

The duchess spotted him too and muttered, "What is *he* doing here?"

Lord Lymington, not having the temperament to understand the duchess' meaning, said, "I'll take a guess—he's exercising his horse. What do you think, Lady Isabel?"

"I am sure you are right, Lord Lymington," Isabel said, biting her lip.

"Your Grace," Mr. Vance said, tipping his hat. "Lady Isabel, Lymington."

"Say, Vance," Lord Lymington said, "did you know that dolphins affect the weather? I just found it out myself."

Mr. Vance's expression indicated he had known no such thing and was not very inclined to believe it. "Really," he said, as more a statement of incredulity than a question.

"Indeed," Lord Lymington said. "They create a disturbance. Makes sense, when you think about it."

"Does it?" Mr. Vance asked.

"Mr. Vance," the duchess said in a regal tone, "I am certain you make your way somewhere. We would not wish to keep you from it."

Isabel winced. While it was true that Mr. Vance could not be considered as eligible, at least not to her particular requirements, the duchess bordered on rude. And this, after Mr. Vance had saved her tiara and she'd not bothered to thank him for it.

"No destination could be more compelling than escorting two fine ladies through the park," Mr. Vance said cheerfully. Though his words were cheerful enough, Isabel thought his expression was one of firm determination.

"Nicely said!" Lord Lymington exclaimed. "How did you think of it?"

"It is only the truth," Mr. Vance said.

"I *see*. The truth. Interesting," Lord Lymington murmured.

The duchess, presumably envisioning no easy method of ridding herself of Mr. Vance, tapped her crop and set Cleopatra on a walk to lead the way. Mr. Vance maneuvered his horse next to Isabel, while Lord Lymington remained on her right side.

"About our discussion of last evening, I do not believe I mentioned, Lady Isabel," Mr. Vance said. "that even a lowly baron might put together a very generous jointure as a cushion against any disaster that might occur. It really does not have to be arrived at by considering a dowry, a gentleman is free to arrange the thing how he wishes. I can only say for myself that I would be inclined to settle at least five hundred a year. At least."

Well, he had jumped right back into that conversation. And right in front of Lord Lymington, who appeared rather lost.

Isabel had not expected him to mention the matter again after she had made herself so clear.

As she had spent so much of her waking days thinking about the security of her future, she had of course thought deeply on the subject of jointures and settlements.

However, she also thought she understood their limits. To account for a lifetime of a decent house, servants, necessities, a carriage, horses, stabling, and all the other things that might be unexpectedly required, a man would need to be rich as Croesus to create a settlement to meet those needs. Two thousand a year might do it, and yet so few gentlemen would consider such a sum, much less be able to provide it.

Especially when one considered that the jointure amount did not increase from year to year. As prices rose, the lady's poverty would increase with it.

No, she had seen what really happened in such cases. The lady lived in reduced circumstances and was the pity of her neighbors. She would not starve and might even have the luxury of a cottage, but nobody would know what to do with her.

If she were given quarters in a relative's house, she was invariably a burden. She was the odd number at a dinner. Or she found that a neighbor had issued an invitation to the family, quite forgetting she was in residence. Or somehow she found she was slowly drifting into being a servant—working as a companion or entertaining the children.

If the lady were lucky enough to live independently, she would not have the funds to maintain a carriage and horses. Her neighborhood would be left wondering if they ought to ask if she needed a ride to a dinner, or would that be embarrassing? If nobody enquired, did she have the means to hire a carriage? Or, would she just decline the invitation as the transport was beyond her means?

Isabel had *been* that person for the past year, as the carriage was in disrepair, the only horse they still had was her father's, and her gig had been sold long ago.

She was not unaware of the irony of her bringing no dowry but what the duchess would provide, while at the same time having strict requirements as to the financial situation of her future. Ironic, perhaps, but true all the same.

Isabel had not answered Mr. Vance's fanciful plans, but Lord Lymington did. "Are *you* the lowly baron, Vance? Are barons that low, though? I hadn't known. I'm to be a duke."

"Everybody knows you're to be a duke," Mr. Vance said.

"Do they? Yes, I suppose they would."

"I only say, Lady Isabel, that for every problem there is a solution. If one wishes to find it."

"Enterprising!" Lord Lymington exclaimed.

"Here we are at the gate," the duchess called. "Good day, Lord Lymington. Mr. Vance."

Isabel had no choice but to bid them goodbye as well and hurry to catch up to the duchess.

As she trotted forward, she heard Lord Lymington say, "Vance, about this solution that solves every problem. What is it?"

Mr. Vance had answered, "Ah, Lymington."

As she and the duchess made their way back to Hanover Square, droplets of rain began to fall.

The duchess peered up at the sky and said, "Shame on those dolphins."

⇥⟫⟨⟨⇤

HARRY WATCHED THE duchess and Lady Isabel trot away while Lymington nattered on about something having to do with dolphins and the duchess' butler.

Had he said enough? Had he convinced her? Or had he at least raised questions in her mind?

She could not still be considering Lymington. Could she?

"Anyway," Lymington said, "Lady Isabel was very specific about my not talking about my horses anymore, so I suppose talking about the weather is as good as anything else."

"Lady Isabel requested that?" Harry asked.

"Just last night," Lymington said, nodding vigorously. "She's the only lady who has told me what to do, so I expect I ought to follow it. Well, wait a minute, that's not entirely true. Miss Rightstone told me to shut up once—gad, she drinks a lot. But Lady Isabel gave me orders *nicely*."

Why would Lady Isabel give pointers to Lymington?

What a stupid thing to ask himself. He perfectly well knew why. She attempted to make him into something she could tolerate. Which meant she was considering him very seriously.

"Do you court the lady, then?" Harry asked.

"Court? Like marriage?" Lymington asked, his face screwing up in great concentration.

"Yes, like that," Harry said.

"Court. I hadn't thought…it's a rather good idea, though. You have done me a service, old fellow!"

Blast. The fool had not thought of it until he put the idea into his head. Lymington was not the only fool then, he had himself just done something extraordinarily idiotic.

"My mother goes on and on about marriage," Lymington said. "Every time I go home, my father and I are having a comfortable conversation about the stables and in she comes with *well, is there anybody?* I say no, she says what are you waiting for, I say I don't know, she says do something, I say do what, she says court a lady, I say which one, she says I no longer care, I say neither do I, she says I feel like hitting you over the head, I say you always say that, she says I just might do it, I say use a pillow, she says I wish your brother was the heir, I say me too, she says…well you get the idea."

"I believe I do," Harry said drily.

"*But* if I court Lady Isabel, the conversation would go entirely different!" Lord Lymington said. "She'll say *well, is there anybody?* I'll say yes there is, *she'll* fall on the sofa in a dead faint, I'll throw water on her, she'll wake up and say are you serious, I'll say yes, she'll say who did you talk into it, I'll say Lady Isabel Beauford, she'll say what's the dowry, I'll say I don't know, she'll say oh who cares, I'll say not me, she'll say…well, you get the idea.

Harry stared at Lymington. He'd like to throw a bucket of water on *him* at this moment.

"Now, I just have to look into this whole courting business. I've never tried it, you know."

Harry looked him in the eye and said, "I would continue to talk about the dolphins, it seemed of particular interest to the lady."

"The dolphins, of course! Great tip."

"The pleasure is all mine," Harry answered. "You might also send a posey, though only if you understand her favorites. Otherwise, it will cause offence."

"I don't know anything about them! What a dunce I am, I should have asked, but I was too busy thinking up a question about the weather."

"I happen to know she favors columbine, lavender, and marigold."

Lymington counted out on his fingers. "Columbine, lavender and marigold. Excellent!"

"And if you mean to show her that you're serious, you'd better write a poem."

"Gad, that's tricky," Lymington said. "I've never even read poetry."

"I have," Harry said. "If you like, I'll help you write one."

"Good man!"

Harry smiled. Let Lymington talk about dolphins and send a bouquet that claimed his feelings were folly, distrust, and sorrow, and deliver a poem that was the most wretched and hopefully offensive ode ever written. For himself, he would send primroses to communicate his consistency.

Lymington was a fool to think him a good man. He was not a good man, he was a man determined to knock him out of the way.

He was certain the duchess would not like his primroses. She might even throw them out. But the message would have been delivered, nonetheless.

When a woman like Lady Isabel Beauford hung in the balance, it was an all-out war and he had no intention of taking prisoners. Lymington had better watch out for himself.

THE FOLLOWING DAY, Isabel watched Carlson enter the drawing room carrying an exceedingly odd arrangement of flowers in a porcelain container. The columbine and lavender were of similar color and almost paired in some sensible fashion, but then the yellow marigolds seemed to have been placed in the wrong arrangement.

As well, if one were to consider their meanings, it was a rather disturbing collection.

"This just arrived, Your Grace," Carlson said, holding the container out with straight arms as if it would suddenly make a grab at him.

"What nonsense is this?" the duchess asked. "Who would send such a message? Do not tell me I have made an enemy somewhere and they dare tell it to me. My enemies are usually in the habit of staying very sensibly quiet lest they incur my wrath."

The duchess paused and whispered, "Oh, no. I know who it is. Lady Rembly. She was so angry over Mr. Vance. Apparently, Miss Rightstone had some sort of fit and broke half the dishes after the guests left her ball. This is Vance's fault."

The duchess took the card. Her face registered some confusion. "It is addressed to you, Isabel."

"To me?" Isabel asked, feeling as if a stone had settled in her stomach. "Why should Lady Rembly be angry with me?"

"I have no idea, but we'd best find it out," the duchess said, opening the card.

The duchess read the card. "Hmm, very odd," she said.

"What does it say?" Isabel asked, her voice no louder than a whisper.

"It is from Lord Lymington," she said, handing over the note.

Lady Isabel—Your favorite flowers for courting. Lymington

"I do not understand," Isabel said. "Marigold is sorrow and Lavender is distrust. Though, I have forgotten the meaning of columbine."

"Folly," the duchess said.

"Sorrow, distrust, and folly? Perhaps he did not take my counsel about his modes of conversation as well as I had thought. Perhaps he thought it over and was offended."

"But he mentions courting," the duchess said, "so let us not jump to a conclusion. Perhaps Lord Lymington did not understand the flowers' meanings?"

Isabel looked at them. "Then you think he might have chosen this combination for its…beauty?"

"I hope not," the duchess said staring at them.

A footman arrived to the drawing room doors and signaled to Carlson. Another arrangement had arrived.

This one was very lovely. An abundance of pink primroses. Pink for a new interest and primrose for consistency. Isabel hardly need inquire who sent them. It must be Harry Vance.

The duchess did not seem to guess it so easily. She opened the card and frowned. "Really, I do not like this at all. First, he loses my tiara, then he ruins my plans for Miss Rightstone, and now he shoots higher than he has a right to. Primroses. Pink. Oh, look at this, he writes—*Constancy can be relied upon.* What a notion. No, Mr. Vance, you flatter yourself; you are worthy of a candle's flame and yet you aim for the sun."

Isabel did not answer, though she had to admit the arrangement gave her a little thrill. A very wrong, not sensible, going nowhere, sort of thrill.

Not for the first time, she cursed the fates for having made him so well but put him in circumstances lacking in any real stability. If only, if only if only…

"If only I could drive him off," the duchess said. "I must be careful though. There is too big a risk of gossip regarding Miss Rightstone's disappointed hopes—that young lady is hardly discreet and there must be more than a few people who were told there was to be a match with Vance. My friendship with Lady Rembly is on shaky ground as it is."

"I am sure nothing need be said," Isabel said encouragingly.

"Yes, you are right, of course. Mr. Vance might send flowers all day long, but he will not get anywhere with it."

That was the real shame, Isabel thought. That he could not get anywhere with it.

"We must chin up and go forward," the duchess said. "I cannot think what on earth Lymington means by that monstrosity, but we will know more when we encounter him on the morrow."

"At Lord Ryland's mystery ball?" Isabel asked.

"Yes, it is a ridiculous sort of evening, but one must go. It is Lord Ryland, after all. Gracious, Anne does make a spectacle of herself on that night, year after year. I used to think her losing at the game was unfortunate for all the complaining she did about it. Now though, I am certain her winning is far worse. First the brooch, then came that absurd walking stick and now that she's got hold of a cipher, she's been sending letters in code. Do any of us know what they mean? No, we do not. She might have informed me that she was being held captive somewhere and I'm none the wiser."

"Lady Featherstone told me there is a blade inside her walking stick," Isabel said.

"Oh yes," the duchess said acerbically. "If she ever gets into a knife fight, she is prepared."

As if speaking the name Ryland had summoned one of that family from the ether, Carlson announced that Lady Ryland had come to call.

They rose to greet her and the duchess said, "Lady Ryland, how gracious of you to call during what I am certain is a busy time."

Lady Ryland laughed and said, "If you mean the ball on the morrow, I can assure you that my husband has things well in hand. It is his evening, after all, and he has planned it down to the silverware."

The duchess nodded. "He is a careful host. Carlson, do bring a tea tray in for Lady Ryland and Lady Isabel. I will leave the two young ladies to themselves, as I ought to write a note to Lady

Rembly. And perhaps send flowers…or something."

The duchess sailed from the room and Carlson sent a footman for a tray before closing the doors behind him.

"It really is very good of you to call, Lady Ryland," Isabel said.

"Nonsense," Lady Ryland said, "and you'd best call me Prudence. We, along with four other ladies, will be forever bound together as being the projects of *The Society of Sponsoring Ladies*."

"It still is very kind," Isabel said, "and do call me Isabel." She had not yet made a female friend in London, and she found she missed the intimacy of exchanging given names and sharing confidences.

"Tell me, how does it go for you, and I will be astonished if there is not some upheaval to discuss. All of us projects have been settled through the most unlikely of situations."

Isabel had not imagined that she would say what was really on her mind to such a new acquaintance, but the lady had all but said there must be a problem. She'd hinted that every one of the ladies sponsored by the society had encountered some difficulty. Of course, it would be such a relief to unburden herself and hear what another would say of it.

"I do not know how much of my circumstances you are aware of," Isabel said. "My life with my father has been one of privation, as the estate does very poorly. In truth, I have never known what's to happen next nor whether there will be adequate food on the table. As that has been my experience, I have vowed that I will make a sensible choice of a husband. A choice that is unassailable…so that I never have to fear such again."

"That sounds entirely sensible," Lady Ryland said. "So why do I have the feeling that there is something that disturbs you about that firm resolve?"

Isabel was silent for some moments, searching for just the right words to articulate the problem. Finally, she said, "I am afraid that my head is all firm resolve, but my heart leans in another direction."

"Ah, your heart leans toward someone not so unassailable."

"Yes."

The drawing room doors opened, and Carlson and a footman came through with the tea trays.

Isabel and Lady Ryland were silent until the tea things were laid and the doors shut once more.

As Isabel poured the tea, Lady Ryland said, "I will presume your heart does not lean toward some sort of jackanapes or somebody society would shun?"

"Goodness no!" Isabel said. "The leaning is toward a gentleman. A fine gentleman in fact, who will inherit a title. But his circumstances are not as…predictable as I would wish. They are not for certain safe. At least, they are at this moment, but I cannot be absolutely sure of what the future might hold."

Lady Ryland nodded and said, "Only you can decide of course. However, I will just say that I resisted my own heart's inclinations out of fear."

"Fear of Lord Ryland? But he is a marquess. I would have imagined his circumstances very secure."

"Oh yes," Lady Ryland said laughing. "He will never be short of money and will always have a place in society."

"But then—"

"It was not his circumstances I feared. I was afraid of losing myself in marriage. From a past experience, I was terrified of marrying a gentleman who would be forceful and take over my opinions. Therefore, I came to Town fully resolved to look for a lamb, and Lord Ryland is rather more like a lion."

"I see," Isabel said slowly. "How did you decide to change your mind?"

"I did not really decide—I was in love and that was all there was to it. As it turns out, I was right about him. He is forceful and irascible, and he takes orders from nobody. That is, nobody except me. He is an absolute lamb with me. I had to take a leap of faith to find it out, though."

"So you are happy?"

"Exceedingly so," Lady Ryland said. "All I say is, remember

that it is all well and good to use your mind and be sensible, but fighting your heart is a difficult matter. A heart is not the weak creature you might imagine it to be."

This was not the sort of thing Isabel wished to hear. She would have been buoyed in her confidence if Lady Ryland had agreed that she must think only of safety.

"Goodness," Lady Ryland said, eyeing Lord Lymington's bouquet, "that is…original."

"Lord Lymington sent them," Lady Isabel said, "we are hoping he does not know what they mean."

"Ah, Lord Lymington," Lady Ryland said. "Perhaps his horse picked them out?"

Isabel laughed despite herself. "It could be so. Though, I have had a talk with him about at least broadening his conversation to include other topics."

"Did you? Brava, my friend. It is high time somebody did so." Lady Ryland paused, then she said, "I suspect he is the sensible but not pulling on heart strings choice."

"Yes."

Lady Ryland's eyes drifted toward the primroses. "And who sent the other?"

"Mr. Harry Vance," Isabel said.

"I see," Lady Ryland said. "Oh yes, now I see."

CHAPTER ELEVEN

ISABEL DID NOT respond, as she thought Lady Ryland did see well enough. She only wished she could herself see with such clarity. Or if not see, then *feel* with clarity.

They went on to talk of more usual things, and Isabel learned a great deal about the proceedings at Lord Ryland's mystery ball and supper. Including, Lady Ryland's advice on what to do if Isabel did not find it convenient to think about a murder. She advised thinking of a book she knew well and silently repeating it to herself. Shakespeare, in particular, was recommended.

That might come as a handy strategy, as she was not so certain she did wish to consider a murder. She could recite *Henry V* and *Othello* by heart, and *As You Like It* nearly so. Among her various instructions to herself garnered from her father's library, she had studied Shakespeare quite thoroughly. She'd once heard Lord Bertridge quote from *King Lear* and had become convinced that the plays must be a typical subject of conversation in London. She did not wish to come up short on it.

As they moved to other topics, Isabel heard the door knocker in the distance. The drawing room doors opened and Carlson announced Lord Lymington.

Lady Ryland rose to take her leave, presumably imagining that the lord would wish to take advantage of the opportunity to have a private conversation with the lady he visited for as long as it took for the duchess to hear of his arrival and hurry into the room.

That was, the lady imagined it until Lord Lymington said, "Ladies, no, well, I just poked my head in to say hello. I've come to see Carlson. About the weather."

"About the weather?" Carlson asked, quickly glancing out a window, lest there be some sort of unexpected conditions developing.

"Yes," Lord Lymington said to Carlson. "The duchess said you'd teach me everything you know. About the dolphins and such."

"She said that?" Carlson asked.

Isabel thought Carlson looked not quite as enthusiastic about the prospect as the duchess had imagined he would be.

"How about the library? That's where one goes to learn things, I believe," Lord Lymington said, "I am sure the duchess will not mind it."

Carlson, seeming to have no defense ready to fend off the request, sadly nodded.

Lord Lymington bowed to Isabel and Lady Ryland and then followed the dejected butler down the hall.

Lady Ryland looked enquiringly at Isabel. "Dolphins?"

Isabel sighed. "Carlson has some interesting ideas about the weather. Now I am afraid Lord Lymington is going to have them too."

HARRY HAD BEEN cagey upon arriving at Ryland's ball. He knew the duchess was irate with him regarding Miss Rightstone, and probably even more so since he'd sent the primroses to Lady Isabel. For all he knew, she'd also discovered that he'd advised Lymington to send columbine, lavender and marigold, in which case her very hair might catch fire from the blistering heat of her temper.

He had bided his time before approaching Lady Isabel.

But then his opportunity arose. The duchess' back was turned and she was in deep conversation with Lady Heathway. He'd stealthily approached and got on Lady Isabel's card.

He wrote himself down for the second—the first was already taken, as was supper. The supper was claimed by Lymington of course. That was irritating enough, but since he'd arranged with Ryland to have Lady Isabel at his table, that meant Lymington would be at his table too. He supposed the fellow would at some point leap up and cry, "Everybody! I think the horse did it!"

As for Harry's military campaign to sneak into enemy territory and capture the lady's card without her bad-tempered general spotting his incursion, Harry was certain Lady Isabel, herself, knew exactly what he was doing.

He was glad. He *wanted* her to know to what lengths he would go to secure her.

Though, he could not read her feelings on the matter. Was she happy? Maybe a little. But she also seemed a little sad.

Worried, perhaps? Yes, that was probably it.

Now the second dance had come round, and Harry was determined to allay her fears. He really did think there was something between them, if he could just remove her ideas about who would be suitable. Then, she could be free to follow her inclinations and he was all but sure her inclination leaned toward himself.

Though, how to allay her concerns, as her fears were not entirely unjustified. He would not lie to her, he never would, but he must somehow convince her.

"Have I mentioned what's gone on with Lord Melburton, the Duke of Canavan's only son?" he asked.

"Of course you have not, Mr. Vance," Lady Isabel said, "though I am certain you will mention it now."

"Well, I only say, a duke's family might seem rather unassailable, but it turns out not to be true. Melburton has fled to the continent and nobody knows what's to be done about it. His wife has been relegated to a ramshackle cottage on the duke's estate."

"I see," Lady Isabel said. "And what dreadful thing has Lord Melburton done to cause such a flight and the mistreatment of his wife?"

"What *hasn't* he done? First, he gets in far too deep with gambling. You know that sort of gentleman, the deeper they get the more desperate they are for a big win and then the deeper they get. I, myself, do not gamble, as I think it a stupid pastime. Whatever my estate produces is ploughed right back into it. I just bought some neighboring land to expand what I already have."

Harry watched Lady Isabel's expression carefully. Was she struck by the story of Lord Melburton compared to his own habits? He could not tell.

"Surely, whatever debt the lord has got into, the duke can get him out if he wishes."

"Perhaps that might have been the case. But it seems Melburton was desperate and took to the bottle and then made a series of rash decisions that ended very badly."

Lady Isabel waited for him to go on, though she looked at him rather dubiously.

"The man who held the debt was a gentleman farmer from the neighborhood. Melburton went to his house very drunk, there was some sort of scuffle, and the man fell and hit his head on the corner of a desk. He is dead."

"Dead?" Lady Isabel whispered.

"Dead," Harry confirmed. "Melburton returned to his own house, admitted what happened to his wife, and then stole off to the continent. I do not suppose he'll ever come back, lest he be hung for a murder."

"But why should the duke send the lord's wife to live in a rundown cottage? She had nothing to do with it."

"Because the magistrate interrogated her ruthlessly, until she could not hold up anymore. She ended by telling him the truth of what happened. The duke will never forgive her for it."

Lady Isabel's eyes narrowed. "Mr. Vance, I believe you have

invented that grim tale. Really, it is too improbable."

"Ask around, you'll see," Harry said. "The news has just arrived to Town, it will not be a day before everybody is talking about it. For myself, I think the moral of the story is that one must rely on a gentleman's character far more than his supposed circumstances. Melburton had every advantage in the world, but he was always a bit of a lout."

Lady Isabel nodded, smiling. He could see that she did not believe a word of it, but she would. It was entirely true and had been communicated to him by his valet, who had heard it from Melburton's cousin's valet. Harry was confident she would be struck deeply when she understood the veracity of his tale.

After all, character was the primary thing he had going for him, and character was the primary thing Melburton had never had.

As he led her through the changes, she said, "I must thank you for the flowers, though they were not at all necessary."

Harry understood her message well enough. *I thank you as a matter of courtesy and gently remind you that there is no hope in this pursuit.*

"I suppose your drawing room is filled with posies," he said. "I imagine Lymington had the same idea."

Lady Isabel said, "He did."

Harry smiled, praying that Lymington had taken his advice and not sought counsel from anybody else.

Lady Isabel seemed to be thinking about something. Then she appeared very decided. "Mr. Vance, you did not happen to advise Lord Lymington regarding his bouquet?"

Harry laughed. "He did it, then? Marigold, columbine, and lavender?"

"Yes, he unfortunately did," Lady Isabel said. "It was unkind to steer him in such a wrong direction as I am certain that was not the message he wished to send."

Harry grew serious. "No," he said, "I do not believe it was unkind. If he has not the sense to find out for himself the meanings of flowers then he deserves to be steered wrong. This is war, Lady Isabel."

She appeared shocked to hear him declare it so bluntly. Let the lady be shocked. This *was* war and Lymington could take his lumps.

⤜⤜⤜⋙⋘⤛⤛⤛

ISABEL'S MIND WAS in a whirl and would not settle in any rational manner. Mr. Vance was getting more and more direct and seemed to be not at all put off by her determination that it was useless.

He said it was war.

She had been deeply moved by it, she could not deny that fact. Never had another person wished to fight for her. Nobody had ever expressed a wish to go to war on her behalf. She had always fought for herself. It almost made her cry to think of a person wishing to fight for her.

Isabel was determined to put it aside, to think of it no more.

She *did* keep thinking about it though, through the various dances. Isabel did her best to attend to a gentleman's conversation and provide suitable answers to their questions. But her mind kept going back to that moment.

This is war, Lady Isabel.

Then, she had danced with Lord Lymington and casually asked, "My lord, are you acquainted with Lord Melburton?"

Lord Lymington had shaken his head and said, "That's a bad business. I never liked him, he always sneered at me, but I never thought he'd kill a man."

"Then it's true?" she said, rather shocked that it was. "He's escaped to the continent and left his wife behind to suffer?"

Lord Lymington had nodded. "Poor Lady Melburton. I knew her as Miss Mayrondale. She is an earl's daughter. She was rather nice, actually. I expect you would have been friends. I don't know why she married him."

"Perhaps for a position?" Isabel asked.

Lord Lymington laughed. "What a position she's in now though, eh? By the by, did you know that Carlson is concerned there is a particular pod of whales just now causing havoc in the North Sea. Watch the weather—he says anything could happen. Anything at all could happen."

Isabel nodded gravely, though she privately thought *anything at all could happen* was very convenient for Carlson. Whichever way the weather went, he would be right.

Now they had made their way to the dining room. It was positively enormous and Lady Ryland had told her what she might expect. Two couples would be seated at each of the small square tables, a bevy of footmen showing everybody where they were meant to be.

Lady Ryland had explained that her lord took a great amount of time arranging the seating. She had given Isabel some sort of amused look when she'd told her, though Isabel did not understand it at the time.

She thought she might be beginning to understand it now, though.

A footman led her and Lord Lymington to a table where Mr. Vance and Miss Thompson were already seated. She was the daughter of a viscount and after the introductions, Isabel said, "Mr. Vance, did you happen to arrange this seating with Lord Ryland?"

"Of course I did," Mr. Vance said cheerfully.

"Well done, Vance," Lord Lymington said. "I'd no idea a person could do that. Good to know."

Miss Thompson was a very genial lady that Isabel had prior met at the Remblys' ball. She seemed delighted to see Lord Lymington and she was very soon engaging him in conversation.

Much to Isabel's chagrin, Lord Lymington was just now outlining the various pieces of information he'd picked up from Carlson. She could not imagine what Miss Thompson thought of hearing that the whales were throwing any kind of weather predictions up in the air, but the lady only murmured, "Fascinating."

Isabel was facing the doors and watched various people, known and unknown to her, stream into the dining room. She was charmed to see Lady Featherstone sweep in, her emerald brooch in place and her walking stick in hand. The lady nodded graciously to acquaintances as she passed them by.

While that was an amusing sight, an alarming sight soon followed. The duchess, who looked not at all pleased to note that Isabel sat at a table with Mr. Vance.

The duchess marched up to Lord Ryland and spoke hurriedly, glancing at their table, but the lord only smiled and shrugged. She stormed off to rejoin Lord Marbeal at her own table.

The duchess would not be pleased at all. Though, as it turned out, that was not the *most* alarming sight.

Miss Rightstone, escorted in by a callow-looking gentleman Isabel was not acquainted with, broke away from him and made her way to the sideboard. She grabbed a decanter of a white wine and poured herself a glass.

Her gentleman partner and the footman who had been leading them to a table looked on in disbelief. Miss Rightstone caught her eye and, if Isabel was not mistaken, the lady was irate.

She looked rather terrifying.

As Isabel watched the lady come toward their table, Mr. Vance talked on about character and dependability.

"Mr. Vance," Isabel said in a cautioning tone.

He paused his campaign. "Yes?"

At that moment, Miss Rightstone reached their table. She dumped the glass of hock in Mr. Vance's lap and said, "Oh dear, how clumsy of me. I *do* apologize, Mr. Vance." Then she slammed the glass on the table and walked off.

Not everyone in the room had seen what occurred, but some certainly had. Their eyes followed the lady until she was safely in her chair, lest she circle back to the sideboard for a second glass and they also get doused.

"Well," Mr. Vance said, dabbing up the spilled wine with his napkin, "at least it was not claret."

"Gad, she's clumsy," Lord Lymington said. "She spilled wine on me once, too. And Mr. Groadstone last season, now that I think of it."

"I suppose accidents do happen," Mr. Vance said.

Lord Lymington nodded and turned back to Miss Thompson to continue his thoughts on the whales in the North Sea.

"She is exceedingly angry," Isabel said, as that had certainly not been an accident.

"I do not have any argument with the lady, though she has an argument with me. She *ought* to have an argument with the duchess, as it was the duchess who created false hopes. But then, I do not suppose she has the daring to spill wine on a duchess. I presume you are aware of the lady's outrageous and highhanded plan to marry me off?"

"Um, she did mention the possibility of an advantageous match," Isabel said vaguely.

"Advantageous for who, I wonder," Mr. Vance said. "The poor duchess, she did not understand that I would refuse to be cowed by her lofty title and her own opinion of herself. I will follow my heart instead."

Before Isabel could respond, and she was very glad she did not need to respond to such forthrightness, Lord Ryland strode to the front of the room and dinged his glass.

"Ladies and gentlemen, welcome to my annual ball and mystery supper. As you know, I come to you this year as a married man." He saluted Lady Ryland with a raised glass. "My wife has been indulgent with me and allows me to continue on with this tomfoolery. So, let us begin. The clues are under your plates and the prize is exceedingly interesting. Let us find out if anybody can prevail over Lady Featherstone this year."

All eyes turned to Lady Featherstone, who nodded like a queen to her subjects. The duchess, just at the next table over, gently touched her tiara, as if to point out that there were far more emeralds on it than could be found on Lady Featherstone's brooch.

As Isabel took her sheet of paper from under her plate, Mr. Vance said, "I suppose we should get started, though I am never any good with these things."

Lord Lymington said, "Neither am I—I can never seem to make heads or tails of the thing."

"I cannot believe that true," Miss Thompson said to Lord Lymington. "I am certain you are very clever."

"Really? Why?" Lord Lymington asked.

"How could I think otherwise after what you have already told me about your study of the weather?" Miss Thompson said encouragingly. "Now, let us put our heads together and see what we can make of it."

Mr. Vance seemed rather pleased with Miss Thompson's maneuvering. He said, "Then I suppose *we* ought to put our heads together and do the same."

Isabel did not answer, though Lord Lymington answered for her. "Good thought, Vance."

Isabel sighed and opened the paper.

CHAPTER TWELVE

A HUSH FELL over Lord Ryland's dining room as his guests read through the case he had prepared for this year's mystery supper. If Isabel could hear anybody speaking aloud at all, it was only Lady Featherstone.

"Oh, I see, well, yes, of course, it could not be more clear, I believe I begin to see how it was," the lady said, lorgnette firmly applied to her eyes.

Isabel began to read her own paper, fairly certain that she would *not* be able to see how it was.

Mrs. Lydia Roberts, age 46, was found dead in her garden on the afternoon of July 14, 1813. She was discovered there by her housekeeper, who had been out doing an errand for her mistress. Mrs. Roberts was found with her lower torso on the ground, and her upper torso hanging over the side of a fountain, her face submerged in the water. Dried blood splatter was noted on the edge of the fountain.

Mrs. Roberts had been widowed for 18 months, having been the longstanding wife of the local doctor. They had no children.

The housekeeper, Mrs. Jenkin, age 55, pulled her mistress from the water and then ran to get help. As she passed by the doors to the dining room, she made a second gruesome discovery. One of Mrs. Roberts' suitors, Mr. Elliot Greg, age 52, was slumped in a chair at the table, and was also expired.

The magistrate was called in and made a thorough report

on what he observed upon entering the scenes of both deaths, which was as follows:

The first scene was the garden: thirty feet wide and forty feet deep, it was filled with a variety of flowering plants, including the foxglove clutched in Mrs. Roberts' hand, amaryllis, lilies, monkshood, dog roses, sweet peas and delphiniums. A path led from the kitchens to the fountain, and then made a circle round the fountain. Smaller offshoots of graveled walkways led to all four corners of the garden. The entirety of the garden was surrounded by a five-foot stone wall. Behind the wall was forested land with no neighbors in view.

The second scene was the dining room: of usual size for a well-laid out cottage with a table to accommodate eight persons. There were two place settings on the table, as well as a platter with a small roasted beef gone cold, salt, pepper, a small dish of horseradish, a wilted salad, and a cheese board. The plate in front of Mr. Greg was half-eaten roasted beef, horseradish, a buttered roll, and a thick slice of cheddar cheese. The other plate situated at the head of the table was clean and unsullied.

On the day of the gruesome discoveries, the magistrate could get little from the hysterical housekeeper. All she was able to communicate was that her mistress had sent her to the butcher. The butcher frequented by the household confirmed that fact and though he had not been in attendance when the housekeeper came and went, his assistant remembered taking her custom.

In the ensuing days, the housekeeper was able to provide a few more salient facts, including that Mrs. Roberts had two suitors. One was Mr. Elliot Greg found dead in the house, the other was Mr. Jonathan Lamprey, age 51.

The deceased Mr. Greg had been suitor the longest and had been calling on Mrs. Roberts for above six months. He was an accountant from town and himself a widower of two years.

Mr. Lamprey was new to the area, having just purchased a dairy farm three miles out of town. He had never been married and had been courting Mrs. Roberts for approximately two months.

Both gentlemen saw the other as competition and their rela-

tions were exceedingly strained. They had, just weeks before, come to blows in the middle of the street.

The housekeeper felt that Mr. Lamprey was the superior of the two men and had a few discussions urging her mistress to see it. If Mrs. Roberts were to marry Mr. Lamprey, they might all move into his comfortable farmhouse, while Mr. Greg only rented a house and would surely wish to move into Mrs. Roberts' current abode. This, the housekeeper thought, would only lead to an inevitable disaster with a certain gentleman named Mr. Clyde.

One of the townspeople, Mr. Clyde, age 32, had been harassing Mrs. Roberts to sell up for years. He had the idea that he could add to her house and turn it into an inn for travelers, as it was ideally situated nearby the turnpike road.

The housekeeper was certain Mr. Clyde would never give up the idea and it would eventually lead to bloodshed between Mr. Greg and Mr. Clyde, were Mr. Greg to take over the house.

The housekeeper has since moved out of the town and went to her sister in Lambeth. She gave the magistrate her forwarding address and has been reliable in answering any questions he might have through written correspondence.

The house was sold, along with one cameo brooch and a set of silverware, those things being the items of value discovered by an inventory. The proceeds from the house and belongings are currently being held in trust by the magistrate as Mrs. Roberts did not have children and more distant relatives have not yet been located. There was no will found.

The cause of death was initially suspected as a death by misadventure, it being concluded that Mrs. Roberts slipped, hit her head and then, in an unconscious state, slipped into the fountain and drowned before she could regain her senses. It was supposed that Mr. Greg, being of typical age for such, died of a heart attack as he waited for Mrs. Roberts to return from the garden.

Upon further examining the facts herein, the magistrate entered his verdict as murder. Who killed Mrs. Roberts and Mr. Greg? Why and how was it done? Was it Mr. Lamprey, the other suitor? Or perhaps it was Mr. Clyde, so that he might get hold of the property before there was a husband installed in it? Or perhaps it was the housekeeper, in a fit of rage over some household matter? Or perhaps it was a stranger not yet identified that the clues must point to?

Mr. Vance had slowly laid down the paper. "What kind of neighborhood is this?" he asked.

Lord Lymington, who had been hunched over his own copy muttered, "It does not say—nearby York perhaps?"

Isabel had failed to ask Lady Ryland if these murders presented by Lord Ryland were actually true. She certainly hoped not.

"It seems like it must be the other suitor, Mr. Lamprey, who killed Mr. Greg," Isabel said. "Though why would he kill Mrs. Roberts too?"

Mr. Vance traced his finger along the paper. "If Mr. Greg did not in fact have a heart attack, what killed him? Indigestion from the roast beef?"

"It must have been poison," Mrs. Thompson said. "One could cover up any sort of taste with horseradish."

"Clever!" Lord Lymington said.

"I do not understand this at all," Isabel said. "It would seem that if there is only one murderer, they would have two different motives for two different people. For example, Mr. Lamprey may have wished to kill Mr. Greg, but not Mrs. Roberts."

"Mr. Clyde, the one who wanted the property to turn it into an inn," Mr. Vance said, "he might have wished both of them dead."

"Perhaps," Isabel said. "But only if they were married, which they were not. Mr. Greg had no claim on the house that Mr. Clyde so eagerly wished to purchase. As well, the methods do not make sense. How would Mr. Clyde gain admittance to the garden? Did he climb over the wall? And even if he managed that, how does he convince Mr. Greg to consume poison?"

"How does he manage to cook a roast beef to serve the

man?" Mr. Vance said.

"I wouldn't know where to start with a roasted beef," Lord Lymington said. "I am not even certain how to get to my own kitchens. Things just arrive."

"Wait a moment," Isabel said. "The housekeeper was sent to the butcher. *Why*, if there was already a cooked roast beef?"

"Because it was not cooked yet," Mr. Vance said. "And who had access to the garden, where there was foxglove and monkshood growing? And who could convince Mr. Greg to eat a plate of roast beef with horseradish?"

"The housekeeper," Isabel said.

"Oh no," Lord Lymington said. "That cannot be right. You see, a housekeeper would never harm anybody. Our Mrs. Kelton is such a jolly soul."

"She sounds marvelous," Mrs. Thompson said to Lord Lymington. "I suppose she slipped you cakes and biscuits with a wink when you were a boy?"

"Yes, she still does!" Lord Lymington exclaimed.

Footmen came round with decanters of wine and while Isabel was grateful to have a glass herself, she was rather worried about what Miss Rightstone might do with one.

Dishes followed, though the mystery distracted everybody from making much of it. At least, Isabel was distracted by it. It seemed Lord Lymington and Miss Thompson were becoming distracted by each other. The lord was going into some detail regarding his housekeeper's good qualities, one of which was cheering him up when he was downhearted after a talk with his mother.

Lord Lymington's housekeeper might be all sweetness and light, but Isabel was certain it must have been Mrs. Roberts' housekeeper who was the murderer. But why would she do it?

Isabel could imagine the how of it, but not the why. There had been some argument in the garden, and then a scuffle. Perhaps it had even been accidental, just as Lord Melburton certainly had not meant to actually kill his neighbor.

Then, Mr. Greg arrived for a late luncheon and the housekeeper provides some excuse for why Mrs. Roberts is not present, she is ill perhaps, and then she insists that her mistress wishes him to proceed with the roast beef.

Then, with both dead, she runs out for help as if she's just arrived to the house and found the disaster.

It could be done. But why?

Mr. Vance was bent over and writing like mad across the blank side of the paper. He said, "I believe you are right, Lady Isabel. It was the housekeeper."

"Why though?" Isabel asked. "What could have been her two different motives for killing those two people? I understand that she might have had a disagreement with her mistress and that of the two suitors she favored Mr. Lamprey, but it does not explain murder."

"It does, though," Mr. Vance said, continuing to write. "Why did the housekeeper so favor Mr. Lamprey over Mr. Greg? It would seem to me that a housekeeper would enjoy living in town, she must have friends she visits and shops to stop into. I will guess she had lived in that house for some time and had established a life there. Why was she so eager to move to a dairy farm three miles out of town?"

Isabel did not answer, because she did not know.

"And what of the estate? Mrs. Roberts was a widow of just eighteen months and there is only a cameo and some silver? Her husband had been a doctor, surely he left more than that. Where is the wedding band, for instance?"

Isabel had not noticed the lack of a wedding band. Now she began to see its' absence as significant.

"The housekeeper so favored Mr. Lamprey *because* he was new to town and he was a farmer," Mr. Vance said. "She did *not* favor Mr. Greg because he knew Mrs. Roberts' history, he'd known her late husband, he would have known what was likely to be in the estate, and he was an accountant. The housekeeper had been robbing Mrs. Roberts' blind and if the lady married Mr.

Greg, she would be found out."

"And so," Isabel said, "Mrs. Roberts somehow discovers the theft, confronts the housekeeper in the garden, and then she is attacked."

"She had foxglove in her hand," Mr. Vance said.

"Perhaps she suspected the housekeeper would use poison and took it from her," Isabel said.

Mr. Vance nodded. "Mrs. Roberts also likely gave away that she'd told Mr. Greg of her concerns, sealing his fate too. The housekeeper leaves Mrs. Roberts dead in the garden, and she serves the roast beef that was meant for both her mistress and her suitor, claiming Mrs. Roberts was indisposed but would be greatly saddened if he did not go on with the lunch."

"Yes, I believe that must have been what happened," Isabel said.

Mr. Vance wrote out a few more lines and folded the paper. He stood and said, "Lord Ryland, I believe Lady Isabel has solved it."

As Lord Ryland approached, Isabel said, "Mr. Vance! I did not solve it. *You* did."

"We solved it as a team," Mr. Vance said, "because we are a remarkably suited team."

Lord Ryland read through the solution, nodding.

"This is not right," Isabel whispered to Mr. Vance.

"There is everything right about it," Mr. Vance said. "At least, I feel so."

"Mr. Vance is correct—Lady Isabel has solved it," Lord Ryland announced loudly.

As Lord Ryland explained to his guests that it was the house-keeper and how and why she did it, Isabel felt her cheeks grow hot. She did not solve it and did not wish to take the credit for it. However, the situation had become like a stone rolling downhill. There was no way to make it go uphill again.

There was a round of applause for the solution and Isabel glanced around. Lady Featherstone appeared in disbelief. Isabel could not precisely read the duchess' emotions—proud of her charge? Delighted that Lady Featherstone had broken her winning record? Something like that.

A footman carried a silk-covered pillow with a small velvet box atop it to Lord Ryland. He took the box and opened its hinges, revealing a stunning blue topaz ring surrounded by two rows of chip diamonds.

It was dazzling.

"Lady Isabel," Lord Ryland said. "You have won this topaz ring once belonging to the House of Hapsburg. It has lived its life on royal fingers, and so it is fitting that its next owner arises from the House of Plantagenet."

Lord Ryland had removed the ring from the box and held it out, intending to put it on her finger. There was not much she could do at this point, so she held her right hand forward.

Slipping it on, Isabel felt the magnificence of it. She'd never owned any sort of jewelry of value—her mother's jewels had been sold long ago.

Though it was a thing of beauty, she was also not unaware of its presumed monetary value. If the worst came and her father was on the verge of losing the estate, she would sell it.

Mr. Vance whispered, "And so I have managed to give you a ring. Though it be on the wrong hand."

Isabel stared at him. Mr. Vance only laughed and said, "It *is* war, you know."

⇉⇉⤜⇇⇇

HARRY HAD WHISTLED all the way home, trotting through the dark streets. Ryland's ball could hardly have gone better. He'd won Lady Isabel a ring and had made several points about his reliability that must have made some inroads.

He'd been so bold as to point out that he'd given her a ring, though she wore it on the wrong hand.

She liked him, he was sure of it. And tonight, it appeared as if Lord Lymington was being taken out of the running. Miss Thompson had very helpfully engaged the man throughout the supper. No utterance of his was to go by without Miss Thompson remarking on how interesting, or kind, or insightful it was.

Lymington was certainly an original, though Harry had to admit that his talk about the weather was a vast improvement over his horse stories. At least the farfetched theories about whales, dolphins, and crows were entertaining.

As Smith took his coat, his valet said, "Well, what now? Have you got the lady in your pocket?"

"Lady Isabel will never be in anybody's pocket," Harry said, "but I have made progress."

"What next then?" Smith asked.

Harry thought for a moment. He *had* made progress, he knew it. But was he to go along like this, wondering when the next Lymington would turn up? For that matter, Miss Thompson may have made a great fuss over the man during one evening, but Lymington was so dense he might not even see it, much less pursue it. After all, it had been Harry, himself, that had put into his head that he might court Lady Isabel.

"I have asked her in hints and innuendos," Harry said, "now I must ask her directly. Formally."

"Will she go along with it though?" Smith asked, not appearing entirely convinced about the idea.

"I think she might," Harry said. "She just might."

"Right then, how will you set the stage?"

Set the stage? He'd not got so far in his thinking as to imagine setting the stage.

"The Tredwells' masque," Smith said. "It is in two days' time. You can disguise yourself as some romantic hero or other."

It was not a bad idea. In a costume, it would be far easier to approach Lady Isabel before the duchess even discovered who he was.

"Very well," Harry said. "Secure me a romantic hero costume. But, make it a *reliable* hero. Do not make me a Romeo, who cannot even be counted on to confirm whether his lady is dead or not."

"No Romeo," Smith said nodding.

"And make me something warrior-like. A romantic soldier, if you like."

"A romantic soldier," Smith said nodding.

Harry contemplated his future. He'd gone through season after season with no urge to ask anybody anything. Now he would ask Lady Isabel about the rest of her life. She just must say yes.

⇛⇚

Isabel did not get much sleep after Lord Ryland's ball and mystery supper. If her head and her heart had been at odds before last evening, they were now wrestling for dominance.

Oh, how she wished she could give in to her feelings! She had even gone so far, sometime in the middle of the night, to consider Mr. Vance's points.

The story of Lord Welburton had been confirmed. That gentleman had every credential—the eldest son of a powerful duke, heir to a large estate. The lady who married him must have gone into it with full confidence that she had made a sensible choice. The most sensible choice possible, really.

And now look what had happened to the lady! Her husband was being sought in a murder and her husband's family had thrown her off.

Mr. Vance had said character was a more reliable predictor of the future. Had he been right?

Isabel could not help but reflect on her own father. A more sensible man would have made something of the land he'd been given.

She had very vague early memories of when her mother had

lived and the house had been different. There had been servants of all sorts and she thought she remembered a fine carriage. She did not recall going to bed hungry.

Isabel supposed her father had just taken what he was given and then spent it without bothering to try to produce more.

She was fond of him, in her own way. But she often found herself frustrated regarding his lack of industry.

What of Lord Lymington? Did he have the character to provide an unruffled future? That gentleman could be reliably counted upon to not kill anybody, but might there be another sort of trouble he might fall into?

Still, in the end, her rational mind would charge in. Melburton was *one* duke's son gone astray. That did not prove that seeking a high position and the protection it afforded was the incorrect way to proceed. If she were to be privy to all the examples in the world, she was certain that far more had gone wrong for ladies who'd married on shaky ground than the one lady who'd married a duke's son who brought disaster.

When she'd arisen in the morning, Betsy had taken one look at her tired features and red eyes and promptly put a cloth soaked in cool water over her eyes and lectured her on the necessity of sleep.

She'd since got up and dressed and felt more like herself. Her resolve, which had been so shaken, began to firm up again.

Now, the duchess came into the drawing room and sat down in front of the tea tray that had just arrived via Carlson.

"What do we think about the Tredwells' ball on the morrow, Carlson?" the duchess asked. "Are our costumes to become dampened and limp by inclement weather?"

Carlson, who at these moments generally looked like he was staring down the barrel of a gun, said, "I do not believe so, Your Grace. Though, it is the season when we have dolphins on one side and whales on the other, both getting up to all sorts of mischief, so naturally we must be prepared for any eventuality."

"Dolphins and whales," the duchess said dismissively. "Those creatures are very irritating, and I do not see why they believe themselves so important as to meddle with my weather."

Isabel stopped herself from laughing, as the duchess certainly regarded *herself* important enough to claim the weather as her own.

Carlson retreated under this genial assessment of where things lay. The duchess said, "My dear Lady Isabel, you do not wear the ring so handily snatched from the claws of Lady Featherstone last evening."

"Indeed, I do not," Isabel said. "It is safe in its box above stairs."

"Just as well," the duchess said, nodding. "On no account allow Lady Featherstone to get it from you."

"Would she try?" Isabel asked in some surprise.

"She might," the duchess said. "Her devastation last evening was embarrassing to behold. Apparently, she thought another housekeeper nearby was the murderer. What other housekeeper? Where did she come from?"

Isabel of course did not know.

"She proclaimed loudly," the duchess went on, "for all her neighboring tables to hear, that she was convinced of it because it is a well-known fact that housekeepers become jealous of one another and could even be driven to murder."

"But if that were the case, why would not the other house-keeper have murdered Mrs. Roberts' housekeeper, rather than the lady herself and her suitor?"

"Why, indeed. Do not attempt to follow Anne's logic, it will only lead to madness," the duchess said.

"I am sorry that she was disappointed," Isabel said.

"I am not," the duchess said acerbically. "Had she won that ring, I would have found it waving in front of my face forever-more. Now, to other subjects. I understood perfectly well that Mr. Vance arranged to have you seated at his table. It was no coincidence. He really does push things."

"Yes, I know he does."

"I have a mind to write Lady Tredwell and ask her to disinvite him from her masque."

Isabel was disappointed to hear it, though she should not be. His absence would give her heart a rest and allow her mind to think more clearly. She had begun to notice that when she was within range of him, her thoughts muddled. When she was not, they cleared. Or if not cleared, then at least her rational mind stepped forward and took the reins once more.

The duchess sighed. "I cannot ban him, though. Especially not after Miss Rightstone very publicly poured a glass of wine in his lap. Were he to be suddenly absent, the two circumstances would instantly be connected. What was that girl thinking?"

Isabel did not respond, as she did not imagine anybody could guess what Miss Rightstone had been thinking. Or if Miss Rightstone had been thinking at all.

"I had the misfortune of being within hearing distance of Miss Rightstone's table and she did not stop there," the duchess said. "She went on to pronounce the mystery stupid, her partner stupid, Mr. Vance stupid, and the footmen stupid for failing to procure her the necessary amount of wine."

"Lady Rembly must be very distraught," Isabel said.

"Oh yes, poor Lady Rembly has been distraught for years. On top of that shame, Miss Rightstone has insisted on going to the masque as a queen, which is quite ridiculous as she has no claim to it. Now, I did think I might outfit you as a Plantagenet queen, but the headdresses, they really do not suit a young lady. Therefore, *I* will go as a Plantagenet queen in your stead, and you will go as Helen of Troy, she was a great beauty, you know."

Isabel did not answer the winding logic of the duchess going as a Plantagenet queen in her stead, while poor Miss Rightstone was to have no claim to it. "I have never attended a masque, it seems like great fun to wear a costume," Isabel said.

"Some do it well and some do not," the duchess said. "*We* do it well."

As always, Isabel was rather in awe of the duchess' supreme

confidence in her judgments. Perhaps that was what it was to be a duchess. Perhaps she would find out.

"Now, this evening we will go out, but it will be a quiet sort of affair. Cards, at Lady Fitzwallen's house. Lady Heathway and I will play against my duke and Lord Heathway. We do so on a regular schedule and we always trounce our poor husbands. I'm afraid Lord Lymington will not have been invited, he is known to be rather dreadful at cards."

Isabel could imagine poor Lord Lymington *would* be dreadful at cards. He had not the head for it. But what of Mr. Vance? Would he be there?

She should not wish it, but she could not help wondering about it.

"At least I will not have to foist off any more of Mr. Vance's impertinences," the duchess said. "I have never seen him at Lady Fitzwallen's annual card party. Does a tradesman's grandson even play whist? One wonders."

So there it was. He would not be there. She should be grateful for it, though she was no such thing.

CHAPTER THIRTEEN

HARRY HAD CONVENIENTLY found Lymington at White's. He was not surprised. Lymington was a creature of habit and was there every morning for coffee in case anybody wished to talk about horses. Surprisingly, the fellow found such conversations more often than one might imagine, especially if a significant race loomed. Lymington might not be a scholar, but he did know his way around a horse.

It was time to deploy the next incursion in Lady Isabel's war.

"What say you, old fellow?" he asked when he found him in a near-desolate coffee room. "Are you ready to write that poem we discussed?"

Lymington slowly nodded. "I suppose. So you say it is absolutely necessary in the courting business, then?"

"Quite," Harry said. "How else is the lady to know your feelings?"

"Why, I might just say, you know, gad, Lady Isabel, you're a very nice sort of person."

Harry stared at Lymington. "You might," he said, "but a lady likes to have things written down, where she can read them privately and reflect on them."

"Do they? They're rather deep creatures, eh?"

"Very deep. Now, I've brought all the writing materials. But first, before I can help you, you must list for me all the things you like about Lady Isabel."

Lymington nodded slowly and began to count on his fingers. "She's pleasant, she doesn't tell me to shut up. And…well her hair is red, that's nice. And then…well that's all that comes to mind actually."

And what a mind it was. Harry took out his quill from its case and dipped it in ink, poised to compose the most wretched poem possible.

> *The lady is pleasant*
> *Her hair very red*
> *The charms of a pheasant*
> *That has been well-fed*
> *There is no 'be quiet'*
> *That I have heard*
> *Just the gentle diet*
> *Of a new hatched bird*

Yes, indeed. It was perfectly ghastly.

"All right," Harry said, "I've managed to work in the images of birds, which is just what you'll want to say."

"Birds?"

"Yes, birds," Harry said. "They communicate interest and fidelity. Pheasants, in particular, represent the home's hearth and new-hatched birds speak of new love. Both of those are always very popular ideas with ladies."

Lymington rubbed his chin. "Who knew?"

Who indeed.

"Clever of you to whip out a whole poem like that. Now what do I do?" Lymington asked.

"Sign it and send it to Lady Isabel. She will be positively bowled over."

As Lymington signed that monstrosity of pointless verbiage, Harry thought if that did not put her off him, nothing would.

THE DUCHESS HAD called an emergency meeting of *The Society of Sponsoring Ladies* and she had gone so far as to commandeer Lady Featherstone's drawing room. This was not terribly unusual, as the duchess looked upon any drawing room she was in as practically her own.

She had decided not to call the ladies to her own house, as she did not wish Isabel to be aware that anything was amiss.

After they were all gathered round Lady Featherstone's tea tray, sans only Lady Easton who continued on at her nephew's estate, they looked expectantly at the duchess.

"As you know," she said, "I have set my mind to a match between Lord Lymington and Lady Isabel. It is to be a glorious marriage of two houses—one a dukedom, and the other The House of Plantagenet."

"Your expression just now does not convince me that all runs smooth in that direction," Lady Heathway said, with perhaps the tiniest note of glee.

"It does not," the duchess said. "There is somebody attempting to get in my way."

"Goodness," Lady Redfield said, appearing as startled as if she had been just accused of it. "Who would dare it?"

"Mr. Vance, that is who would dare it," the duchess said, her tone a veritable deep freeze.

"Oh, Mr. Vance, I feel sorry for him sometimes," Lady Featherstone said. "You know, tradesman grandfather and all that. He is very pleasant though."

"I found myself next to him at your dinner, Theodosia," Lady Heathway said. "He provided more rational conversation than I had expected. He has some educated views on the development of children."

"Oh, children!" Lady Mendleton nearly cried. "Did I say that Daisy speaks in sentences now? She tried to call me grandmama, but I said, dear Daisy, I do find *Bwandbaba* so charming. Call me that, as you always have done."

The duchess looked around at her friends with nothing short of incredulity. It seemed to her, and not for the first time, that if there were a way to get off track, they'd all be racing toward it as fast as possible.

"Rather than sing Mr. Vance's praises, or," she said, looking darkly at Lady Mendleton, "revisit the irritating subject of *Bwandbaba*, perhaps you would like to know what he has done."

This was said in the duchess' most regal and noble tone, effectively communicating that her simmering temper was in danger of going on the boil.

Lady Redfield looked near faint. Lady Featherstone examined the inside of her teacup.

"All right, tell us," Lady Heathway said, the only lady who was not cowed by the duchess whether she was simmering or boiling.

"First, Carlson brought me this note from Lord Lymington," the duchess said, passing it to Lady Heathway. "Naturally, as her guardian it is my duty to review any communication coming from a gentleman. I had hoped for something that hinted at a proposal."

Lady Heathway had read the note and appeared ready to guffaw. She passed it on to Lady Redfield, who held it out as if it had been dipped in poison, then it went on to Lady Featherstone, who whispered, "What an idea," and then ended with Lady Mendleton, who only stared at it wide-eyed.

"You see how bad it is? I thought, what is this about well-fed pheasants?" the duchess asked.

"Or the gentle diet of a new hatched bird?" Lady Heathway said, snorting into her napkin.

"As you can imagine, I had no intention of allowing Lady Isabel to view such drivel. But that was not the end. No, not the end at all."

The ladies leaned forward to hear what more was to come.

"My duke came home from his club, and it seems that Lord Harrington was in the coffee room reading his paper this morning. The duke was told all about how Lord Lymington and Mr. Vance were in there together over a sheet of paper. It was not Lord Lymington who wrote this, it was Vance, convincing the poor lord that the mention of birds had some sort of romance to it."

Lady Featherstone erupted in laughter. The duchess glared.

"Come now, Theodosia," Lady Featherstone said. "It is rather funny."

The duchess did not see anything funny in it at all.

Lady Heathway shrugged and said, "Well, Lymington is a bit of a dolt, and it seems Mr. Vance is an enterprising sort."

"I do not wish Lady Isabel to become interested in an enterprising sort. I wish her to take on Lord Lymington," the duchess said. "The question is, what am I to do about Mr. Vance?"

Though the ladies so often had much to say on this or that subject, none of them had an idea to put forth on this particular problem.

What on earth to do about Mr. Vance?

NOT FOR THE first time, Harry reflected on the value of being a single gentleman with a willingness to assist a hostess. He'd just received a note from Lady Fitzwallen, a personage he was acquainted with but did not know well.

It seemed her card party was this evening and Lord and Lady Langley had been called away on the queen's business. Would he mind stepping in? Miss Thompson's mother had already been attending and so would bring her daughter, leaving just one spot open for a gentleman.

He was at loose ends this night, and this might provide an opportunity. He might find the chance to hint to Miss Thompson that if she wished to get anywhere with Lymington, she would have to be direct about it. No, that was not even the right description. She'd have to hit him over the head with it.

Miss Thompson's overtures, coupled with the worst poem ever written in the history of time, might be enough to tip the scales in his favor. Miss Thompson could gently pull Lymington away from Lady Isabel, while the poem should act as a shove to assist her.

Harry of course wondered if there was the smallest chance that Lady Isabel would attend the card party, but he doubted it. At Ryland's ball, he'd asked her about her engagements, determined to muscle into some affair she would go to if there were a way to do it.

The next thing she would attend was the Tredwells' masque on the morrow.

He supposed she stayed in with the duchess this evening.

Harry could not imagine anything more tedious. The lady would likely spend hours talking about how wonderful Lord Lymington was and how awful Harry Vance was. She'd probably be sinking under that outsized tiara while she did it.

No matter, he would have his own say on the morrow.

LADY FITZWALLEN'S HOUSE was well-appointed and the mistress of it a rather jolly sort of woman. Isabel had been introduced to her and the lady had said, "Ah, the Plantagenet girl I've heard so much about. Very charming."

Isabel had been certain she'd colored. If anybody had heard anything at all about her family's long and winding history, it was most assuredly from the duchess. It always caused a sort of embarrassment. It presented her as this elevated creature, all the while failing to mention her real circumstances.

How charmed would Lady Fitzwallen be if she understood

that Isabel had no more means than a laborer's daughter and had often gone hungry or depended upon the charity of others to avoid it? Or that her household did not employ servants, other than a butler who ought to be retired and the occasional day hire from the village? Or perhaps the lady would be interested in the idea that she had no horse and carriage and her clothes, were it not for the duchess, were more repairs than original? Isabel felt a fraud at such moments.

Upon entering the drawing room, she noted the card tables set up, each with fresh packs of cards and stacks of paper and graphite to keep the scores. There was a sideboard running along the side of the room, piled heavy with sweets and savories, hot and cold dishes, an enormous cake, bottles of Canary wine, a punch bowl, and both a tea and coffee service. The evening would not likely be wildly entertaining but, however it was, she would not go hungry.

Just as she was considering whether a fruit tart or slice of cake would suit, she saw him. Harry Vance.

He was just this minute talking to Lord Ryland. Then he saw her too.

He excused himself from Lord Ryland and came toward her.

"Oh, why?" the duchess muttered.

"Your Grace, Lady Isabel," Mr. Vance said, bowing. "I did not expect to find you here."

"Your surprise could not possibly match my own," the duchess said drily.

"It seems Lord and Lady Langley bowed out," Mr. Vance said. "I am only an afterthought as a replacement. Do you play piquet, Lady Isabel?"

"Yes, of course," Isabel answered.

Before the duchess could interrupt any further inquiries, Lady Fitzwallen blew through the room. "Duchess, you'll want to be over there, with your duke and Lord and Lady Heathway—I remember the rivalry between you ladies and your husbands and fully expect you will trounce the gentlemen. Mr. Vance, what is your preferred game?"

"Piquet, my lady."

"Ah, perhaps Miss Thompson—"

"Lady Isabel prefers piquet as well," Mr. Vance said.

"I did not hear the word *preferred*," the duchess said, looking very irritated.

"Lady Isabel?" Lady Fitzwallen asked.

"Wherever you would like me to be," Isabel said, not certain where she herself wished to be.

"Piquet it is, then," Lady Fitzwallen said. "There is a table for you right there."

Isabel could practically feel the steam coming from the duchess. Though, it was too late now to do anything about it.

For his part, Mr. Vance looked rather amused at her fury. He really must be the only person in London who had not the slightest care for the duchess' opinions. Her disapproval seemed as water off a duck's back.

"This way, Lady Isabel," he said cheerfully.

They made their way to the table Lady Fitzwallen had directed them to. Mr. Vance said, "What would you prefer from the board? Tea, punch, wine?"

"Wine, I think," Isabel said. She might have been inclined to tea under different circumstances, but being so near Mr. Vance made her nerves jittery. Wine might go some way to calming them.

He returned with the wine and broke the seal on the deck. They drew cards and the deal went to Mr. Vance. He said, "I find myself glad that looks and frowns cannot physically injure a person. Else, I'd surely be dead by now, a victim of the duchess' narrowed eyes."

Isabel could not help but laugh. It was true the duchess was staring at him like he was the devil himself.

Perhaps he was, a little. Who but the devil could tempt one to overthrow a carefully laid out and eminently sensible plan the way he did?

Isabel examined her hand, discarded three and took from the stock. Mr. Vance discarded four and picked up. They then proceeded to call for point, sequence, triplets or fours.

Isabel put all her concentration on what Mr. Vance was calling. Piquet was impossible to win if one's mind wandered.

It seemed, at least for now, that he had not been dealt a very wonderful hand.

The preliminaries were got through and now the play began. Isabel laid down a card. Then Mr. Vance. She took the trick.

Mr. Vance said, "I had a friendly word with Miss Thompson regarding Lymington not a quarter hour ago."

Isabel did not respond. She did not wish to discuss Lord Lymington with Mr. Vance.

"She likes him, you know. Really likes him. She finds his bumbling about and awkward conversation rather endearing."

Isabel had of course noticed that Miss Thompson seemed to admire Lord Lymington at Lord Ryland's mystery supper. She had not known if it were genuine, or if Miss Thompson was only flattering a gentleman who would be a duke. She did not know Miss Thompson well enough to make such a judgment.

"Have you met Miss Thompson's father?"

"I have not," Isabel said, not at all clear what Miss Thompson's father had to do with anything.

In a lower voice, Mr. Vance said, "At the moment, he is very fortunately laid up with gout."

Isabel looked up from her cards in some surprise. What a thing to say. "Surely, Mr. Vance, you do not wish illness on another person."

"A man like that is best laid up, so he does not have the strength to cause trouble," Mr. Vance said. "Everybody knows what he is."

"I cannot comment on the gentleman," Isabel said, "as I certainly do not know what he is." Though, she wondered what it was that everybody knew.

"Well, I *can* comment, and it is a stretch to even call Viscount

Merdon a gentleman. He is a philanderer and a brute. But the reason I mention it is I believe that is why Miss Thompson finds herself so fond of Lymington. He can be a very great fool, but there is nothing brutish about him. As for philandering, I cannot imagine he would even notice if the opportunity somehow presented itself."

"Mr. Vance, I take exception to the idea that Lord Lymington is a fool," Isabel said, feeling a very great need to defend what might be her future husband.

"You know perfectly well that he is," Mr. Vance said, taking his first trick. "I do not hold it against him, he is a jolly enough fellow. But dolphins affecting the weather? Where on earth did he get such an idea?"

Isabel sighed. "That is not entirely his fault. I encouraged him to broaden his conversation, and he settled on weather and…I am afraid he got that idea from the duchess' butler, Mr. Carlson."

Mr. Vance appeared as if he might roar with laughter. "Of course he did, where else would he get such a notion but from that lady's household?"

Isabel was well aware that Carlson's theories were absurd, but she would not dream of admitting it.

"People are free to believe what they want," she said, the defiance in her voice evident to her own ears. And sounding rather stupid in the process.

"Certainly," Mr. Vance said, failing to conceal his amusement. "One may choose to believe the earth flat and fear sailing over the edge of the world if they wish, assuming they are not averse to being wrong. In any case, Miss Thompson was very forthcoming. She does singularly prefer Lymington."

"I suppose a lady can prefer whoever she likes," Isabel said. "Though I am surprised she would admit to it. It might lead to…"

"Disappointed hopes?" Mr. Vance asked.

"Yes."

"A risk, of course. But you see, I am determined that Miss Thompson's hopes are not disappointed. Both for her sake and Lymington's…and your own."

Isabel was rather shaken by that sentiment. It was exceedingly highhanded, and it meddled with her future!

"You have no cause to presume what would be for my sake. I would ask you to refrain from being so bold in your speech, Mr. Vance," Isabel said, her cards shaking in her hand.

"I cannot help it, perhaps it is the tradesman's blood in me that speaks so plainly. Miss Thompson is half in love with Lymington already. She adores his gentleness and doesn't give a toss for his missteps. I cannot think it fair for Lymington to miss out on someone who holds real affection for him. I cannot think he would rather prefer being only somebody's security net."

"I am certain Lord Lymington is well able to conduct his own affairs without your interference," Isabel said, her cards bending under the pressure of her fingers.

"Are you? Because I am not. I informed Miss Thompson that although Lymington is unflaggingly genial, he can be dumb as a rock. If she wishes to get anywhere with him, she's going to have to communicate her interest very directly."

Is this what it had come to? Was Mr. Vance really attempting to interfere with her future in such a manner? It was exceedingly rude and misguided. And dangerous.

What if he were to sink every suitable match that came her way? What if he were to be around long enough to weaken her defenses?

They were coming to the last few cards and Isabel willed herself to focus on the game and not Mr. Vance's various conversational outrages.

He took the last three tricks.

Isabel stared at the table as she began to comprehend how he'd done it. He'd held back during the calling, choosing to forgo those points so that he might hide their existence in his hand and leaving her to guess they were still in the stock.

It was a daring play, and not often done.

"Did you sink those cards?" she asked.

"I did," Mr. Vance said smiling. "It seems I always have a trick up my sleeve."

CHAPTER FOURTEEN

HARRY COULD NOT have been more delighted with the happenstances of the evening. First, he was unexpectedly invited to Lady Fitzwallen's card party, then he had the opportunity to speak plainly to Miss Thompson, and then Lady Isabel had miraculously appeared and he'd maneuvered himself as her partner.

He'd found Miss Thompson worlds away from a shrinking violet. He'd asked her for her opinion of Lymington and he'd got it. She found the fellow handsome in his own particular way and thought his seemingly always rumpled appearance had a certain charm to it. She found his way of being in the world delightful. Further, she was a keen horsewoman, as was he. He might not be a renaissance man, but he knew horses.

Harry had been hard-pressed not to laugh when she said, "I saw him in the park today and we spent a good half hour discussing how MacBeth was managing to throw shoes so often. I advised him to stop blaming MacBeth and get a new farrier."

That was a rather good thought.

Miss Thompson went on. "He was delighted with the advice, though he also told me he is not to speak of horses in certain quarters. Only the weather, which he is being educated on by some lunatic of a butler who thinks fish have something to do with it."

"Oh yes," Harry had said, "the dolphins."

"You know, when he spoke of it at Ryland's ball I assumed it was a passing fancy and was amused by it. Today, when I realized he was intending on making it a permanent topic, I gave him some advice. I told him, there is not a thing wrong with talking about horses and I am always happy to do it. He seemed very relieved to hear it."

Harry had appreciated Miss Thompson's forthright speech and said, "While Lymington may have certain charms, understanding subtlety will not be one of them. My advice is, hit him over the head with your interest."

Miss Thompson had laughed and said, "You mean, club him and drag him into my cave."

Yes, Miss Thompson, that is exactly it.

He'd proceeded to apprise Lady Isabel of where things stood. She might be willing to ignore her own heart, but then she might have more of a care for Lymington's.

He'd flustered her all the way through cards, he knew that.

Harry did not wish to cause Lady Isabel pain or upset, but she must see where she was going wrong! A person could not arrange their entire life around only safety.

He was not immune to the feeling of wishing to be secure. He'd worked hard to see that it was so on his estate. But that could not be the one and only driving force of a life.

No. It was not enough.

He'd beaten her handily at piquet. He had, for a moment, thought of allowing her to win. But then, he'd decided that it would be better for her to see how clever he could be when he put his mind to it.

He'd sunk three cards and she had not seen it coming.

After he'd had the difficult conversation regarding Miss Thompson and Lymington, he'd moved on to another topic—his estate.

He described every aspect of it in great detail. Perhaps in making it real, he would also make real the idea that there was nothing to fear. It was prosperous, and he made the point that he followed Lord Bertridge's method of stewardship—diversify, expand, carefully maintain, buy land when the opportunity arose, hire the best people, and pay them fairly.

She was that lord's neighbor and must be well aware of his success.

Harry thought he'd made some important inroads this night.

Now, his valet was taking his clothes from him.

"Well," Smith said, "dare I ask for highlights?"

"You always dare ask," Harry said, laughing. "Miss Thompson was talked to and set straight, Lady Isabel was there, much to my surprise, and I partnered with her in piquet. Finally, the duchess would like to murder me."

"All in all, a success," Smith said.

"Yes, I rather think it was."

CARLSON STARED GRIMLY out the window. The rain came down in sheets, just in time for Lady Tredwell's masque. The whales and dolphins were at it again. Why could they not settle themselves and act as proper animals? Instead, they were gallivanting about, throwing the weather topsy-turvy and very carelessly inconveniencing everybody.

He stopped himself. Were they, though?

He was beginning to fear that he was slowly going mad. Somehow, he was starting to believe the theories he posited about dolphins and whales and crows and foxes. He could almost see the whales and dolphins frolicking and causing a weather disturbance. It could be true, after all. Nobody had ever proved it was *not* true.

But somewhere in his mind there was that small voice, that still sane voice. It said, *You know perfectly well it is all stuff and nonsense. You've never seen a dolphin in your life and have no idea what they get up to.*

Had this spiral into insanity been what had happened to his

old mentor, Lord Ingraham? Had the gentleman developed his theories until it seemed they must be real, and he was, for all intents and purposes, a madman?

It was all well and good for Lord Ingraham to go mad—he could afford it. But what of a mad butler? Would he end his days in Bedlam, attempting to convince his jailors that the rain was the dolphins' fault?

Fortunately, or unfortunately depending on who was looking at it, the duchess had descended into madness right along with him. If he said dolphins were to blame, she cursed the dolphins. As for the servants, they did not dare say anything about it.

With one notable exception, it seemed. That new lady's maid—Betsy.

Oh, she had plenty to say. She was, *allegedly*, a farmer's daughter. She went on and on about seasons and *alleged* types of clouds and wind direction. All things *allegedly* taught her by her father.

What did a farmer think he knew about the weather? *If* she was really a farmer's daughter at all.

That unpleasant lady passed by him just now and whispered, "Those awful dolphins!"

Wrong, Betsy, *allegedly* the farmer's daughter. It is *you* who are awful!

⇒⟫⟫⟫✳⟪⟪⟪⟸

SMITH HAD COME through as always. He'd secured Harry a costume for Lady Tredwell's masque that would say what he wished to say. He was to be Henry V, battling impossible odds to victory and then wooing his new bride. He would be no idiot Romeo, killing himself before he was even certain his Juliet was actually dead.

He added a black half-masque to complete the ensemble. If the duchess looked closely, she would recognize him. However, he did not plan on giving her the time to do it.

He had got to the Tredwells' early and then bided his time for a full forty-five minutes. As if on cue, a mass of people began to arrive. He weaved this way and that through the crowd, always looking out for Lady Isabel and blending in with the sea of people. As of yet, she and the duchess had not arrived.

Though he had come in steeling his nerves for what he planned to do this night, he could not help being caught up short and nearly roaring with laughter at what he just now found before him.

Lady Featherstone stood proudly as a Bow Street Runner, her tall top hat and blue jacket with two rows of brass buttons proclaiming it to the world. That would not have been so striking though. When one's eyes traveled further down, it was apparent that the lady was wearing pants. They were loose and revealed nothing, but they *were* trousers. The whole thing was capped off by men's shoes. Harry would not be surprised if, after the ball, Lady Featherstone leapt on her horse and set out across London to run down criminals.

To complete the comedy, Lady Mendleton, dressed as a Madonna holding a lifeless baby by means of a doll, was staring wide-eyed at the costume while Lady Redfield swiveled her head right and left like a bird looking for an open window.

He moved closer beside them as he would be delighted to hear their conversation.

Lady Redfield, dressed as a Dutch lady of old and stumbling around in wooden shoes, said, "Goodness Anne, that costume is rather, that is…the lower half of it is…well…it seems…brave?"

"Brave?" Lady Mendleton said. "But it is pants."

"Yes, so it is," Lady Featherstone said confidently. "It is more important that the costume be accurate than to bow to any notion of false modesty. My lord has had nothing to say against it and so you can have no cause to either."

"Lord Featherstone approves this," Lady Mendleton asked in some wonder. "It is exceedingly liberal of him."

Lady Featherstone had an obstinate look on her features. "He *would* approve. If he knew. He is at Newmarket just now."

Lady Mendleton peered at her closely. "I am afraid I know what has happened to you, Anne. You have experienced some sort of breakdown over Lord Ryland's mystery supper, haven't you? You think that topaz ring Lady Isabel won should be on your own finger."

"I think no such thing," Lady Featherstone said, drawing herself up. "I do, however, believe that the wrong housekeeper was arrested. I have dedicated hours of my life to studying these matters and I have a keen instinct about them."

"Who was the other housekeeper, though?" Lady Redfield asked, beginning to tip over and grabbing hold of Lady Mendleton's arm to stay upright.

"That, right there, is the *real* mystery," Lady Featherstone said.

"Oh dear," Lady Mendleton said. "Anne, might I suggest you go to the card room and sit down and then do not get up? Perhaps not too many people will notice this…aberration. Which I am certain is only temporary."

Lady Featherstone sniffed at this suggestion. Lady Redfield, always the peacemaker, said, "Excellent notion, though. Cards are so pleasant, are they not? And you, Louisa, tell us about your costume."

"I am the Madonna," Lady Mendleton said, gazing down at the doll in her arms as if it were an actual baby. "I thought, what is most important to my life? Who am I, really? Of course I knew that it must be motherhood, or grandmotherhood." Lady Mendleton suddenly laughed and said, "I am the Grand-Madonna!"

"Well! That is…pleasant," Lady Redfield said.

"Cecilia," Lady Mendleton said, "Might I suggest you and Anne go to the card room together? I fear you will not stay upright for long in those wooden shoes."

"Goodness, I did have doubts about them," Lady Redfield

said, peering down at them. "It was Lord Jeffries' idea, he's to come as a dutchman and he did say he wished to escort a Dutch lady round the floor if I would consider matching."

"I am afraid you will twist your ankles," Lady Mendleton said.

"I *am* a bit unsteady," Lady Redfield admitted. "I fell in my bedchamber and then again in the drawing room before I even got out of the house. I did not wish Lord Jeffries to be disappointed, though, and I did imagine I would somehow get used to them."

"Of course you will. Do not allow your confidence to be shaken," Lady Featherstone said to Lady Redfield. Despite the lady's stalwart defense, she suddenly paled as she looked toward the door.

"It's the duchess," Lady Redfield fairly squeaked out.

Harry whipped his head around toward the door. There was more than one duchess batting around London, but based on Lady Featherstone's white face, he was certain which duchess he would find. There was only one duchess *he* was interested in, and that was the particular one who escorted Lady Isabel.

Finally, there was the lady he waited for.

Lady Isabel was magnificent as a Greek, possibly as Helen of Troy. That would be very apropos. She had, after all, started a war.

She was dressed simply in elegant white folds of material that draped. The shoulders and waistband were done in gold embroidery and a gold silk sash was gathered on one side and knotted on the shoulder. Her glorious auburn hair hung loose in soft flowing waves, topped by a gold crown.

Harry had not seen her hair undone before and he imagined that was what it looked like when she rose from her bed. He had the urge to run his fingers through it.

As for the duchess, she added to the hilarity he had already witnessed from her friends, as she had clearly styled herself a Plantagenet queen. The awful emerald tiara plunked atop a floor-sweeping lace veil drifting down her back, the rich fabrics, the long outer cape glittering with paste jewels all told the tale.

For once, the lady did not wear brocade, but had chosen a purple velvet to announce her royal status. It seemed she had taken on Lady Isabel's rarified blood as her own.

Harry made certain his mask was in place and then strode by the duchess and Lady Isabel. Making his voice deeper and growly to disguise it, he said, "Lady Featherstone is in trousers."

It had the desired effect.

Like a falcon diving down after prey, the duchess pulled her cape close and flew toward the Bow Street Runner.

Harry circled back around and caught up to Lady Isabel who had, at least for the moment, been left behind.

"Lady Isabel," he said.

"Mr. Vance," she said, seeming a bit flustered. He was pleased though, she had instantly recognized his voice.

Then she said, "Wait a moment, did you just send the duchess on a goose chase?"

"I sent her, but it was no ruse. Lady Featherstone really is wearing pants. I did not even bother to mention Lady Redfield teetering on wood shoes and Lady Mendleton carries a doll, as the duchess will discover that for herself."

"Goodness," Lady Isabel said.

"Good for me, I think. May I put myself down on your card?"

"Should you?" she asked.

"Yes," Harry said with determination. "I most definitely should."

Lady Isabel gave him her card, albeit reluctantly. She was such a contrary creature. He was certain she liked him and yet she was always trying to push him away. All because of her wrong-headed ideas. No matter, when it came to it, he was certain she would not refuse him. Frightened she might be, but she would not throw her future away because of it.

He took his opportunity and wrote himself down for her supper. The duchess would not approve, but he did not much care.

She saw that he had done so and said quietly, "Oh."

"Yes, I know. The duchess will be as mad as a large bull in a small pen on a hot day," he said. "I have every confidence she will not die of the feeling, though."

The duchess returned to Lady Isabel and Harry glanced behind him to see if Lady Featherstone had been reduced to tears or whether Lady Redfield had yet tipped over in her wooden shoes.

Lady Redfield was now hanging on the arm of Lord Jeffries to remain standing. Lady Featherstone had her chin up in an expression of firm resolve. Lady Mendleton clutched her doll as if the duchess had threatened to make off with it. Which she probably had.

"Mr. Vance," the duchess said.

Harry attempted not to smile. Her words might only be *Mr. Vance*, but her meaning was closer to *Get away from my girl this instant you nobody of a person.*

The duchess reached for Lady Isabel's card, and she slowly handed it over.

"Supper? Really, Mr. Vance. I cannot have this, I just cannot—"

She was interrupted in whatever awful thing she planned to say by Lord Lymington, who'd just lumbered over to them.

If his tight doublet and even tighter breeches were not enough to stun the senses, his hat would complete the job. It was a squat cap sporting an alarmingly long yellow ostrich feather that waved enthusiastically back and forth as if it attempted to catch somebody's attention.

"Lady Isabel, Duchess, Vance, how do you do? Duchess, what weather! The dolphins are at it again, eh? Contrary creatures. Lady Isabel, may I?" he asked, holding his hand out for her card. Then, seeing no card, he looked about confused.

The duchess handed it over with a sigh.

"Vance! You devil! You got on for supper. Well, that's all right. I'll take the first. Lady Isabel, I've written my mother all about things here in Town—you, the dolphins, weather in general, no more horse talk! I've made that clear. She'll like that, she's always telling me to shut up about MacBeth."

A silence lingered then, as nobody quite knew what to say about Lord Lymington's mother telling him to shut up.

The duchess finally cleared her throat and said, "Tell me of your costume, Lord Lymington."

"Romeo. You know, from the play," Lord Lymington said. He paused and looked as if something troubled him. "Though, that poor fellow really ought to have called a doctor instead of just deciding she was dead. Juliet, you know. I cannot like it. I've always thought that was a mistake."

Harry pressed his lips together tight. Romeo had made a *mistake*? Rather!

"What do you think, Vance?" Lymington asked him. "Did he not make a mistake there?"

Harry was doing all he could to maintain some appearance of seriousness. "It seems they did not have a lick of sense between them," he said.

"That's true!" Lord Lymington said. "It cannot be right to kill oneself with so little thinking over."

"Certainly not," Harry said, his stomach beginning to pain him from holding in his laughter.

He bowed and then bowed out before laughter overtook him. It was likely well that he did so. If he lingered, he would end up laughing. Or worse, the duchess might come up with some idea to thwart him.

For now, he was on Lady Isabel's card for supper and not a duchess or an ill-advised Romeo could get him off.

This was his moment. His future was within reach.

As Henry V said, *unto the breach.*

ISABEL HAD SEEN clearly enough that Mr. Vance was holding in his laughter. She could not entirely blame him, Lord Lymington did sometimes say the most confounding things. There were times when the most obvious thing in the world seemed to strike him as a new and novel idea.

Well, she supposed it was fortunate that if Lord Lymington *did* ever have such an unfortunate moment as to contemplate killing himself, he had made the firm decision to at least pause to think it over.

After both gentlemen had moved off, the duchess said, "I am finding this evening getting off to a very irritating start."

"Because Mr. Vance has put himself down for my supper," Isabel said.

"Yes, that is certainly one of the things I do not like. He is very bold and I do not care for it. I think sometimes he is secretly laughing at me, which I *really* cannot countenance. If people take to laughing at those superior to them, where will we be?"

ISABEL DID NOT speculate on where they would be, as she rather thought they were already there. Deriding those located up the chain seemed to be a favored English sport. It was only that Mr. Vance did not particularly hide his amusement.

"If there is any comfort to be had," the duchess went on, "I can assure myself that Mr. Vance's stratagems will get him nowhere. You have far too much good sense to be swayed by his smarmy manners and mien of savoir faire. The facts belie his veneer of polish. He cannot dodge his tradesman grandfather or his lack of connections."

Isabel had not answered that opinion, but the duchess was right. Mr. Vance might be the handsomest man in the room, he might be entertaining, he might have some sort of undefinable and undeniable pull on her. None of that changed the facts of him.

"As if Mr. Vance were not maddening enough," the duchess said, "I should at least be able to count on my friends not to represent themselves as a collection of lunatics," the duchess went on, narrowing her eyes at Lady Featherstone.

Isabel could not possibly answer that. To agree would be to insult the lady's friends and to disagree would be to insult the lady herself.

"Lady Featherstone is in trousers, and it shall be the talk of every drawing room on the morrow. Of course, she is already known as an eccentric. But eccentricity is not the same as madness! The lady has lost her faculties."

Isabel glanced over at the lady in question. It was true, she was drawing an unusual amount of looks.

"And then Lady Redfield," the duchess went on, "staggering about like a sailor searching for his sea legs. How long will it be before she hits the floor? What was Lord Jeffries thinking to suggest it?"

Isabel could not imagine what Lord Jeffries had been thinking as he did not look all that steady in his own wooden shoes.

"And the icing on the cake is Louisa. Oh, at first glance there seems nothing amiss. But then one notices the doll. Apparently, her costume is meant to be some sort of Madonna. What is she to do with that baby at a card table? Or at supper? Throw it under her chair?"

"I suppose designing a costume every year can prove challenging," Isabel said vaguely and for lack of anything else to say.

"Not for anybody with sense," the duchess said. "Well, at least you look lovely. Despite the setbacks, let us attempt to enjoy the evening."

And so, the duchess' account of her friends ended on that happy note.

ISABEL'S DANCE WITH Lord Lymington was by turns strange and illuminating. He kicked off the conversation with some new ideas about the weather and whales that he was planning to discuss with Carlson.

Could it be that when they spouted, the force of it pierced the clouds and set the weather in a new direction?

Isabel had replied that, of course, anything was possible. Though really, she did not think *that* was particularly possible.

Then the lord had seemed dejected and explained that if he were correct about the whales, what in the world were the dolphins doing?

"Perhaps you might expand your topics of conversation, Lord Lymington," she said, hinting that he should not only speak of weather, whales, and dolphins. Or never speak of them, which would be preferable.

The lord did not seem to know where to go with the hint.

Isabel said, "Perhaps you might read a book?"

"*Is* there a book on weather?" Lord Lymington asked. "Carlson has not mentioned any."

Isabel was rather afraid that Carlson had created a bigger problem than the one she'd attempted to solve. Lord Lymington's penchant for talking about his horses had been a little tedious, but it had not been as strange as his new interest in whales and dolphins.

"No, I mean a book about some new topic, like geography, or philosophy."

Before Lord Lymington could express any feelings on the matter, they were suddenly bumped into rather hard. Isabel did not fall, but she did stumble. Lord Lymington had teetered back and forth, and it looked as if he might go over, but he thankfully regained his balance.

Isabel turned to discover what had happened and could not quite believe what she was looking at. Like a set of dominoes, people were going down across the floor. One person hit the next, who hit the next.

CHAPTER FIFTEEN

I SABEL GAZED ROUND in some confusion at the dozens of people who had either fallen on the ballroom floor or were currently on their way to that location. Medieval ladies struggled with their head pieces gone askew, men in dominos became twisted in their capes, a milkmaid rolled over a bishop, a jester staggered and fell on an abbess, a magician landed in the lap of a splayed Cleopatra, and Lady Mendleton's doll sailed overhead, landing on a sultan's fez.

Amidst the chaos, Isabel thought she suddenly spotted the culprits of this bizarre circumstance.

Lord Jeffries crawled toward one of Lady Redfield's wooden shoes, which was just now situated some distance from the foot it was meant to be on. The lady herself was on her hands and knees, staring at it as if she could will it to come back to her.

"Sorry everybody!" Lord Jeffries shouted.

The fellow grabbed the wooden shoe and got it back on the foot it had so recently abandoned. He struggled to his feet and proceeded to pull Lady Redfield to her own feet. They staggered and weaved off to the refreshment room together.

Goodness, Lady Redfield and Lord Jeffries had taken down half the ballroom.

The dancers, some shocked and some amused, depending on how they had been affected, began to get to their feet. Some rearranged themselves back into order and worked to determine where they'd left off dancing. Others appeared to have their fill of the activity and limped off the floor.

"I think it was their shoes," Lord Lymington said. "Too coincidental for both people to fall down at the same time while they were both wearing strange shoes. It had to be the shoes."

"I believe you are right," Isabel said, willing herself not to laugh. Poor Lady Redfield—the duchess would have steam coming from her ears.

They carried on with the dance, though the looks on other people's faces gave Isabel the idea that Lady Redfield's and Lord Jeffries' shoes would be alongside the appearance of the Bow Street Runner and Lady Mendleton's doll as a topic of conversation on the morrow.

As she was contemplating how the duchess would take it, Lord Lymington did an abrupt about-face in the conversation. He began discussing the letter to his mother, and then his estate, and then his costume. It seemed these things were all somehow related, though Isabel was not at first clear how.

Then it became far more clear.

"My mother wants me to marry, she's very set on it. So, Romeo. Right?"

Lord Lymington did not come out and ask for her hand, but he was leading up to it. Isabel had begun to become adept at unraveling the lord's unique way of expressing himself. It probably helped that she'd had so much experience unraveling her father's own unique way of talking. A proposal was definitely where Lord Lymington was going.

"I did not tell *your* duchess, but I've heard back from *my* duchess already," Lord Lymington said, looking very pleased with himself. "She and the duke will come to Town in a fortnight. You know, to look things over."

By things, Isabel was certain it was herself to be looked over.

"After that I guess I'll go to Hertfordshire!" Lord Lymington said, alluding to a meeting with her father.

This had got very serious far more quickly than she'd thought possible. He'd made some sort of declaration to his parents and now they would come to meet her.

It was hard to know what to think of it. It should not be hard, it was what she wished for. But it was hard to take in all the same.

On the one side, a marriage to Lord Lymington would fulfill all her requirements. His estate was on safe ground, and she would have the protection of a vast network of well-established and powerful relatives.

As for the lord himself, it was very unlikely that he would ever bring disaster down upon her head. He was no Melburton, she could not imagine him ever violent. He did not seem a gambler or to drink to excess. His worst vice would likely be buying too many horses. And then talking about them. And the weather.

He was a cheerful sort of fellow and, while he did not touch her feelings in the slightest, she liked him as a friend well enough.

On the other side was her stupid heart. How self-indulgent she was becoming. How lacking in discipline and logic and good sense! How absurd that she should wish for all that Lord Lymington could provide *and* a man that made her heart beat faster.

The truth was, that man did not exist. She would have to choose, to prioritize. She could not have everything she wished for.

Isabel had been silent as Lord Lymington lumbered her around the floor. She imagined herself far into the future. How would her life have been? How did it all turn out? Why could she not be told for certain—this way is your only course?

She would not be told, though. The future was a mysterious and shrouded thing, only to be guessed at. It seemed either way she went, she would leave a regret behind her.

What would she regret more? Following her heart into a possible disaster, or following her head and leaving her heart behind?

Isabel took in a deep breath. She knew. Finally and with surety, she knew what she must do.

IT HAD, SO far, been a strange sort of evening. On the one hand, Harry had been endlessly entertained and diverted by the antics of the matrons of *The Society of Sponsoring Ladies.*

He had been fortunate enough to be in a position to see Lord Jeffries determinedly stumble through a quadrille, with Lady Redfield gamely swerving with him. La Poule had proved too much for the couple. One of Lady Redfield's shoes had shot off her foot like a ball out of a cannon and the couple had promptly gone down like a sack of potatoes.

It would have been hilarious enough had it only been their own misfortune to meet the floor in such a surprising fashion, but they'd inadvertently set off a chain of knock-overs across the ballroom like so many bowling pins. He'd only narrowly kept his partner from being one of them.

The final touch to the comedy had been Lord Jeffries shouting, "Sorry everybody!" as he crawled along the floor after Lady Redfield's shoe.

As all of that went on, though, he could not forget his purpose this night. He was to ask the momentous question every gentleman must eventually ask. He'd put it off from season to season, waiting for *her.* Now, she was here, and he'd got to do something about it.

He'd never, in imagining the moment, thought of any difficulties that might come with it. But then, was not Lady Isabel worth some difficulty?

She liked him. He knew it. She might even love him, if he was not flattering himself to think so. He could see it in her eyes.

Of course, he was rather more sure of his own feelings. He was stupidly in love with the lady.

She must say yes. She must cast aside whatever worries she

had for her future and grab hold of the future she was meant to have.

IT WAS WITH resolve that Isabel allowed Mr. Vance to lead her through the dance before supper. It was with a firm eye on her future and a decided opinion on where that future must be.

There must be no more nonsense and vacillations. It was time to stop her girlish thoughts and become a woman who managed her fate with logic and determination.

She did find it, as always, disturbing to be so close to him. Perhaps she always would find it so. But the feeling would not destroy her. She could live with it. Most likely.

Mr. Vance said, "I can only find it fitting that you have come as Helen of Troy, the greatest beauty that ever walked the earth. So beautiful that she could start a war."

"The duchess chose my costume and I am sure she did not entertain any such notions," Isabel said, wishing him to stop being so charming.

"Poor Helen," Mr. Vance went on, "the writers of old could never agree on her motives. Did she love Paris or Menelaus? Did she love Troy or Sparta?"

Isabel turned her face away. Mr. Vance was clever and she understood his meaning. If she were Helen, where was her heart really? With a new-minted barony or a longstanding dukedom? With Mr. Vance or Lord Lymington?

He could not know that her head was in one location and her heart in another. He should know, though, that she depended on her head's judgment. She had made that clear to him.

Though she may have vacillated at times, she had done so silently. She had not given herself away. She did not think. Now, she'd made her firm and final decision.

It was confounding that he should broach such a conversation, though. It had wit and spoke to his intelligence and education. It was thrilling to hear him speak so. It was also a very wide leap away from whales and dolphins.

But Lord Lymington had summoned his parents. He would ask for her hand. Everything she wanted was within reach.

"Personally," Mr. Vance said, "I think Helen was only confused. Which way should she turn? Where did she really belong?"

If that were what Helen was faced with, then they were indeed very similar. It had been a mighty and exhausting struggle to decide to go one way or the other. But she *had* decided which way to go, and it was no matter that she could not be entirely happy with it. It was a decision of sense. Joy and happiness were not the only yardsticks with which to measure.

She had finally understood that there was a price to pay for everything. She had decided what she wanted, and she would pay for the choice.

Mr. Vance led her back to their place and another couple took their turn.

He leaned over to her and whispered, "But I would ask this Helen to choose and would point out that her fears are no more substantial than a morning fog that burns off in the sun. If only she will see it."

Isabel was frozen. Except her heart, which was nearly bursting. Her eyes welled and she willed them to stop it.

"Lady Isabel," he said, "will you choose me? Will you consent to become my wife?"

He'd said it. He'd asked. He should not have asked!

Isabel bit down hard on her lip to stop herself from sobbing. In a shaking voice that hardly sounded like her own, she whispered, "I am grateful for the courtesy, but I must regretfully decline."

Mr. Vance did not answer, but she could feel the heat coming from him, as if he would explode.

It was terrible and terrifying, and she had done it. She had wrought this. She should have been more firm in pushing him off all along. It was her own fault that she'd been not firm enough, that she may have given him the idea that there was a chance, even if only a small one.

She'd not been able to be so firm. The regret she anticipated as a result of making the sensible choice washed over her like a rogue wave that could sink a ship. She could hardly catch her breath.

This was the moment. This was the moment she had chosen a path to follow and she would leave her heart by the side of the road, never to be examined more.

"Nobody could love you more and instead you will run and hide. Your entire life will be guided by your fear. You will end up regretting it," Mr. Vance said gruffly.

Isabel recoiled from his words. She had thought he would protect his dignity by acting as if her refusal was no great matter. She'd understood that was what a disappointed gentleman did. He had not though. He spoke of her future regret. It was perhaps not the most appropriate sentiment, but there could hardly be a truer one. She regretted it already.

Though her mind was being battered from all sides from her heart's urgent signals, she was at least clear on one thing. She could not dine with Mr. Vance as if nothing at all had happened.

She pinched herself to stop from blubbering on the ballroom floor. Gathering all her resolve, she said, "In light of the…circumstances, it may be well for me to develop a headache and retire."

"Agreed," Mr. Vance said sharply.

His anger nearly took her breath away.

The dance came to an end.

Everything came to an end.

Isabel curtsied and hurried away to find the duchess. She must leave this place before she could no longer contain herself and made a very great and hysterical scene.

⤜⤜⤜•⤛⤛⤛

HARRY CRASHED THROUGH his front doors, not waiting for a footman to open it. His butler took one look at him and stepped aside. He jogged up the stairs and stumbled into his bedchamber.

Smith was on his heels, his valet hearing the commotion. The man went right to the decanter of brandy and poured him a large glass. "I do not know what has happened, but it is surely terrible. Please tell me you do not have some appointment at dawn lined up."

"She refused me," Harry said, draining the glass of brandy and slamming it on a dresser. "She still cannot see that she is preventing her own happiness!"

"Then, you are convinced that she loves you, but not enough to overlook your rather recent entry into the *ton*?"

"It's the connections," Harry said. "Her father has been bailed out who knows how many times by his network of deep-pocketed relatives."

"So she wishes for the same guarantees," Smith said. "Perhaps there will be another lady some time in future who will not come with such a damaged psyche?"

Smith said the words in a hopeful tone, though Harry knew well enough that neither of them held out such a possibility.

"There will not be another lady of any sort of psyche," Harry said. He knew it to be true. He'd been looking for her and had found her and that was that.

"What shall you do, then?" Smith asked. "You must have an heir, or your cousin—"

"Yes, I know. My idiot cousin will run the estate into the ground until it is worth nothing," Harry said.

He paused. Why was he giving up so easily? Did no gentle-man ever make a second run at it? Certainly, they must have.

"I could ask again. And then again. And again if necessary."

"Ah, wear the lady down," Smith said.

"Yes. No. I don't know. No, it won't work. The only thing that would work would be to fix the underlying problem."

"Which is?"

"Her damn father!"

"How do you propose to fix her father?" Smith said, beginning to look alarmed.

"Pack me a bag, and one for you too. We leave for Hertfordshire in the morning. And get me pen and paper. I will send a message to Bertridge by fast horse. He is that idiot earl's neighbor."

ISABEL HAD SEARCHED the card room for the duchess and then blurted out some nonsense of having a terrible headache. The duchess had most likely paid more attention to her general state than she did her words and hurried her to the front hall. The carriage was called, a vinaigrette waved under her nose, and a glassful of sherry was pressed into her hands.

Once inside the carriage, Isabel could not control herself any longer. The duchess was by turns frightened at the violence of her outburst and angry at whoever had caused it.

That was, until Isabel was able to choke out the real case of it. Lord Lymington had hinted that his father and mother soon came to have a look at her, and she was certain he would ask. Then Mr. Vance *had* asked, and she'd been sensible and refused him.

She could see well enough that, while the duchess was all kindness over her upset, she did not really understand the cause of it. To her, Mr. Vance was an unimportant inconvenience. To Isabel, he was the man who broke her heart. And she had broken his too, she suspected.

They had reached the house and the duchess had hurried her charge upstairs and sent Betsy for a hot cocoa.

As the maid hurried off, Isabel sat on the bed sobbing. She'd cried all the way home and was still crying. It felt as if she might weep all the rest of her life, though surely the tears would run out at some point.

"I know you feel the sting of it now, my dear," the duchess said. "I have never approved of Mr. Vance, but I will give him his due. He is well-spoken and can be charming and is very pleasant to look at. I say nothing against all of that. Then, Lord Lymington is rather…Lord Lymington. But you have made the sensible choice, as all women must. Determining who to marry is determining the course of your life. We have no other card to play."

Isabel nodded. She knew the duchess spoke the truth. In fact, she'd articulated it better than any of Isabel's thoughts ever had. She'd made the right choice. It was her only card to play. It just felt terrible to have played it.

Betsy bustled in with a tray. Though the duchess had only asked for cocoa, Betsy had loaded it with the cup of cocoa, biscuits, and a brown bottle of some sort.

"Laudanum," the duchess said. "Very good thought. It will help you to sleep, Isabel. Sleep is what you need just now."

"If you don't mind me saying, Your Grace," Betsy said, "I'll get Lady Isabel into her nightclothes and sit with her until the spoonful has taken its effect."

"You are very good, Betsy," the duchess said. She squeezed Isabel's fingers and said, "Put yourself in the hands of your maid. Trust that you have used your head to make a rational decision. Things will not seem quite so awful in the morning."

Isabel had nodded, though she did not have particularly high hopes for the morning. For now, she would be comforted to cry on Betsy's shoulder.

And she did cry. Two hours later, a second dose of laudanum was given and that finally did have an effect. Her mind grew foggy as she watched the scenes pass by, all of the future she'd regretfully left by the side of the road. Her head had prevailed, but had broken her heart in the process.

LORD BERTRIDGE FOLDED the note that had only minutes ago been given to him and went in search of his wife.

He found Caroline in her dressing room, resplendent in the last stages of her pregnancy. He was certain she grew more beautiful by the hour.

"Bertie," she said, "I understood you were to set off early to have a look at how the new cheese-making equipment gets on."

"So I was," he said, kissing the top of his wife's head. "However, I just got a note from Harry Vance. I have no idea what is coming our way."

He handed the paper to his wife, and she unfolded it.

Bertridge—

The Earl of Somerdon must be straightened out once and for all. I do not know the details of how that gentleman has chosen to carry on, but I do know that he has done untold damage to his daughter. I will not stand for it. I will not tolerate it. I will see that irresponsible fellow set right myself.

Harry Vance

"Oh, I see," Caroline said smiling. "Mr. Vance is in love."

"Is that what it is?"

"Most assuredly," Caroline said.

Seeing the rather befuddled expression on her lord's face, she said, "Do not fret over it. Mr. Vance is certain to come to us and give us a more detailed explanation of what has occurred. It's bound to be fascinating—not every gentleman is so bold as to confront a lady's father."

Bertridge nodded. "No doubt, he is bold. Though, how he expects to straighten out Somerdon is a mystery."

"And there, we are in full agreement, my love."

"Now what do you do, closeted away up here?" Lord Bertridge asked. "Dare I hazard a guess you are hiding from my aunt?"

"Let us not call it hiding," Caroline said, laughing. "Let us call it staying out of her way. I have heard from my maid that Lady Easton is on a rampage about organizing and labeling the spices in the kitchens. Cook's assurances that she knows what everything is without a label on it has fallen on deaf ears and that poor lady is fanning herself in a corner somewhere."

Lord Bertridge sighed. He was very fond of his aunt. He just wished she was not so organized. Or so energetic. Or so interested in the workings of his house.

⇶⇷

HARRY HAD RARELY been in such a temper. As a usual thing, he was not inclined to anger. If a circumstance did set him off, which was rare, the feeling did not linger. He was of an optimistic and cheerful temperament.

Not so now.

Now, he'd already spent a full night seething. Everything that had led up to Lady Isabel's refusal of his suit could be laid at her father's door. Therefore, all of his anger had turned in that direction.

They'd left London at dawn and he'd seethed on horseback all the way to Hertfordshire. He only seethed more as the day grew brighter and he turned down Lady Isabel's drive. The lane was so overgrown as to be half its original width. He did not think his anger could possibly bloom any larger, but on approach to the house, it did.

Missing windowpanes, shingles from the roof scattered across the drive, a fountain that did not look as if it had been operational in a decade—the place was crumbling around the earl's ears.

If there were anything edifying about the scene, it was that it had transformed what he understood about Lady Isabel. He had intellectually known perfectly well that her fears were rooted in what she had lived. Now, he'd seen it with his own eyes. Now he'd *viscerally* felt it, as she would have done. Now, he began to see why she could not put aside her fears.

My God, if the earl could not afford servants, he could have very well walked out here himself and cleaned this mess up.

Smith looked about and muttered, "Apparently there is no broom on the premises."

Harry was ready to throttle the earl before he reached the front doors.

He and Smith dismounted their horses. Harry was not surprised that no groom came running. They found the stables themselves, and he and Smith discovered one lone horse inside that ramshackle building. They rubbed down their own horses, found some oats and hay, and watered them.

Then, they went back to the front of the house and Harry pounded on the doors.

CHAPTER SIXTEEN

AFTER WAITING WHAT seemed to be a full five minutes, Harry pounded again. Finally, the earl's doors slowly swung open.

Before him stood a butler as old as Methuselah. Harry got the idea that his knocks might have been heard the first time, but it had just taken the fellow that long to get to the door.

"Mr. Harry Vance, here to see the earl," he said through gritted teeth.

The butler looked very confused, and Harry wondered if he were suffering from an age-related dysfunction of the mind.

"He expects you?" he asked, in a high, breathy voice.

"He does not," Harry said. "Though he ought to have been expecting *somebody* to call him on the carpet about this mess. I have no intention of leaving without an interview. I can stand here all day."

This seemed to have the desired effect. Harry was certain the man could not remain upright for long and so would be the inevitable loser in a standoff.

The butler shrugged and turned, shuffling to a nearby bench, where he promptly sat down with various creaks and groans.

"In the breakfast room. That way," he said pointing down a corridor.

Harry should have known this particular earl would be so lackadaisical as to be breakfasting so late in the morning.

He set off down the corridor, with his valet on his heels.

Harry noted the cobwebs in every corner and dirt on the stone floor. He was sure a mouse had just darted away. There were stains on one wall, as if somebody had tripped carrying a tea or coffee pot and spilled its contents. The place had not been cleaned anytime this year.

He found the breakfast room, and he found the earl in it. From the looks of it, breakfast consisted of toast. There was no sideboard, no warming trays with meats and eggs. No smell of coffee brewed. Just toast.

The earl looked up in surprise. "What? Two strangers let in? *Who?*"

"Lord Somerdon, I am Mr. Harry Vance, this is my valet, Smith. I have a few words to say to you."

"Words? To me?" the earl said looking rather incredulous. "Here? *Now?*"

"Yes, to you, here and now," Harry said, thinking the earl was a little less articulate than expected. No matter, he was prepared to plough forward.

"Lord Somerdon, do you realize that you have so damaged your daughter's mind that she is prepared to marry herself to a big lump of a fellow rather than myself? Do you understand that, through your inattention and neglect, the lady has been living in fear of poverty and privation all her life? Do you comprehend that she is on the verge of making herself miserable through an unsuited marriage, and it is all your doing?"

Harry thought all of that would be easy enough to understand, but he began to have doubts.

The earl nodded as if he'd just been delivered good news. "Married. That duchess said so. All right then. *Done.*"

"No, it is not done! That's the point—it is not yet done. There is still a chance to save her from herself. To alleviate her fears."

Now the earl looked confused.

"Pull yourself together, man!" Harry practically shouted. "You've got to fix all this," he said waving his arms.

The earl looked about himself, as if searching for what *all this* was that Harry said must be fixed.

"Your estate," Harry said. "It's a wreck and that must be rectified."

The earl had nodded as if he comprehended the point, though what he said next made Harry wonder if the man understood any point at all.

"No. Things turn up, don't you know. Always do. *Last minute*," the earl said complacently.

Harry was beginning to think the man made it a habit to speak so inscrutably. He made a guess that *turns up last minute* was meant to convey that some relative or other would bail him out of the worst of his circumstances before he was entirely undone. He made a guess that the earl had been operating in such a fashion all his life.

"Turns up last minute," Harry said. "Yes, you are quite right. Somebody has turned up. *I* have turned up. This heap of an estate is going to right itself and you'll not get rid of me until that is accomplished."

"No—"

Harry cut the earl off before he could compose any more of his nonsensical phrasings. "Smith, find us suitable rooms. I will make a tour of the place to see what is to be done. After the horses are rested, I will go and see Bertridge. He'll know where I can find people to employ to clean this place up."

The earl, who had looked rather satisfied with himself, looked less so now. He dropped his toast.

Harry stared down at him and said, "You, earl, had better prepare yourself to be more energetic than you have been. This estate will be brought back to what it always should have been. Lady Isabel will see that I am capable of such things and will no longer fear the future. Furthermore, do everybody the courtesy of speaking in full sentences!"

Harry turned on his heel and strode from the room.

He ignored the earl's parting words—

"What? *No.* Go away."

ISABEL HAD DRIED her eyes, though they still retained a telltale redness and puffiness. Her bouts of tears had ended and she'd been left with an odd heaviness. It was as if she carried more weight on her bones than she had before. Her arms and legs felt tired though she'd done little and they should not be so exhausted.

She sat in the drawing room mechanically embroidering and considering that this new feeling would likely linger. She would never be entirely happy again—she had traded that feeling for a guarantee of safety and protection. Lord Lymington's parents were coming in the next weeks to have a look at her.

Isabel presumed she would pass muster, her only real deficiency was a lack of a spectacular dowry amount. She did not know how much the duke and duchess had put by for her, but she was certain it would be modest. But that was no matter. If a very large dowry had been important to Lord Lymington's parents, they would not be coming.

She would be a duchess and she would have an enormous cushion of money and connections.

As Isabel mulled over what sort of life she would have with Lord Lymington, she heard his voice in the hall. Carlson opened the drawing room doors but did not escort him in.

"Lady Isabel," he said, "Lord Lymington has come to call but, as you know, the duchess has gone out. Might I suggest sending in Betsy to chaperone?"

"Yes, of course," Isabel said.

She folded her embroidery and put it back in her sewing basket. It was not too long a time before Lord Lymington was shown in, followed by Betsy. The lord held out a pot of Columbine and said, "I remembered! One of your favorites. Actually, my butler wrote down what I sent before, and *he* remembered."

Carlson went off to arrange tea while Betsy sat herself discreetly on the far sofa.

Isabel said, "Lord Lymington, I am afraid Mr. Vance was playing a joke on you regarding the flowers."

"Really? What's the joke?"

"Regarding the meanings of the flowers he suggested to you," Isabel said gently. "Columbine represents folly."

"Does it?" Lord Lymington said. "I've never paid much attention to such things. So *that's* why my butler kept saying, 'Columbine again? Are you certain?'"

"You might borrow a book on the subject from the duchess," Isabel said encouragingly. "Then you would know what messages you were sending."

"Excellent idea. I have books, you understand. It's just there all…"

"About horses?"

"Yes!" Lord Lymington paused, as if he were mulling something over. "Vance. He steered me very wrong about flowers. What about the poem, though?"

Isabel was not certain what the lord alluded to. "The poem?" she asked.

"The poem Vance helped me write. Actually, he wrote it, I didn't know where to start. He said it was necessary so a lady could keep it and reflect on it and so I signed it and sent it."

"I am afraid I did not receive it," Isabel said, confounded as to why Mr. Vance would have helped Lord Lymington write a poem.

"No matter, I can tell you the gist—I said you were nice and had red hair. Then I compared you to a well-fed pheasant, because of hearths, you know. And then I ended with something about a gentle diet for a bird."

Isabel could not make heads nor tails of this mishmash of words. Until suddenly she could. Among Mr. Vance's other enterprising strategies, he'd written out a ludicrous ode and convinced Lord Lymington to send it. Isabel suspected the duchess had opened it and then promptly set it alight.

"I am afraid Mr. Vance may have played another joke on you regarding that poem. As you describe it."

"It's the well-fed pheasant part, isn't it?" Lord Lymington said, looking rather dejected. "I thought that couldn't be right. I really ought to follow my own instincts more often."

"If your instincts lead you away from such ideas, then I heartily agree."

"I'd have a word with Vance about this. If I could."

"Oh, I do not think it necessary to mention anything to him," Isabel said.

"I could not anyway. But next season! If I remember. Or my butler remembers."

Isabel was not certain of his meaning. If he was determined to say something, why would he wait until next season?

"Funny thing about Vance," Lord Lymington said. "I was at White's last night and they say he's disappeared along with his valet."

"Disappeared?" Isabel said. "What does that mean?"

"Well, Crandall saw him leaving town at dawn, on horseback with only his valet. Crandall was on his way home you see, long night of gambling. He hailed Vance and asked him if he was off to Cornwall. That's where his estate is, you understand. But Vance says no, and Crandall says where then? Vance says he doesn't want anybody to know where he is going. Is that not odd? Why the secret? You see? He accepted invitations and then did not turn up and his trip is a secret."

Isabel gripped the arm of the sofa; her head was spinning and she felt a little sick. Where had he gone? And worse, wherever he'd gone, she was afraid she was the cause.

"I suppose a gentleman might choose a hundred different places to go at the spur of the moment," she said, though she did not think she sounded very convincing.

"Oh, yes," Lord Lymington said, nodding. "But why is it a secret? Rendridge speculated that he was off to Gretna Green but then he could not come up with the name of the lady meant to have gone with him. James said it was likely a tryst with an actress—well never mind what *else* he said about that idea. Barclay said he might have gambled too high and got himself in trouble. But I've never seen Vance gamble, so I don't know…"

Surely he was all right. Surely.

But if he wished to leave Town, why did he not go home? Why did he not tell any of his friends where he was going? Or send his regrets regarding invitations he'd accepted? Why did he not pack up his household? Why only leave with his valet?

Perhaps that was it. He'd only taken his valet because wherever he went was to be a short trip. Of course that must be it. There was no sinister mystery. There was nothing wrong. He'd probably gone off to see a relative somewhere. Her mind only panicked because, well…

But why was it a secret?

Carlson came in with the tea tray and laid out the things.

"What do we think, Carlson?" Lord Lymington said. "What do we make of the weather just now? Will the sun stay out?"

Carlson glanced out the window. "It is hard to say, my lord. Things are calm at the moment, but one never knows when a disturbance might erupt."

Lord Lymington took his teacup and nodded knowingly. "Dolphins," he said.

HARRY HAD SPENT hours walking through the house and touring the estate to see what the potential might be. It was almost enraging to note the resources the earl had at his disposal and not a one of them had been utilized. There was good land for farming, room for a sizable dairy, and a vast forest full of good wood and plentiful game.

The earl was either an idiot or the laziest man in England. Or both.

Now, though it was becoming very late to turn up unannounced, he'd ridden to Lord Bertridge's estate.

He was shown into the drawing room and found Bertridge and his wife, as he expected he would find. He had not expected to find Lady Easton there too, but could easily enough guess the cause. Lady Bertridge must be soon going into her confinement and Lady Easton would not like to be left behind on such a matter. Not when they'd all heard so much from Lady Mendleton about her astoundingly advanced grandbaby and now Lady Heathway had her astonishingly alert grandniece. Lady Easton would require an equally original infant of some sort.

"Vance," Bertridge said. "Come in, we got your letter and were expecting you to arrive at some point."

Lady Bertridge said, "You are very welcome here, Mr. Vance. Do excuse that I do not rise in my current condition."

"Do not tire yourself on anybody's account, Lady Bertridge, least of all me," Harry said. He turned and bowed. "Lady Easton."

"Mr. Vance, I have seen the odd communication you have sent. What does it mean? What are you here to do?" Lady Easton asked with her usual directness.

"I am here to rectify the Earl of Somerdon's deficiencies and had hoped to speak to Lord Bertridge privately about the situation, Lady Easton."

Lady Easton frowned. "But why should you involve yourself with the earl? What connection can there be?"

"I have become acquainted with the earl's daughter, Lady Isabel, and it has come to my attention that his behavior has affected her deeply and scarred her psyche."

Lady Easton shook her head. "What should you know of the lady's psyche? Dear me, no. If there is anybody who should rectify the earl's situation, it ought to be somebody…"

"Somebody related? Or somebody she is engaged to? Like Lymington?"

"Are they engaged! I hadn't known," Lady Easton said, her delight all too apparent.

"They are not, and I pray they never will be. Now, if I might be so bold, Bertridge, may we step out somewhere? I am at a loss as to how to even describe the shambles I found in the earl's house. Work must begin immediately."

Lord Bertridge nodded. Lady Bertridge only looked amused.

"A shambles, you say?" Lady Easton asked. "What sort of shambles?"

Harry was not certain precisely where Lady Easton's interest lay though he, along with everybody else in the world, knew of her obsessions with both time and order.

He said, "There is not an inch of the place that is not covered with dust, the larder appears to be bare, there is only one servant in the house and the fellow is eighty if he is a day, there are windows broken, roof tiles falling, linens molding, very little silver in the drawers, no decent tea or coffee service, the tea chest itself is empty, birds are nesting in the attics, rats roam the cellars with impunity, and there is not a clock in that house that is set to the right time."

Lady Easton appeared rather staggered to hear of this description. She nervously grasped at her fichu. "How many clocks has he insulted in such a manner?"

"I counted five," Harry said, though he had not really paid much attention to them.

"Five clocks out of time," Lady Easton murmured. This seemed to prompt some sort of internal struggle, her expressions changing with great rapidity. Harry thought she was hard-pressed to fathom such a thing and her fingers itched to set those clocks right.

Finally, she said, "I do not see why you and Richard must secret yourself away to discuss the plans," Lady Easton said. "You may discover that I have some very sound advice. You will not be aware of it, Mr. Vance, but I run a very tight ship in my own household. Very tight."

"It is true," Lady Bertridge said. "If there were anybody to go to regarding getting things in order, it must be Lady Easton. You ought to consult her on everything *inside* the house, and Bertie for everything *outside* the house."

Harry was not so certain that he wished to have any consultations with Lady Easton at all.

"We dine shortly, Mr. Vance. You must stay and we will review the whole thing over a good dinner," Lady Bertridge said.

"I could not impose to such a degree," Harry said.

"Nonsense, Mr. Vance. You have ventured out to seek order and you have found it," Lady Easton said. "My nephew and I will guide you with our expert hands. If, as you say, Lady Isabel's psyche has been affected, then it is my duty to step in as a member of *The Society of Sponsoring Ladies*. The duchess would expect it of me."

Harry nodded. Though, he did not think the duchess would thank Lady Easton for assisting Harry Vance in anything, much less a bid to win Lady Isabel. Fortunately, it seemed that Lady Easton did not really comprehend that point. She was so blinded by thoughts of dusty corridors and wrong-set clocks that it had clouded what ought to be a fact waving a flag right in front of her.

From the amused expression Lady Bertridge currently showed, it did not seem as if that fact had escaped *her* notice though. Harry suspected she would be rather an ally than not.

In any case, he would not mind dinner at all, as he did not think there would be much at the earl's table when he returned. When he found the opportunity, he would ask Bertridge to pack him something to take back for Smith, who was unlikely to be a subject of the earl's hospitality. If there was any hospitality at all to be had.

OVER THE NEXT two hours and a very good dinner, they saw rapid progress on the plan for the earl's estate. It seemed that Bertridge had already mapped out a strategy some time ago, though it had been rejected by the earl. Judiciously cut down wood and sell it for ready funds to pay for servants and the purchase of livestock, then build a dairy and prepare fields for wheat, barley, and vegetables for the next growing season.

Harry had thought renting to tenants an obvious plan, though he was swiftly apprised that the earl could not keep a tenant long-term if his life depended upon it. It would be best to hand the whole thing to a competent steward and leave tenant relations out of it. The steward could house the workers in the old tenant cottages and eventually rearrange the terms so the workers would *become* tenant farmers, with the earl no more the wiser. In that way, the workers could improve their circumstances without fear of the earl knocking on their doors looking for more rent.

This time around, the earl would not be asked his opinion on the plans for his property, but would be carried along by the waves of activity that would shortly hit his shores.

Bertridge would lend some servants until permanent hires could be made. Lady Bertridge insisted that whoever would be tasked with it would receive double their monthly wages. Lady Easton had thought that excessive, but Lady Bertridge had only to gently lay her hand over her expanding stomach and the point was handily won.

There had been some debate as to the likelihood of transforming the earl himself into a creditable landowner, with Bertridge exceedingly doubtful of it. It was decided that what was really needed for the long-term success of the estate was a hardnosed steward who would pay little mind to what the earl thought of anything. One who could hold the purse strings and not allow the earl to do anything stupid with the money coming in.

It turned out they might have a bit of luck there—Mr. Browning had been longtime steward to Viscount Ledbetter, but the estate had been entailed. Browning did not at all approve of the new viscount, who was exceedingly coarse. Bertridge knew Browning well, as they had often compared notes on this or that estate matter. He thought Browning could be lured away with the right salary and that the fellow might relish the challenge of upending the obstinate earl and righting the estate.

As for the feelings of the new Viscount Ledbetter upon losing his steward, it seemed Browning was not the only person disliking that person. As Lady Bertridge said, "We had him here once, and that was quite enough. His table manners are more suited to a barn than a dining table."

After the question of the steward was settled, it was even suggested that they might be able to make off with the viscount's cook too. Mrs. Redman was an excellent woman and while Bertridge could not positively know her feelings about her new employer, he could guess at them. As well, he'd often suspected that Browning and the cook were great friends, possibly more. He would ask Browning to speak to the lady.

Lady Bertridge suggested asking a person named Bemmy if she might not put a hand in to supervise the housemaids. This turned out to be Lady Bertridge's one-time lady's maid who had since married and managed Bertridge's cheesemaking with her husband. Bemmy, if descriptions were true, was an energetic and enterprising soul who would not be the least put off by any rantings and ravings from the earl.

The poor old butler, Rogers, was considered and Bertridge was in total agreement that the man must have a pension so he could retire. Harry took that on himself. He had a cottage nearby the house on his own estate that was currently empty and would do very well. He would see that the old fellow was made comfortable. They would advertise for a butler and a cadre of footmen.

As for the finances to be arranged before the estate was back on its feet—Bertridge proposed a loan split between them, but Harry was prepared to foot it all. Lady Isabel would come to be apprised that *he* had done what was necessary, and nobody else.

Lady Easton had all sorts of questions Harry could not an-swer about the details of the workings of the house. Finally, she said, "There is nothing for it, I will have to go and see for myself first thing in the morning."

Lady Bertridge had nodded and said all sorts of encouraging things about the idea of Lady Easton splitting her time in such a fashion. Harry got the sense that the lady would not mind her husband's aunt exiting the house for at least a little bit of time each day. If not exiting altogether permanently.

He left with Lady Bertridge's good sense following him back to the earl's estate by way of a carriage filled with things that were required immediately. There were two plates of sliced ham, boiled potatoes, and green beans and two berry tarts. One would be for Smith, and the other for Rogers, who looked decidedly underfed.

There was tea, coffee, bacon, eggs, a side of beef, fresh-baked bread, biscuits, butter, cream, various sweetbreads, pounds of cheese, and two pies. There were three cases of wine, two bottles of port and two bottles of brandy.

Until they had a cook, Harry had no idea how any of the food would get prepared. He did not think Rogers up to the task and he was the only servant there. He supposed he and Smith could try their hand at it—how hard could it be to cook eggs?

He did not know, but he would find out in the morning and hopefully they would not burn the place down while they were at it.

His valet was waiting for him at the door when he arrived back to the earl's estate. He took hold of Harry's horse and said, "There is nothing for you to eat, nor was there for me. There was a quarter of a chicken and some boiled beans a woman brought from the village and the earl left not a crumb behind."

Smith glanced at the carriage now stopped on the drive. "Please tell me you did not bring back guests. I am so hungry right now I might boil and eat one of them."

"Get the name of that woman who brought the chicken and employ her as a temporary cook. In the meantime, you will not starve, the carriage is full of food, not people."

"Praise the heavens," Smith said. "I was on the verge of lighting a torch and going out to forage for mushrooms and berries."

Harry ignored his valet's rather fanciful claims. He was certain Smith had never foraged for anything in his life. "What has the earl had to say for himself this evening?" he asked.

"What did he say? Let's see. Something along the lines of: "*Him*. What? Here, don't you know. Change. *No*. Dreaming? Could be. Deuced awful. Go away. Chicken is mine. *Paid* for. Rogers so slow."

CHAPTER SEVENTEEN

THE DAYS AND weeks were passing in a blur for Isabel. The duchess had been busy going round the town to tamp down talk about Lady Featherstone's Bow Street Runner trousers, Lady Redfield's calamitous wooden shoes, and Lady Mendleton's doll-baby.

Isabel had thought the presence of the doll would be the least of it. And it might have been, had Lady Mendleton not named it Margaret and took to explaining Margaret's personality to fascinated onlookers at supper. Margaret, despite the duchess' prediction that she would end up under a chair, had been given her own place at the table.

Despite Lady Featherstone's assurances, it turned out Lord Featherstone had been rather floored to discover his lady had been gallivanting about the town in pants. The duchess said he'd extracted a solemn promise that she would never do so again and then stolen out of the house with the offending item of clothing. She assumed he'd had the trousers burned.

Lady Redfield and Lord Jeffries got through things rather better despite taking down half the ballroom. Everybody admitted that a costume could go wrong in untold and unexpected ways. Did they not all recall Lady Davida's six-foot train years ago? The poor Prince of Wales had inadvertently stepped on it and rode on it a few feet as the lady walked forward. Until the inevitable happened—either the Prince or the fabric must give way. As the Prince had grown rather substantial in his person, it was the fabric that had given up the ghost. After a loud tearing sound, Lady Davida found her bodice ripped from her in a most alarming fashion.

In any case, the *ton* seemed far more interested in the idea that Lady Redfield and Lord Jeffries had both been bruised from head to toe and spent most days recovering in Lady Redfield's drawing room over pots of tea.

When the duchess was not, as she termed it, *cleaning up her friends' messes*, she and Isabel took their horses to the park each day. At least when Isabel had her mare at a gallop, she did not have heavy thoughts upon her.

They sometimes encountered Lord Lymington in the park, and he called at the house too. He had read a book on the meanings of flowers and had begun bringing daffodils to hint at his regard.

He also took another run at poetry. He was determined to write one himself that did not include any well-fed pheasants. One afternoon he stood in the drawing room and said:

Shall I compare thee to a summer's day?
Thou art more lovely and more temperate:
Rough winds do shake the darling buds of May—

Isabel had quickly interrupted him and said, "Lord Lymington, you did not write that yourself."

He'd hung his head and said, "No, I found it in a book. It's nice though, isn't it?"

He was a dear of a man, bumbling though he was. He aimed to please though he had few personal resources to do so. She had not had much success getting him off the subject of weather, and the even more unfortunate topic of *dolphins* and the weather. Every time he came to the house, he managed a conversation with Carlson.

Isabel had begun to wonder if she ought not be clear with

Lord Lymington on why she would consider him as a future husband. She did not wish to fool him into believing she had romantic feelings where there were none. Theirs would be more the sort of friendship upon which many successful marriages were built.

She had told Mr. Vance that she would be transparent about her wish to be settled safely and she had meant it.

Isabel especially felt the urgency of it now. His parents would arrive soon and, on top of that, she had begun to sense that Miss Thompson had a real interest in Lord Lymington. She seemed to find him vastly amusing and appeared very indulgent of him.

She wondered if Miss Thompson would have revealed that she already knew Sonnet 18 by Shakespeare and that Lord Lymington certainly did not write "Shall I compare thee to a summer's day." Or perhaps the lady would have allowed him to have his little ruse.

Mr. Vance had come out and told her plainly that Miss Thompson had set her cap. Though, Isabel had preferred to see for herself.

She *had* seen it—both at Lady Redfield's musical evening and once when she and the duchess had encountered them deep in conversation in the park. They had been talking of horses, and Miss Thompson had seemed delighted to be doing so.

Of course, Lord Lymington would not have noticed the lady's particular interest. He did not pick up on such things and Isabel thought that might be because he was exceedingly modest.

Isabel had brought up Miss Thompson in conversation and he'd only said, "She's very nice!" He'd then paused for what seemed like a full minute and looked very much like he was ashamed of himself. He broke the silence by saying, "I know you will not approve, but she does like to talk about horses."

Was she doing Lord Lymington a grave disservice by being in the way of a lady who had a real affection for him?

She'd even mentioned the idea to the duchess. The duchess had said, "My dear, the marriage mart is no less brutal than a

Roman colosseum. Step aside for nobody."

What if she were to cause a lost chance for Lord Lymington in finding real love with Miss Thompson? But then, what if she were to cause disaster for herself in stepping aside?

She must allow Lord Lymington to decide for himself by understanding where she stood. The problem was, how to apprise the lord of her feelings, or lack thereof? It would be far too presumptuous to broach the conversation before there was a proposal. And yet, after a proposal seemed too late. Was such a thing communicated *during* a proposal?

As if that was not confounding enough, she'd been hearing more and more talk about the disappearance of Mr. Vance. It seemed to be a topic of endless speculation, particularly because he'd said he did not wish people to know where he'd gone.

The duchess claimed it was a matter of happenstance. The *ton* was fickle, and some stories grew without merit while others faded though they be far more significant. Mr. Vance was discussed because he was a favorite of various hostesses who appreciated his good humor and willingness to reliably turn up and dance all evening.

The speculations were many and varied. One heard he'd gone to Germany as he owned an estate there. Another heard he'd gone to America to grow tobacco. Another heard he'd been spotted in Ramsgate, while still another said no, it had been Eastbourne. Worst of all, it was widely rumored that a lady had thrown him over and he was nursing his wounds in a remote location. She had not heard whether her name had been mentioned in association with that idea.

Isabel prayed he'd only gone to the assistance of a relation who had summoned him.

Wherever he went, she felt on edge about it.

HARRY HAD BEEN surprised by how quickly the estate was in hand. Of course, there was a long way to go to secure the future of it, but plans had been set in motion. It was on the right road and need only continue going forward.

Mr. Browning had been lured away from his ill-favored new viscount, and Mrs. Redman had come with him as the new cook. Mr. Browning had announced his intention of marrying the lady and refused to budge unless they were suitably accommodated. Rooms for such an arrangement were located and prepared, with a cottage to be built in future.

Those two reliable people, along with Bertridge, the ever-outraged Lady Easton, and the indefatigable Bemmy, had set balls rolling in every direction.

Wood was cut, laborers were hired for the fields, the beginnings of a dairy were going up, grooms employed, the stables were repaired, and more horses and a carriage brought in.

Lady Easton confronted the clocks and their sadly out of time states and then turned her attention to every corner of the house. Maids swept through the rooms with brooms, mops and pails, Lady Easton ever driving them forward. Linen was laundered and aired. What was left of the silver was cleaned. Every stick of furniture was polished.

Footmen were hired and put in suitable livery. A butler had been advertised for while Rogers had taken to sitting out in a back garden in the sun, having been told his retirement was secured.

As for the earl himself, he had gone through various shades of temper in finding his house invaded and his habits upended. He had made several attempts to throw everybody from the premises, though his less than articulate speech had not assisted him in the effort.

"You. Terrible person. Go, *now*," he'd shouted at Bemmy.

For his trouble, he'd only got a smile and the cheeky response of "Do not be such a goose, Lord Somerdon."

The steward took the earl's tempers in stride and said things like, "We can't have *that*, now can we?"

Lady Easton was perhaps the most frightening to Lord Somerdon. Whenever he attempted a complaint within her earshot, he was told in no uncertain terms that she would not soon forget the state of his clocks. She accused the earl of keeping time by looking at the sun and hazarding a guess as if he were some sort of caveperson.

The earl, finding himself helpless against so many determined people, took to sulking and refusing to eat. This did not last long, as the earl's character was not built for such self-discipline. One breakfast come and gone had cured him of it.

Finally, Lord Somerdon was resigned to what was happening around him. Harry found him much easier to manage in such a state and had begun to instruct him on how to actually get his thoughts out of his mouth. He had become convinced that there was not a thing wrong with the earl that prevented it, other than exceedingly lazy habits.

Just now, they were in the breakfast room, that place now sparkling from vinegar and water applied with a scrub brush. Lord Somerdon said, "Rogers. Retired now, don't you know. *Here?*"

"My lord," Harry said, "that is just what I've been pointing out to you. There are a lot of words missing in those expressions. Try again."

The earl stared off into the room as if he might find those missing words floating in the air. He cleared his throat and said, "Rogers. *He* retired *here?*"

"Excellent effort, and no he does not. He will go to my estate in Cornwall and take an empty cottage there. I will pay his pension."

"You? *Why?*"

"Try again."

"Why *you?*"

"Close enough," Harry said. "I have every intention of marrying your daughter, therefore, I feel it my duty to care for your people, as you are not yet up to it."

"Her married. To you? *Why?*"

"Why? Because I love her, that is *why*," Harry said. "Though it has been necessary to get this house in order first. Do you not see what has happened? She's grown up in poverty and squalor and with the estate entailed what will she be left with? She has no dowry and nothing to fall back on. When you die, what is she to do? Become a governess or companion to a rich relative? Because of this, she believes that if she does not choose the safest course she will have doomed herself."

"Entailed? Stupid idea, don't you know." the earl said.

Harry was caught up short. Of all that could have been examined in his speech, the earl had taken up the mention of an entail. "What did you say?"

"What?"

"About the entail. Do you mean to say the estate is not entailed?"

The earl nodded. "No. Issy and Margy. *Them.*"

"The estate will go to your two daughters?" Harry asked, rather incredulous.

"Yes. *Them.*"

Harry was certain Lady Isabel had not the first idea of it. Had she, she would not have lived in such fear of the future. She would have seen that quite a lot could be made of the place, even if her father had not chosen to do any of it. She would have known that she could take the estate in hand. She would have known she was not to be left with nothing.

The impediments that had weighed on her had never really been there—all because her father could not even find the energy to communicate in any rational manner.

Further, once she saw that the estate was in order *now* and her father had been roped into sensibility, she must throw off her fears.

She would see it. She would marry him. He was certain of it.

LORD LYMINGTON'S PARENTS had come to Town and much to everybody's surprise, they had located themselves in the duchess' house. Neither Isabel nor the duchess had any notion of them doing so until a letter arrived the day before they did.

It had said that they did not see the reason to go to the trouble of opening their own house for what was to be a short trip. As Lord Lymington only took small apartments when he was in town, they must look elsewhere. They were certain the duchess would not mind if they imposed upon her hospitality.

As it happened, the duchess minded very much, but she was also very desirous of a match between their son and Isabel, so she was determined to put a good face on it.

The Duke and Duchess of Hastings had arrived late on the evening before and by the time their rather extensive collection of trunks had been got into the house and they and their servants settled, it was after eleven o'clock.

Isabel had been briefly introduced to them, he a squat fellow who resembled Lord Lymington, though his son was much taller, and she a thin and pinched-looking lady.

Isabel had found herself relieved that they were both very tired and would retire, only requesting trays sent to their rooms.

Now, she sat with some embroidery in the drawing room. It was still early, and she did not expect to have company for another hour or so.

That was fortunate, she needed time to think.

It seemed every day brought her one step closer to the future she had chosen. Every step meant less chance to turn back. It was like choosing snow-covered paths through a forest. Eventually, the decision became permanent because to backtrack would no longer be possible. One's tracks left behind had since disappeared in the snow.

She had been wise and considered and she'd employed sound

judgment regarding her choices. And yet, her decision being made certain and permanent shook her to her core.

What had been abstract and logical was becoming real and terrifying.

Amidst those roiling feelings, she had not the first idea what were they to do with these people in the house. She had thought there would be a dinner or some such event, a thing that would last a matter of hours and then be done. This seemed too much.

But here they were, regardless of how she felt about it. How long would they stay? What did they wish to see from her?

To her surprise, Carlson opened the door and said, "Her Grace, the Duchess of Hastings."

Lord Lymington's mother sailed in and said, "Carlson, do bring my breakfast on a tray in here—I cannot abide a breakfast room. Two eggs, soft-boiled. Toast, marmalade, tea."

Isabel had risen and curtsied. "Your Grace, it was unnecessary to come down, a tray could have been brought up to you."

"Not with His Grace snoring loud enough to blow off the roof. Our rooms adjoin and it is a veritable series of thunder claps up there. At home, I've got him at the other end of the corridor."

Isabel nodded, as there was no possible comment to be made on such a description. In truth, she had really rather not know anything about the duke's sleeping habits.

The Duchess of Hastings settled herself and said, "Lady Isabel, I must inform you that I am a direct sort of person. I say what I mean with no dancing round the thing."

Isabel felt some trepidation growing, as why would a person make such a statement unless they were on the verge of delivering some very direct bad news?

But certainly, she could not have formed an unfavorable opinion from only the very short introduction of last evening?

"I am not blinded, as some mothers are," the lady went on, "as to the qualities or lack thereof my eldest son may possess. He's a bit of an idiot, as you could not have failed to notice unless you are an idiot too. In which case, I would fear for the state of any children you might produce. Presuming you are not an idiot, I must surmise that your motivation in this proposed match is to become a duchess. Have I read the situation correctly?"

Isabel was at once frightened and insulted. What a speech!

Blessedly, Carlson came in with the lady's breakfast tray and the duchess fell silent, giving Isabel time to think.

She could not deny that Lord Lymington was not exactly an incisive mind. Though, he had other good qualities. She also could not deny that she was motivated by his title and all the protection it would provide.

But such things were not spoken of! At least, not as the duchess had spoken of them.

Carlson retreated and shut the door behind him.

The duchess spread a thick layer of marmalade on a piece of toast and said, "Do not be bashful, Lady Isabel, just lay out the facts as they are."

There was nothing for it. She *would* lay out the facts. They were the facts she should have already laid out to Lord Lymington himself.

"Ma'am," she said, "you have been so kind as to dispense with any roundabout conversations, so I will attempt to be as direct as you have been. My father, primarily through his own mismanagement, has not two farthings to rub together. It has always been so. Now his estate is mortgaged. I have lived on the edge of catastrophe my entire life. You are correct, I do seek a position like the one Lord Lymington can provide, though it is not through any desire for the social powers of rank. I would not care if he were a baronet, as long as there had been long-term stability to show and vast connections to call upon. I wish to ensure my future and never live with the fear of poverty again."

The duchess looked at her critically. "You know he only talks about horses? Oh, he wrote to me about some strange thing regarding whales and weather, I cannot say what that is about, but his mind is always on horses."

"I did notice that," Isabel said.

"Very well," the duchess said. "I see no impediment, as long as you know what you're getting yourself into. My advice—when you tire of hearing about horses, just tell him to shut up. It's effective, I've used it on my duke for years."

Isabel felt her cheeks burn. The lady's words might be flaming torches thrown in her face. Her skin was on fire, though it was not from embarrassment. It was from shame.

Is this what marriage to Lord Lymington was to look like? When she tired of his conversation she must only tell him to shut up?

She could not imagine such a thing. But then, where had *this* duchess started? Had she come into the marriage with the same ideas Isabel had and then found the years wearing down any civility she might have brought with her?

If she were to go forward, might she turn into a woman like this?

She could not bear to think of it.

"I have wondered," Isabel said slowly, "how I might express the nature of my interest to Lord Lymington. It has not seemed possible while he has not declared himself, though it seems too late if he does and then I explain it."

"Goodness, he's not *that* much of an idiot," the duchess said. "He will not imagine you've fallen in love with him."

"As to that," Isabel said, pressing on, "I believe there is a lady who has. Though I do not think Lord Lymington has perceived it. I wonder—"

"A lady in love with Percy," the duchess said with a chuckle. "What an idea."

HARRY HAD GONE to Lord Bertridge's estate in the afternoon, leaving the earl to contemplate his new circumstances on his own. One could only take so many *What? Who? Here? Why?*

conversations. He had not got very far with attempting to pull words out of the earl's head. What went on in there, he was almost afraid to imagine.

Though the invitation to tea had been welcome, he was surprised by it. Lady Bertridge appeared as if she would burst and certainly her child would arrive any day. Or any hour, really.

He found her in good spirits though, and he found Lady Easton in her usual spirits. Which were always somewhat less good.

They were around a tea tray in the drawing room, discussing the progress on the estate, when Lady Bertridge suddenly said, "Mr. Vance, I find I must inform you of something. I maintain a regular correspondence with the other ladies that have been assisted by Lady Easton's society."

"Of course she would," Lady Easton said. "They are all very grateful for the help we have provided. Though, do not let the duchess hear you call it *my* society. It would set her hair on fire."

"Lady Langley, as you may know, is just now in London," Lady Bertridge went on. "She has written me that Lord Lymington's parents are in Town."

Harry set down his cup. Was he too late? Had Lymington proposed and been accepted?

He would not have thought Lymington would take things in hand so quickly. He'd imagined the fellow would need at least another season to get to it.

Lady Bertridge, no doubt sensing his fears, hurried on. "There has not been anything announced," she said.

Harry breathed a sigh of relief. An announcement was the only thing that could not be undone. Or at least, not undone without causing a very great scandal.

Lymington's parents had probably arrived for an entirely different reason.

"I expect we will hear any day," Lady Easton said. "The duchess has been quite set on Lord Lymington, right from the first."

"But it is not the duchess who would marry Lymington," Harry said. He knew it was a step too far, but it was out before he could decide to keep it in.

"He is to be a duke," Lady Easton said with a sniff, as if that were really all that need be said about it.

"Mr. Vance," Lady Bertridge said. "It appears that Lord Lymington's parents are staying with the duchess."

Harry leapt up. "Then an announcement is in the works," he said.

"That is what I fear," Lady Bertridge said.

"You ought to go tomorrow," Lord Bertridge said. "See if you can stop the thing."

"Tomorrow?" Harry asked, his voice incredulous. "I'm going *now*."

He looked toward the doors, hoping to find a butler or footman lurking there so he could don his coat and be off.

"The sun will set before you reach London," Lord Bertridge said. "You will not do Lady Isabel any good if you're lying dead on the side of the road, having encountered highwaymen. Set off at first light."

"First light?" Harry asked. "What are they doing tonight, though? All having a cozy dinner? No, I will go now and explain to Lady Isabel that her family ship has been righted. Then, I will explain to Lymington that he is to cease being a fool and marry Miss Thompson."

As he strode from the room, he heard Lady Easton say, "And who, pray, is Miss Thompson?"

"I do not know," Lady Bertridge said laughing, "but I believe she is shortly to become Lady Lymington."

As the front doors were opened for him, he thought he faintly heard Lady Bertridge say, "In any case, I have sent a letter ahead of him."

CHAPTER EIGHTEEN

I SABEL HAD JUST come in from shopping with Betsy. She fully intended to rest for an hour or so before going downstairs again. The duchess was out making calls with Lord Lymington's duchess. Isabel thought they must make a formidable pair, and she also thought their squiring about together would set tongues in motion. People would say there was to be a match and people would be right.

The Duchess of Hastings had come right out and told her that her son would propose at the Willistons' rout this evening.

She had said, "I've told him to stop dithering and go forward. He'll do it, he does not like to cross me. Though, do not expect to be swept off your feet. If he can manage to just get the words out, it will be a job well done."

Isabel had thought silently that there were no words Lord Lymington could compose that would sweep her off her feet, even if he had been the sort who could compose something elegant.

She did not love him. She was quite sure she never would. The cause was not his person, but that her heart had already been given.

Still, she would do what was sensible. Far into the future, when she had grown used to the idea that she no longer need fear poverty, she would appreciate that she stood on such steady ground. She would thank herself for doing what was necessary to get there.

There would be so much else besides romance to engage her. There would be children and society and amusements. There would be a household to manage. A real household. Not one that only consisted of poor old Rogers breaking teapots right and left.

Of course, it would be a trial to get to all those things. She did not relish what must be done with Lord Lymington to get those children. She *really* did not relish that the Duchess of Hastings had insisted they spend their first married years in her house.

She found the lady overbearing and did not look forward to her company.

Betsy hurried in with the various packages that had been gathered from a full day of going in and out of shops.

"This came," she said, holding out a letter.

Isabel took it, always wondering if her father had any intention of writing her as, so far, he had not answered any of her letters.

It was from Lady Bertridge. Perhaps to say that the baby had come, knowing her father would not bother to mention a new addition to that family? Or not bother to mention anything at all?

Isabel opened it and scanned it. Then she read it again, as none of it seemed real. And yet, it *was* real. The lady had written in the plainest terms.

It was as if the whole world had suddenly blown apart. The reality she had painfully pieced together, bit by logical bit, was upended. Black seemed white, up was down, north was south, and nothing was as it had been.

"Oh no," Isabel said softly.

"What is it?" Betsy asked. "Do you feel the beginnings of a headache?"

Isabel handed Betsy the letter.

My dear Isabel—

We miss you greatly in our little neighborhood and I miss our confidential conversations over tea. I had not thought I would have news to send you, other than the arrival of the baby, which has not yet occurred.

However, I was quite wrong in that assumption and must apprise you of the activities going on at your father's estate. Mr. Vance arrived some weeks ago with the notion of putting your father to rights. Bertridge and I were not certain it could be done, and please excuse my bluntness for saying so. But Mr. Vance was determined and so we joined in on the scheme. You would not recognize your house as it is not at all as you left it.

Rogers has been retired and a full staff brought in, including Mr. Browning as the steward and Mrs. Redman as the cook. The stables have been repaired and stocked with a coachman, grooms, horses, and a carriage. Wood is being cut and already a great lot of it has been sold to provide ready money. Fields are being prepared for the next growing season and a dairy is being built.

The house sparkles from attics to wine cellars and the estate is a hive of activity.

All of this is due to Mr. Vance, who will not take no for an answer. Lord Somerdon has resigned himself to the idea that his steward is now in charge, and he causes far less trouble than he did in the beginning.

I write you all of this so that I may come to the most direct part of my letter. Mr. Vance has done all this because he is in love with you, and he is a fine man. I have heard via letter from Lady Langley that Lord Lymington's parents stay with the duchess, clearly portending an engagement in the works. Isabel, do not make a mistake in this.

You have always been so sensible. Perhaps too sensible. Marriage is more than a contract and love is not to be underrated. I would have married Bertie if he were the local farrier and would have been happy to have done so.

I will see Mr. Vance this afternoon and apprise him of Lymington's parents' arrival. I hope it is not too late.

All my best,
Caroline

"My word," Betsy said, handing the letter back to Isabel. "What will you do?"

"I do not know what to do," Isabel said quietly. It was so much to take in. All the talk of where Mr. Vance might have gone…and all along he had been at her house with her father.

He knew what her fears were, she had not hidden them. He'd got on his horse and gone to Hertfordshire and strode into her father's house to set it right. To remedy what had always haunted her.

So much was happening there! So much that should have been happening all along.

Mr. Browning had been brought on as the steward. If there were one man who could withstand her father's complaints, it was the implacable Mr. Browning.

And then, Harry Vance loved her. She'd known that. Now he'd said so publicly, to a whole neighborhood of people, even though she'd rejected his suit.

Such determination!

"I'll say one thing for Mr. Vance," Betsy said, "that fella has what my ma would call the stick-to-it and step lively about him."

"Yes, he does," Isabel said.

"Well, this seems to be a real crossroads for you, Lady Isabel. Which way shall you go? Lord Lymington or Mr. Vance?"

Isabel's heart pounded. She knew which direction she *wished* to go. Did she dare, though?

She leapt up, filled with a sudden energy. "Of course I will dare!" she cried.

How could she not? This man, Harry Vance, he could do anything. He could achieve anything. Why had she ever worried about putting herself in his hands?

"You dare what?" her maid asked hesitantly.

"Betsy, go downstairs and tell Carlson we require one of the duchess' carriages this instant. We go to Hertfordshire in all haste."

"Now?" Betsy said. "We'll be traveling in the dark by the end of it."

"Only the end, though. We will be close to my own neighborhood and the roads are safe enough there. But we must hurry!"

"I'll have to pack—"

"No, there is no time to pack. I will gather some things and write the duchess a note. Order the carriage!"

Betsy was galvanized by Isabel's renewed energy and rushed out the door.

Isabel scribbled a hasty note to the duchess and threw some clothes into a valise. She then took some minutes composing two other letters and folded one inside the other.

She hurried down the stairs.

Now that she'd made this bold decision, she could not allow anything to stand in her way. She must be off before the duchess arrived home and attempted to dissuade her. Or outright forbid her.

Though, she was of a mood this moment that she did not think the queen herself could forbid her with any effectiveness.

As she reached the great hall, she did not find the duchess there to attempt to stop her, but she did find Carlson.

He was pacing back and forth. "Lady Isabel, this is madness! What will the duchess say? You must stay and hear her thoughts."

Isabel took a deep breath. "It may be, as you say, madness. Nevertheless, I am going. I have been far too sensible for far too long."

She laid her note on the hall table. "Please see that Her Grace gets this as soon as she arrives home. She has been most kind and I do not wish to disturb her peace in any manner. Though I find I must."

She put another note into Carlson's hands. "This is to be sent with a footman right away, delivered to Miss Thompson. She lives in Bedford Square, I do not know the number, but her father is Viscount Merdon."

"It is too dangerous to leave on such a journey now," Carlson said. "You will not have been aware of it, but the weather is to grow very terrible in the next hours."

Isabel glanced out a window and of course there was not a cloud in the sky.

Betsy said, "Not more of your whales and dolphins, Mr. Carlson."

Carlson drew himself up. "If you must know the technical terms, Betsy the farmer's daughter, it is to be a thundering reverse windage. Sea creatures have nothing to do with it. It is a migration of birds that will bring it in!"

"We will take our chances," Isabel said. She heard the clip-clops of the carriage and said, "Let us be off."

As she ran down the front steps, she heard Betsy say to Carlson, "A migration of birds? Heaven help us."

They were into the carriage in a thrice and though Rumson appeared exceedingly dubious on the box, they were off.

⊰⊱

HARRY HAD SET off directly from Bertridge's house. Bertridge, ever sensible, had caught up to him just as he'd leapt on his horse and had loaned him a loaded pistol. If a highwayman were so foolish as to try his luck, it would be the last luck he ever tried.

He had a lady to see in Town and he must see her before it was too late. He could not know the duchess' plans this evening. With any luck, they would be at home—Lady Isabel, the duchess, and Lymington's parents.

He would be direct with them all. Lymington was not the right choice for Lady Isabel and Lady Isabel was not the right choice for Lymington. Then, if Lymington happened to be there, he would send him off to find Miss Thompson.

If they were *not* at home, he'd shake their location out of Carlson and set off after them.

He really did not care what sort of scene he made in the process.

Lady Isabel must be secured, and he would topple over any societal niceties to see it done.

There was not much traffic on the roads and so far he made good time. He'd change horses at the next inn.

As the sun lowered itself beyond the trees and dusk settled on the landscape, a fine carriage barreled past him at top speed. He did not wonder at it. A carriage so well-appointed would not like to be traveling after dark. He hoped for their sake that they reached their destination quickly and were well-armed in the meantime.

Harry turned his attention to what lay ahead.

He had proposed to Lady Isabel once and been refused. He had no intention of being refused again.

This proposal would be far different. This time, he would talk some sense into her head and demand that she stop allowing the fear of poverty to make all her decisions for her.

He would be in Town in less than an hour. He must succeed.

CARLSON DID NOT like to convey bad news to the duchess. She was not a lady who brooked bad news of any sort, as she tended to take it as a personal affront. Even to tell her of some lack in the grocery order could be a trial.

But this? Lady Isabel running off to Hertfordshire?

He did not know the cause of the girl's flight and he dearly hoped it was her father on his deathbed, as he could not see any other reason that would at all satisfy the duchess.

Further, a grave illness or calamity could not be laid at his door. It was not his fault. Even further, he had done his best to stop her. He'd warned Lady Isabel in the strictest terms of a thunderous reverse windage approaching, so if her carriage overturned on the road, that could not be his fault either.

Though, if the note she'd left for the duchess *did* concern a grave illness or calamity, what did Miss Thompson have to do with it? Why was a letter going to *her*?

The idea that her charge had set off with nary a look back would be bad enough for the duchess to take in. But Lord Lymington's parents were here. There was supposed to be a match.

Was it called off?

Carlson had been sitting on the bench in the great hall, attempting to gather his thoughts and fortify himself for what was to come.

No, not what was to come. What was *here*.

The duchess' carriage had arrived.

ISABEL WAS AT once relieved and terrified to be turning down her father's drive.

The relief came from getting off the turnpike road, as it had got very dark. There was only a quarter moon and despite her assurances to Betsy that the roads in this area were quite safe, she was not certain that was entirely true.

Now that her growing fear of highwaymen had abated, a new fear rose up to replace it.

What on earth would she say to Mr. Vance?

It would be to her to do the talking, she thought. It had been her that had refused him and now it was her come to say she'd changed her mind.

What would he make of it?

Certainly, if he'd wished to walk away and think no more of her, he would not have walked right into her father's house.

This first meeting would be awkward though, there was no getting round it.

But who cared for awkward! She was to see him! She must

trust she would know what to say when she did first lay eyes upon him.

The carriage turned down her father's drive and Isabel instantly noticed it was far wider than it had been. All the undergrowth that had been encroaching on it had been cut back. It no longer had the appearance of being abandoned.

The house came into view and it took Isabel's breath away.

Windowpanes were replaced, there were no roof tiles haphazardly scattered on the drive, the fountain had been cleaned and it bubbled with running water once more. On either side, the gardens had been pruned and planted into order and there were new beds planted round the fountain itself.

She thought there might even be fresh paint on the door.

"Look at what he has wrought, Betsy," Isabel whispered.

Betsy peered out the window. "It is a fine house. Though I don't have any prior notion of it to compare to, so I cannot see the changes as you can."

"Everything has changed. Absolutely everything."

To Isabel's amazement, a footman came striding out in a smart blue uniform, replete with glinting brass buttons. Another footman ran off to the stables to find a groom for the horses and carriage.

Rumson had descended from his perch and opened the carriage door. He helped Isabel to the drive, followed by Betsy.

Of course, the footman had not the first idea of who she was and must wonder at this sudden arrival in a carriage emblazoned with a duke's coat of arms.

Another man, dressed in a very neatly tailored suit, came jogging down the steps.

"You will not know me," Isabel said, "I am Lady Isabel Beaufort, daughter to Lord Somerdon."

The footman bowed and said, "My lady, welcome home to Somerdon House."

The man in the suit seemed rather staggered by her introduction. "Lady Isabel? Here? You are not in London?"

"I was in London," Isabel said. "Now I have come here. I wish to see Mr. Vance."

She said it as confidently as she could manage, though she did not feel confident. Her legs felt as if their bones had been left in the carriage. She was unsteady on her feet. Harry Vance was in there somewhere. Had he heard the carriage and wondered who it was? Would he be angry, or happy, or something in between?

Isabel was dimly aware that she ought to be thinking of her father and wishing to see him before anybody else. That was not the case, however.

She wished to see Harry Vance.

"Lady Isabel," the man said, "I am Smith, Mr. Vance's valet. Just hours ago, I received a note from Lady Bertridge—Mr. Vance has gone to London."

That was impossible. He was meant to be right here.

"He is not here? He has gone to Town?"

"Yes, it seemed there was some urgency to the situation, though Lady Bertridge did not say specifically what it was."

Isabel was silent for some moments. She had built herself up to see him and tell him all and now he was not here. He'd been called to Town on some matter. What should she do?

Smith cleared his throat. "Ah, while Lady Bertridge did not say *specifically*, she did mention the urgency as being Lord Lymington's parents staying with the duchess."

Isabel took in a breath, and she might have not been breathing for a time, so welcome was the air into her lungs. *She* was the matter he'd raced off to Town about.

Isabel turned to Betsy. "It is Lord Lymington, he is the urgent situation. Or was, anyway. We have to go back! Let us set off this instant!"

"Now, my lady," Betsy said sternly, "I really will have to put my foot down on that idea. It would be far too dangerous."

"And I put the other foot down," Rumson said. "The only people out on the turnpike roads this late are those with nefarious intentions. Driving the duchess' carriage into such circumstances would be like swinging bait at every highwayman in the county. I won't do it."

Isabel might have been able to sway Betsy, had not her maid been so well backed by the coachman. He stood with arms folded, appearing entirely immovable.

"Very well," she said, defeated. "We will go first thing in the morning. At first light, not a moment past it. You will see that we are ready to go first thing?"

The coachman nodded, though he did not seem enthused to be a part of this foxhunt for Mr. Vance.

That mattered little, though. Harry Vance had rushed to Town to stop her from wedding Lord Lymington.

Of course he had. It was a very Harry Vance thing to do.

⁂

CHAPTER NINETEEN

CARLSON HAD NEVER witnessed such a scene in the duchess' house. Excepting, perhaps, the evening the duke fell asleep with a lit cigar in his hand and set the drawing room curtains afire. They had been a fine yellow brocade and the duchess had been devastated. She had held up far better regarding the burns on the duke's hands and his missing eyebrows.

This night, Carlson had been the reluctant bearer of the note from Lady Isabel. What a note it had been! He had prayed for something along the lines of—'I am afraid I have just been informed that my father is near death and must race to his side.'

But no. What they'd got was—

My dear Duchess, I write this note hastily and then must be off to my father's house. It seems Mr. Vance has been there all along, setting my father's affairs in order and managing the estate. I must go to him.

Lord Lymington's mother, as might be expected, wished to understand more thoroughly who this Mr. Vance was and why Lady Isabel was racing off to his side.

The duchess, had she had time to mull it over, might have thought of some sort of conciliatory if not particularly plausible explanation. She had not had the time though and had only crumpled the note in her hand and shouted, "That girl!"

The next hours had been like flying up and down the Alps in

an out-of-control sleigh. One minute, Lord Lymington's mother would pack and be off. Carlson called for her carriage. Then, she would remember that she had nowhere to be off to and the carriage was canceled. Then, she vowed she would go to her son's apartments in Town and sleep on the drawing room floor if necessary. The carriage was called again. Then she would remember that her duke, still not home from his club, would likely be put out if she were to leave without him. The carriage was cancelled.

Just now, she explained that she could not spend another minute in this house and demanded the carriage. Carlson nodded and left the drawing room. He did not call the carriage, as the lady's coachman had been ready to explode the last time they had communicated.

He heard the clatter of hoofbeats out of doors and praised the heavens—it was one of the dukes finally arrived home. Carlson presumed that gentleman would calm his wife. That would leave only one irate lady in the drawing room as opposed to the current two.

A footman opened the door.

It was not one of the dukes.

It was Mr. Vance.

Carlson felt his chest tightening and he clutched at his heart. Apparently, he had been delusional when he had assured himself that this night could not possibly get worse.

HARRY HAD MADE good time into London and gone straight to the duchess' house. He did not know if he would find Lady Isabel there, or whether he'd have to crash into some ball or dinner to get to her, but get to her he would.

He dismounted, handed his reins to a groom, jogged up the steps, and pounded on the door.

It swung open. The duchess' butler staggered backward at the sight of him. Harry almost looked over his shoulder to see if the devil were lurking behind him, such was the horror on Carlson's face. He also heard rather loud voices coming from the drawing room and one of them was the duchess herself.

They were at home. Lady Isabel was here.

Harry strode into the house. The butler had not yet said anything to him, but was madly waving his hands at him as if to stop his progress.

"Step aside, Carlson," Harry said.

"No, do not go in there," Carlson said in a panicked whisper. "You must not. You must leave this instant! Go! Go on, you! Get out!"

Carlson's eyes were wide, and he was getting very red in the face. Harry was not certain why the butler looked as if anybody going into the drawing room would be murdered, nor had he ever had the experience of a butler attempting to throw him out of a house.

He supposed it did not signify, as he certainly would not leave the house without seeing Lady Isabel.

Harry skirted round Carlson and made his way to the drawing room, ignoring the butler's halfhearted cries of, "Stop, no! Get out!"

He let himself through the doors and bowed.

"Your Grace," he said, "forgive me for arriving without an invitation, but it is imperative that I have an interview with Lady Isabel this instant."

"You!" the duchess said, pointing at him from her position on the sofa.

The other lady, who Harry did not know, glared at him. She whipped her head around to the duchess and said, "*Him?* Is that, is it that person? Vance?"

Of course he should have instantly known who the lady was. In his haste to get to Lady Isabel, he'd somehow forgotten that Lady Bertridge had said Lord Lymington's parents were not just in Town but also staying with the duchess. That was what had drove him to set off so precipitously in the first place. It must be her, the Duchess of Hastings. Though, he could not imagine how the lady had ever heard of *him*.

Harry bowed and said, "I am Mr. Harry Vance. And you are the Duchess of Hastings, I presume. Now, I really must insist on speaking to Lady Isabel."

The duchess was rather red in the face. She said, "Not if I can help it."

The other duchess said, "What does it matter now? I will not allow my son to connect himself with such a lady. She has been positively disgraceful."

Harry bristled. He could not know what had gone on to set these two harridans off in such a fashion, but he would not have Lady Isabel insulted. "There is nothing, and never will be anything, disgraceful about Lady Isabel Beaufort," he said. "I do not care who you are or what sort of standing you have by way of rank. I would not accept such talk from the queen herself."

The Duchess of Hastings, who had been on the verge of standing, fell back onto the sofa. It was apparent to Harry that nobody had crossed her in quite a while. If ever. It was the fundamental problem with a duchess—nobody ever told them a truth they did not wish to hear.

The Duchess of Stanbury, Harry could see well enough, was in a bit of a quandary. She did not like him, she was furious at his arrival. But then, it appeared she could only agree with his sentiments as she also very clearly disliked the Duchess of Hastings and that lady's opinions.

Carlson staggered into the room. Holding on to the doorframe, he said, "Your Grace, Lord Lymington and a Miss Thompson have arrived."

Harry suppressed a smile. He could not fathom why Miss Thompson was soon to be escorted into the duchess' drawing room by Lymington, but the circumstance could only be in his favor.

"Who is Miss Thompson?" the Duchess of Hastings asked.

Lymington came in with the lady on his arm and said, "*She* is, mother. This lady, right here, is Miss Thompson."

Miss Thompson curtsied and said, "Your Grace."

"But I mean, why?" the Duchess of Hastings asked. "Why have you brought this girl here?"

"Oh!" Lord Lymington said, laughing. "I see. Yes, well we are engaged. Not a half hour ago. We wished to tell you straightaway. At least, Miss Thompson, Olivia, said we ought not keep it a secret, though *I* wondered."

Harry was both amused and delighted. Miss Thompson had obviously taken her fate into her own hands.

The Duchess of Stanbury turned to the Duchess of Hastings and said, rather victoriously, "Who is disgraceful *now*?"

"Who?" Lord Lymington asked pleasantly, as if he'd walked into the middle of an amusing parlor game.

"Percy," his mother said, "I demand you explain yourself at once. You were meant to be proposing to Lady Isabel this very night!"

"I *know*," Lord Lymington said. "Funny, that."

The Duchess of Hastings looked rather dumbfounded by her son's less than illuminating explanation and Harry presumed it was an expression she was often afflicted with.

Miss Thompson stepped forward and said, "Perhaps I should explain."

"Please do, Miss…whoever you are," the Duchess of Hastings said with cool condescension.

Miss Thompson opened her reticule and said, "I am Miss Olivia Thompson, daughter of Viscount Merdon. I received two notes from Lady Isabel shortly before departing for the Willistons' rout. One was addressed to me and one I was directed to pass along to Percy."

"He is Lord Lymington outside of the family," his mother said.

Miss Thompson eyed the lady, and it was obvious to Harry

that she was not at all cowed by her. As frigid as ice, she said, "Would you be interested in the contents of these two communications, ma'am?"

"I know I was!" Lord Lymington said.

"Please read us the letters, Miss Thompson," the Duchess of Stanbury said, fanning herself on the sofa.

Miss Thompson unfolded the first note and read it aloud:

Miss Thompson—

Though we do not know each other so well that a communication of this sort is at all appropriate, I find I must dare it anyway.

I do not love Lord Lymington, though I have been led to believe that you do.

I know you will see him this evening at the Willistons' rout. Please give him the enclosed note and I hope to have the opportunity in future to wish you joy.

Isabel Beaufort

The Duchess of Hastings sniffed. "Lady Isabel assured me that she did not need to love Percy. She assured me that a safe position was her primary aim."

Lord Lymington turned to Miss Thompson and said, "You were right! She never did love me after all."

Miss Thompson patted his arm. "You may always rely on my judgment, Percy," she said kindly. "I will not steer you wrong."

Lymington appeared pleased as Punch to hear it.

"And the other one? The one addressed to my son?" the Duchess of Hastings demanded, ignoring Miss Thompson's assurances.

Miss Thompson nodded and read that one too:

Lord Lymington—

I must say some words that you will likely find surprising. I cannot know for certain what your future plans have been, but I am compelled to say what I think they should be. I believe Miss

Thompson, the bearer of this missive, is in love with you. I further believe there could not be anybody better suited to you. Please excuse me to your mother and father if that seems necessary.

As a postscript—if you find yourself confused by what I have written, please consult Miss Thompson on the matter. She will explain it to you.

Isabel Beaufort

"So you see," Lymington said, "I did ask Miss Thompson, I mean Olivia, about it and she did explain it. She's been in love with me all along and I never even knew it. Also, she likes to talk about horses."

The Duchess of Hastings groaned. She muttered, "Or in love with the idea of becoming a duchess."

"Your Grace," Miss Thompson said, "you seem to have the temperament and stamina that would allow you to live a hundred years. So, if I were aiming to be a duchess any time in the near future, it would not be with Percy. Furthermore, he is the kindest, gentlest, most guileless man I have ever encountered. I love him to pieces and that is that."

"That's exactly what she said to me at the Willistons'. She said, *and that is that*," Lord Lymington said, looking very pleased.

Harry cleared his throat. "All my felicitations, Lymington." He turned to the Duchess of Stanbury and said, "Now, I really must see Lady Isabel. Do me the courtesy of having her called."

The Duchess of Stanbury waved her hands as if signaling some sort of defeat. "She is not here. She's gone to Hertford-shire."

Hertfordshire? Harry hardly knew what to make of that information. Was it even true? Or had the duchess had Lady Isabel locked above stairs or in some other way detained? He would tear the house apart if that were the case.

The duchess, seeing his expression of disbelief, held out a sheet of paper. "Read it for yourself."

Harry crossed the room and took it, scanning its contents. She had gone. She had really gone.

Most importantly, she had written, *I must go to him.*

Him. He was him. She must go to Harry Vance.

"Well!" he nearly shouted, "I'll be off to Hertfordshire then!"

"I do not approve, Mr. Vance," the Duchess of Stanbury said. "I do not approve at all."

"But *she* does," Harry said. "And I think her father will too."

"What I say is," the duchess huffed, "you do not have my blessing."

Harry smiled. "Fortunately, Your Grace, I do not need it."

He turned on his heel and left the drawing room. Harry passed by Carlson, who was sitting on a bench with an uncorked bottle of port beside him.

"I'm off to Hertfordshire, Carlson," he said cheerfully. "What's to be the weather?"

Carlson narrowed his eyes and said, "If there is any justice in this world, Mr. Vance, you will encounter a blinding side rain with tornadic gusts and a swerving fog."

Swerving fog. Harry laughed himself all the way out of the house and back on his horse.

He would stop at his house and have Ares saddled. Ares was a beast of a horse who had unbeatable stamina.

It was late, and the ride would not be without dangers. He needed to be on a horse who would not quit were he pursued by the unsavory elements haunting the roads at this time of night.

Most of all, he needed to be on his way back to Hertfordshire this very hour.

WHILE ISABEL HAD been disappointed that she had missed Harry Vance, she could not help but be gratified too. Her carriage had no doubt crossed paths with his horse as he flew to London to stop her from marrying Lord Lymington.

He would be there by now and he would have heard that she'd set off for Hertfordshire. He might even know that she'd thrown over Lord Lymington and proceeded to throw him directly in the path of Miss Thompson.

He would know her real feelings. She prayed he was happy to know them.

She had since taken a tour of the house, she and Betsy escorted by Smith, who pointed out all the improvements.

It was remarkable, what had been done. There was not a speck of dust anywhere, everything had been either polished or replaced. New curtains were on every window, the windows themselves were clear as new ice, and her bedchamber had been entirely remade.

Gone was the leaky ceiling, and in was fresh linen bedding, a new rug, the chimney cleaned so the fire did not smoke. New paint was on the walls, a charming pale blue with matching blue silk curtains. Had Harry Vance chosen the color for her? She hoped so, it was everything lovely.

She had been especially touched that a new pianoforte had been brought into the music room and it was in tune. Harry would have thought of that, as that had been his first inkling from her that all was not well at Somerdon House.

Now, she sat in the drawing room, pouring tea for her father from a new silver service.

"Him. Just turned up. *Changes*, don't you know," the earl said.

"Yes, Father," Isabel said. "Mr. Vance turned up and changed everything. He's put you on the right path."

The earl shrugged, as if he was not certain he'd ever wished to be on the right path. Then he pointed at Isabel and said, "Married? He says so. To *him*?"

"I certainly hope so," Isabel said. "And I know I can count on you for your unreserved blessing."

The earl narrowed his eyes. "Running round everywhere. Too much. *No*."

"Yes, he is exceedingly energetic," Isabel said. "Do not bother saying no, he will ignore the sentiment, as will I."

"You. *Changed*," the earl said sulkily.

"I *have* changed," Isabel admitted. "There is no going back now. I will marry Mr. Vance if I have to ask him myself. We will race off to Gretna Green if necessary. That is my final word on the matter."

Before the earl could counter Isabel's final word with one or two of his own disjointed stylings, she heard the clatter of hoofbeats on the drive.

Was it him? It might be him. It would be very like him to decide not to wait until morning. Had he come to her straightaway from London, braving highwaymen all the way?

Isabel leapt up.

The earl said, "Who?"

"I cannot be certain, Father, but I am praying it is Harry Vance."

She ran from the room and down the corridor, passing a footman hurrying to the sound of an arrival. She flung the doors open.

It was him. He had come.

"Harry!" she cried.

He leapt down from his horse and she ran to him, flinging herself into his arms. She very well knew she was behaving like the boldest little minx that ever lived, but she did not care.

Harry had her in his arms and whispered into her ear, "Finally."

"Yes, I know, I have been a terrible fool," Isabel said softly.

"You certainly have not," Harry said gruffly. "Once I arrived here, I understood everything."

"I'm not going to be afraid anymore, though. I've made up my mind about it."

"Have you made up your mind to kiss me, though," Harry asked.

As it happened, she had made up her mind to do just that. She raised her face to his and he softly kissed her.

It was just as it ought to be. His lips were soft but firm and though she had never been kissed, it seemed the most natural thing in the world.

It seemed a thing she could do all night long, actually.

There were people around them, and Isabel was vaguely aware of their presence. Somebody had taken the reins from Harry and led his horse away. Somebody else, she believed it was Smith, was directing a footman to stop gawking.

She did not think Harry noticed any of them, though. He was far too intent on kissing her. Her lips, her eyelids, her neck—there were such a lot of places to be kissed!

"I threw over Lord Lymington," she said, as Harry made his way down the side of her neck. "I directed him to Miss Thompson."

"Yes, I know," Harry said, nuzzling her neck. "They announced their engagement to both duchesses."

"Were they angry?"

"Furious," Harry said laughing into her hair, which he had somehow undone. "But what care we?"

Harry was right. Of course he was. She would not wish to unduly upset the duchess, but in the end, what care she?

In any case, he had moved back to her lips, and she did find that rational thought was not compatible with kissing Harry Vance.

After he had kissed her long and soft, he said, "Lady Isabel Beaufort, will you finally consent to become my wife?"

"Finally and fully," Isabel said.

Harry reached into his coat pocket and brought out a velvet-covered box. "I have been carrying this around since the Tredwells' masque."

Isabel flinched just a little at the mention of that time and place. She had refused the best man who ever lived. She'd come so close to ruining her life.

He opened it to reveal a magnificent rose cut emerald in a

gold setting.

"Green suits you," he said, "it complements your coloring. Further, the ring will symbolize our intentions."

He slipped it on her finger and it dazzled in the moonlight.

"It is perfect," she said.

"You are perfect," Harry said, drawing her close once more.

She could not be certain precisely how long they stayed in that particular attitude on the drive, but it was long enough that the cool evening air began to make her shiver. Harry removed his coat and put it round her shoulders.

She stared at him and was certain she wore a flustered expression.

"What is it?" Harry asked, looking bemused.

"I have never seen you with your coat off," she said. Now, she was certain her face flamed. Seeing him without his coat brought to mind seeing him without other pieces of clothing on. Her thoughts did not seem particularly ladylike, but they were thrilling.

"Come inside," he said gently. "When we are married, it will be your purview to direct me at all times on what I ought to be wearing, or not wearing, as the case may be."

Isabel's legs felt wobbly as her mind considered *that* idea.

"Let us go see your father and hear what few words he will muster on the subject of our engagement. I have told him of my intentions several times, though he has not seemed enthusiastic about the idea."

"Oh I know. I have already told him that I would propose to you myself if necessary and then he said no and then I said neither one of us would care and we would set off for Gretna Green."

Harry laughed, rich and deep. "You are becoming downright daring, which I find I very much admire. By the way, the estate is not and has never been entailed. It will go to you and your sister."

Isabel froze where she stood. All along, she'd been terrified of being left with nothing, and the estate was not entailed? It would go to her and Margaret? She had been certain it was entailed.

There was some cousin in York who sent Christmas gifts every year and she had assumed…

"Now you are wondering why your father never mentioned it," Harry went on cheerfully.

"Because he does not often mention anything," Isabel said quietly.

"Precisely."

"But that would mean that all along…"

"All along you have feared that which was never to be," Harry said.

Isabel took in a deep breath, as if to clear all those old fears from her mind. "I shall not countenance any more outrageous worries. I will trust in you."

"Please do, my dear lady."

CHAPTER TWENTY

THE EARL, AS was expected, did once more say no to an engagement between his daughter and Harry Vance. Isabel, understanding more and more by the minute how clever and determined Harry was, could only be amused by his strategy.

"My lord," he said, "I would like to be apprised of your reasons against it, if you would be so kind. With words. In complete sentences."

This, naturally, gave the earl pause. He screwed up his face. Then as if it were a great effort to get it out, he said, "*You.* Everything is changed, don't you know. Don't like change."

"So you say," Harry said, not looking the least bit put off. "However, if you will examine the matter more closely, you will see that you actually do like change."

"No."

"Yes," Harry said. "Do you like having your own wine cellar again?"

"Yes."

"Do you like having a full breakfast on the sideboard each morning?"

"Yes," the earl said grudgingly.

Do you like your stables full?"

The earl shrugged.

"Now tell the truth. You do like your stables full?"

"Yes."

"Do you like that a tailor arrives tomorrow to fit you for new clothes?"

"Maybe."

"Do not be ridiculous, of course you will like a tailor. Now, can you explain what it is you do not like about this new way of going on?"

"Browning. *Stern.*"

"Yes, your new steward is rather stern, which is all to the good."

"No."

"Yes," Harry said firmly. "Further, I think you will find me a genial son-in-law."

"No?"

"Yes," Harry said firmly.

The earl shrugged. Then he sighed. Then he muttered, "Yes?"

"Excellent," Harry said. "I'll arrange the banns."

⟫⟫⟩✦⟨⟨⟨

OVER THE WEEKS that the banns were read in both Hertfordshire and Cornwall, Isabel and Harry occupied their time in several ways. They had thoroughly agreed that they would put off a wedding trip—the earl's estate was on its way to success, and they could not allow it to falter now.

Isabel often watched Harry and Lord Bertridge from a window, walking together and managing some aspect of the estate. The cheesemaking operation was to mirror Bertridge's own and the dairy was nearly completed.

Isabel attended to matters inside the house, including continuing with the earl's lessons on speaking in full sentences. It became apparent to her that he could do so when pressed, but that he generally did not feel like it. She began to get the idea that it amused him to speak in riddles and leave it to his listeners to divine his meanings. That, along with his general air of languor, did not bode well for any vast improvements.

It was not all work between the couple though. Many an afternoon, neither one of them could be found. They would tiptoe off with a picnic basket and explore her father's wood. There, they found a charming and meandering stream and would spend hours talking beside it about their plans. Or, if not talking, they were doing *something*.

Were they to arrive back at the house looking rather more disheveled than could be expected from talking, nobody commented on it.

Isabel rather wondered at her old idea that she could have ever tolerated Lord Lymington touching her in such a personal manner. *That* was only for Harry Vance to do. She'd had the notion that she would do what was necessary to get children and it would be simply something to be got through.

Now, though, it was not at all to be got through. It was something to be got *to*.

Fortunately, Harry seemed to have more self-control than she did, else they might have arrived to the church wearing exceedingly guilty countenances.

They were married in the small local church with only a select few from the neighborhood attending, though Lady Bertridge did miss the proceeding as she was at home with her new infant daughter. Harry's father traveled from Cornwall and seemed rather delighted with his son's choice. The baron had helpfully left Harry's coarse cousin behind, and he got on surprisingly well with the earl. They were both men of few words with a fondness for port, and that seemed satisfactory to them both.

The only guest who had not been anticipated was the duchess.

Isabel had written the lady several letters, all expounding on how the dear duchess had made happiness possible for her. Though it had not turned out how the duchess had predicted, and perhaps had wished, it had turned out right all the same. The duchess, if Isabel were to be believed, was the kindest, wisest, most gracious, and dare she say it, *noble* lady in England.

None of those letters had been answered and so Isabel could not have known their effect.

The duchess, having so little experience in resisting compliments, finally capitulated. Being named noble had tipped the scales in Isabel's favor. Once she did relent, she blew into Somerdon House with all the authority of the mistress of the house. She graciously accepted Harry's very heartfelt and abject apologies, which Isabel thought were masterfully done, and became rather sanguine about the whole thing.

Now, some months later, Isabel lounged in bed with her husband at the shocking time of eleven o'clock in the morning. They'd had breakfast sent up after being out very late at a neighbor's theatrical evening.

"I am sure we have caused no end of talk with our rather brazen habits," she said.

Harry pulled her close and said, "They've got to talk about something in the servants' hall."

There was a quick knock on the door.

Before Isabel could alert whoever it was that they were *still* abed, the door swung open and a maid carrying a silver tray walked in.

She saw them and gave out a squeak, before dropping the tray and running from the room, slamming the door behind her.

"Now that will cause even more talk," Isabel said. "A housemaid has seen us en déshabillé and she will not soon forget it."

"Not at all," Harry said, jumping out of bed to pick up the girl's dropped tray and the letters that had been upon it. "She will say nothing of it as she will not wish to be scolded over it."

"That poor girl," Isabel said. Privately, she thought it was rather fortunate that Harry had been beneath blankets when the maid had come in, as he did not have a stitch on. He usually did not when they were alone.

As she was admiring his person, Harry handed her a letter

and Isabel saw at once it was from Lady Bertridge.

"Ah," she said, "perhaps Caroline feels up for visitors by now. I have been waiting for her to signal, though Lady Easton has barred the door like a tiger to guard against anybody bringing disease into the house." She tore open the letter and read it with some amusement, as it was not at all what she had expected.

My dear Isabel—

You will no doubt hear from the duchess shortly about this plan that is in the works. The Society of Sponsoring Ladies intends to gather together all of their projects and their associated husbands so they may revel in their successes. As I have so recently given birth, Lady Easton has decided I must not travel and so the party comes to me. (She intends on quarantining the baby with the nanny and nursemaids while the house has visitors.)

The ladies intend that everybody is to come on the 16th.

By the by, Caro does very well and has her papa at her beck and call. Nanny is forever chasing him out of the nursery. I am delighted to have visitors and introduce you to this little lady, if you dare to call and brave Lady Easton's pointed stares.

Caroline Camden

"Goodness," Isabel said, handing Harry the letter.

"Oh dear," he said, "a gathering of self-congratulations. The poor duchess will have to face down your rather less than lofty choice."

"She is quite resigned that I did not marry Lord Lymington. She says she did not care for his mother one bit and would not have liked to see me having to manage such a creature."

"Ah, the duchess. All her opinions come out right, in the end."

THE 16th CAME on time and the ladies of the society descended upon Lord Bertridge's estate. Harry was only thankful that it was Bertridge's estate and not Somerdon House. He did not have anything against any of those ladies, not even the duchess. Though, when they came together they were rather like a wildly eccentric and unpredictable herd, zigging and zagging their way through society. Once all six ladies were in the same room, the safest course was to exit that room without a look back.

In the great hall leading to Bertridge's drawing room, Harry took Isabel's arm and whispered, "Unto the breach, my love."

His very clever wife instantly noted the reference to Henry V and finished off the speech—"The game's afoot: follow your spirit and upon this charge cry God for Harry, England and Saint George."

"Or just cry," Harry said, laughing.

They entered the drawing room, both of them laughing, as they so often were.

What a sight was before them. The ladies of the society were round a table, the duchess pouring tea and looking for all the world the queen of the group in a stiff gold brocade. It was not even her house, but he supposed that would not have occurred to her.

Scattered about the room, Harry saw them all. There was Gresham with his lady, née Miss Grace Yardley. Then Ryland with his bride, who had been known as Lady Prudence Landry. Langley and Blackwood stood together with their wives, previously Miss Georgiana Wilcox and Lady Arabella Beresford. And then Bertridge, of course, who'd married Miss Caroline Upton. He'd watched all these couples from afar, season by season.

The gentlemen had all wed exceedingly pretty and genial ladies. Of course, none of them was quite as lovely or wonderful as Isabel. None of them could compare to the woman who would become Lady Leighton in the fullness of time.

Harry Vance had waited out the seasons and he had been

rewarded with the grandest prize.

Bertridge's butler brought round a tray with small glasses of sherry. He and Isabel both took a glass, and he suspected they would need them. There was nothing so draining as a group of matrons set on congratulating themselves.

The duchess dinged her spoon on the side of her teacup. Silencing the room, she said, "Now that we are all here, words must be spoken."

Harry had been afraid that words would be spoken. He assumed there were to be a lot of them. At such a moment, he found he almost missed the earl's more economical way of speaking. Harry would do very well with it if the duchess just said what she meant—"Right, always. Noble, don't you know. *Me.*"

The lady rose and said, "More than five years ago, we six aristocratic ladies of the realm came together and committed ourselves to a noble cause. We were certain of our purpose, and we have succeeded. Naturally, there were some…bumps on the road. But we persevered in our noble effort. What noble cause does not have…bumps?"

Harry noted several amused glances between husbands and wives. Lady Bertridge appeared near ready to burst. There were more nobles in her speech than there were wandering round Buckingham Palace.

"We ladies felt it incumbent upon us to reflect on the noble journeys we have taken and so I will begin. As we are among friends, I need not prevaricate on what my wishes had been for my dear Isabel. However, I changed my wishes after meeting the Duchess of Hastings. Really, she is a most opinionated woman, I do *not* recommend her. I now believe that I was right to change my wishes, as Isabel's children will be so far removed from trade as to make the whole problem go away. In the end, my sponsorship of Lady Isabel cannot be viewed as anything less than a rousing success."

Harry had his lips pressed tightly together lest he fall over in laughter. He did not dare even glance at his wife, as that would have been sure to send her into her own peals of merriment. It was so like the duchess to claim that she'd been right all along, while still managing to mention that his grandfather had been in trade.

He could not know the thoughts of everybody else in the room, though they politely clapped. Or perhaps they only clapped to bring this ludicrous speech to an end. In either case, the duchess nodded graciously and once more took her seat.

As they were apparently to take turns going in a circle, beginning to the duchess' right, Lady Mendleton rose, all smiles. "I cannot imagine that anybody's happiness can exceed my own. Why, right from the beginning, Georgiana proved her worth. Imagine, saving my son from footpads!"

Harry noted Lady Langley squeeze her lord's hand and Lord Langley give a little cough. He'd always thought that story rather dubious, and now he was certain that it was. It remained a mystery what had really gone on the night Langley was shot.

"And then, of course, dear Georgiana and Jasper have stayed on with us in their own wing of the house which makes it ever so convenient. Georgiana is a true daughter to me. As for little Daisy, well I know you all laugh at it, but she really is very advanced. I dote on her. I am not ashamed to say it, I positively dote."

Lady Mendleton seemed to have flustered herself in the midst of speaking of her grandchild and sat quickly down and fanned herself.

Lady Heathway rose. "I am not, perhaps, as sentimental as my friend Louisa, though I cannot avoid noticing that my grandniece is rather more alert than is usually to be found in one so young. I have heard that sort of alertness denotes intelligence and that can only be assumed to be right."

Harry gripped the arm of the chair next to him. Lady Heathway had heard that nonsense from himself while trying to placate her at the duchess' dinner. He had not the first idea if it were true, and how did one measure alertness anyway?

"Grace has become like my own daughter," Lady Heathway continued.

Lady Gresham nodded encouragingly.

"It is a comfort to me to know with certainty that I am always welcome in their house, and in fact am pressed to be there more than I can be."

Lady Gresham was still nodding, though perhaps less encouragingly.

"It was my great trial to straighten out Lady Barlow, Grace's sickly mother," Lady Heathway ploughed on, "which I did with remarkable energy and purpose. That lady now has me to thank—she is up and out of bed and happily married to Lord Copeland. I have every confidence that she *will* thank me. One of these days."

Harry heard Isabel choke back a snort. This was all getting too much. Somebody was going to break out into laughter.

"In any case, I know my duty and have done my duty," Lady Heathway concluded. She sat down like a retiring general having said farewell to her troops.

Lady Easton rose to take her turn. "Penelope has spoken of duty," she said. "I could not agree more. It is one's duty to steer young people in the right direction and I hope I can consider my efforts a success. One may notice, if one looks about, that every clock in this place *and* Somerdon House is timed to the second. It has been my pleasure to come into this house and straighten it all out for dear Caroline and my dear grandniece, young Caro."

Harry stole a glance at Lady Bertridge. The lady remained stoic, if one could ignore the slight quivering of her lips.

"I will not shirk my responsibilities for a moment and am here to help for the foreseeable future. *No* amount of time is too much."

Lady Bertridge glanced at her husband with what could only be interpreted as a rather forlorn expression.

Lady Easton sat down, appearing very satisfied by her words.

Lady Featherstone rose, lightly touching her emerald brooch

and handing her famed walking stick to a very perplexed Lady Redfield.

"As you all know," Lady Featherstone said cheerfully, "I live and breathe crimes and mysteries. I have been Lord Ryland's veritable right hand in our Society for Advancing Criminal Knowledge, or SACK as we insiders call it, for some years."

Harry almost bellowed with laughter at the look of surprise on Ryland's face. The fellow had not had the first idea that Lady Featherstone was his right hand, veritable or otherwise. Or that his society had changed to *our* society.

"Naturally," Lady Featherstone went on, "when the Earl of Copeland found his own mystery in his lap, he instantly called on me, and *I* instantly called on Lord Ryland. I do not believe that two minds less incisive than our own would have been able to root out the villain. However, we did it and now Lord Ryland is my dear son-in-law."

Ryland seemed even more surprised to hear of that relationship. As far as Harry knew, Lady Featherstone was a very distant cousin to Lady Ryland. She had no claim of connection to Lord Ryland at all.

"I could not have wished for a better son-in-law, as he treats Lady Ryland exceedingly well. She is protected from all notion of crimes and their villains, as she does not prefer it. Lord Ryland and I carry on with it, we set our minds to it, making England safer day by day, mystery by mystery. Let the murderers and kidnappers and forgers beware—we are looking for you."

Harry glanced at the duchess and then he wished he had not as it nearly sent him over the edge. She was staring at the ceiling as if imploring God to stop Lady Featherstone's crime-solving career.

Lady Featherstone gave one more touch to the brooch she'd won at one of Ryland's mystery suppers in case anybody forgot she had it. Then she took her walking stick, once owned by the legendary French investigator Vidocq, and raised it slightly in case anybody forgot she had that too.

She sat down, nodding graciously to her audience.

Lady Redfield rose in the fluttering way she had, as if she were a robin looking for a branch to settle upon.

Harry told himself to keep his expression neutral. This was turning out to be better than a Shakespearean comedy, but there was just one more speech to go. He just must make it to the end. There would be ample time to laugh about it when he and Isabel were behind closed doors.

"Well, everything that has been said…so uplifting, I thought," Lady Redfield said. "As for myself, well my dear Arabella! So lovely and lively and everything I could have wished for. And dear Peregrine, you have become like a son to me."

Harry could not help himself. He glanced at the duchess once more to see how she would take the news that her son had now a second mother. As the lady's fingers had gone white round the handle of her teacup, he assumed she was not entirely sanguine over the idea.

"And in Town," Lady Redfield continued, "you are both right next door to my own. Did I say how much Lord Jeffries has enjoyed your company when you visit? And he is there? He is there sometimes. When he visits my household. As he does from time to time."

Lady Redfield had gone rather pink at the mention of Lord Jeffries. Was there a December romance in the offing?

"Well, really, what more can I say?" Lady Redfield asked. "Arabella has brought so much joy into my house."

"And other things into the house," the duchess said acerbically.

Lady Redfield nervously crumpled her skirt in her hand. "Well, yes, Theodosia, there was the squirrel. His name was Rusty. He is back outside now. And all those birds, the cocks, they were never inside the house, you see."

Harry was almost crying, his laughter was so ready to burst. Everybody had heard of Lady Arabella's pet squirrel that had made an untoward appearance on the table at one of Lady

Redfield's dinners. Now they were to know that it had been Lady Arabella who'd set free Skeffington's birds ahead of his Welch Main?

"In any case," Lady Redfield said rather hopefully, "Arabella will not be bringing in any creatures to this house?"

Though it ought to have been a statement, poor Lady Redfield could not manage more than a hopeful question.

Lady Blackwood, just now on her husband's arm, gave a noncommittal shrug. "I only mention," she said, "that I did note a rabbit on the side of the drive who may be rather poorly. I will check on the poor fellow in the morning."

That was too much for everybody. As if on cue, the room erupted in laughter. Fortunately, none of the matrons appeared to have any notion that they were a large part of the cause.

Of course they did not. These six indomitable souls could never dream anybody was laughing at them. Harry could not hold anything but amusement and affection for these women— who could do otherwise?

They were confounding creatures. However, they had also, whether they meant to or not, been the means to his happiness.

HARRY AND ISABEL did not go to Town that first season. They'd felt their time was better spent at Somerdon House, ensuring the success of the estate for generations to come.

Isabel saw a good deal of Margaret and her squire, Margaret being as flighty as ever. The idea that the estate was not entailed had made her far more cheerful than she had been. Isabel adored how patient Harry was with her often nonsensical ideas.

She and Harry spent far more time with Lord and Lady Bertridge. Sometimes, they brought the earl along with them, though he was not known to be a great socializer. Still, it amused Harry no end when the earl would catch Lady Easton staring at him critically and he would lean forward and say, *"Staring.* Why?"

Lady Easton usually had the same response. "I was thinking about your poor clocks, Lord Somerdon."

Lord Somerdon sometimes answered and sometimes did not. Though one time he'd pointed at her and said, "You. *Strange."*

Summer came round again, and Isabel and Harry were convinced that Browning had the estate well in hand. They determined it was time to get out of the steward's way and set off.

Though Isabel had been thoroughly convinced of Harry's acumen at keeping an estate afloat, it was only over time that she understood just how well he'd done for himself. He not only had the estate in Cornwall and a house in Town, but another smaller estate in Bedfordshire that was outside of the entail. Harry was determined that a second son would not be forced to choose the military or the church and could live as a gentleman. Should there be a third son, he'd find another estate, and money was already being put by for daughters' dowries.

Harry also happened to own a very charming cottage by the sea.

It was to the cottage by the sea they went.

The little stone house was not located nearby a town of any size and Harry had bought a mile of land on either side of it so there would never be any neighbors in sight. He had a small staff to run it when he wished to be there, and kept them on a retainer when he was absent.

As there was not any neighbors, Isabel and Harry took to their own version of sea bathing. Isabel would wear her shift into the water and then remove it and throw it on the beach to be retrieved by Harry when they were ready to come out.

As for Harry, himself, he simply left his clothes on the beach. Isabel did not know if all men were so used to walking about as unclothed as the day they were born, but her husband was certainly in the habit.

Whatever went on in the water in the meantime was their

own private business.

In the evenings, they ate dinner on the veranda with wine and sea breezes and talked about how to enlarge the cottage should they find their little family expanding.

At night, they slept with the windows wide open, letting the salt air wash over them.

It is often thought that once a danger has passed, the terror of it fades from memory. That was not true for Isabel. Though she did lose her fear of poverty easily enough, she would never forget how close she'd come to making the worst mistake of her life.

She was forever grateful that Harry Vance had not given up.

EPILOGUE

O VER TIME, HARRY and Isabel's little family did expand just as they'd hoped. And as far as Isabel was concerned, she had not only hoped—she had prayed. Once she'd got a look at Harry's cousin, to which the estate was entailed, she fairly shuddered at the thought of being left in his charge, with no young baron having arrived.

That horror was not to be, though. There were two boys and a girl, healthy and in high spirits. Their hair colors were a lovely combination of Harry's dark blond and her auburn—a sandy color with hints of red that glinted in the light. Their personalities, however, were not blending. They firmly favored Harry. They were bold and outspoken and afraid of nothing. It seemed a pinch of Plantagenet blood mixed with a drop of tradesman's blood was a smashing combination.

Led by their eldest brother, they were charmingly determined over any question they considered to be a matter of some importance. They routinely presented justifications for why they should be awake late into the night or have double-dessert or ride out on their ponies to defeat the kingdom next door, otherwise known as the neighbors. They prosecuted their various cases with all the flair and persistence of an appearance in the Old Bailey.

Harry was a bit of a marshmallow when it came to his children, so these prosecutions were generally presented to him in the library, after their governess had been eluded.

Isabel was delighted with her children. She was delighted with her Harry. She was rather delighted with everything.

She had almost given up happiness for a dull, albeit safe, existence. She would have done it too, had it not been for the energy and determination of Harry Vance.

WHEN LORD LYMINGTON had been entirely confused by the letter Isabel wrote him, he, being a cooperative sort of fellow, did as he'd been directed. He consulted Miss Thompson.

Miss Thompson was able to explain the matter thoroughly and wondered aloud if he would not rather marry her than anybody else.

So little was his guile that he'd said, "I rather think I do!"

In the end, though there might not be an overwhelming amount that was sensible about Lord Lymington, he did very sensibly marry Miss Thompson. His mother did not love his choice, as now there were three people out of four in her household who only wished to speak of horses. She did, however, respect her new daughter-in-law's ability to steer her son in the right direction. Miss Thompson did not waste any time in alerting her fiancé that Carlson's theories on the weather were stuff and nonsense and he ought to give up talk of the whales and dolphins.

The couple got on rather famously—the new Lady Lymington cherished her husband's gentle manner and almost childlike innocence. Lord Lymington found himself in a rather unique and surprising position. For the first time in his life, he was adored.

They built their life around horses and spoke of horses. When they were going somewhere that horses could not be the entire conversation, Lady Lymington very helpfully gave him interesting things to discuss ahead of time. Lord Lymington became especially fond of learning interesting facts about other sorts of animals. He remained all his life amazed that pigeons mated for life and thought them very like he and his wife.

Lady Lymington took being compared to a pigeon in all good humor.

THE EARL'S ANCIENT butler, Rogers, was given a stipend and was settled very comfortably in a cottage on Harry Vance's estate in Cornwall. It was a neat and tidy little place, had a garden out front, and was very nearby the main house. He became friendly with the cook and that lady sent over plates of beef, cakes, roast chicken, jars of jam, pickles, and all sorts on a regular schedule. She was even known to knit him a scarf for the cold weather.

The retired butler turned out to be a very good listener and became a favorite with the children of the neighborhood, who stopped by the cottage to pour out their troubles over a cup of tea and biscuits. Sometimes they brought a dog or a cat who also had troubles and required a bit of meat or bowl of milk. Whatever the problem, Rogers' visitors always left feeling better than when they had arrived.

WHEN ISABEL'S SISTER, Margaret, had initially heard of the goings on at her father's estate, she'd made her way there to discover the truth of it. She was, at first, outraged that this interloper by way of Mr. Vance had taken charge of the house and claimed he would marry her sister.

She was far less outraged when she was apprised of the lack of an entail. Later, it was proposed that after the earl's passing Margaret and her husband would take possession of the house, and financial arrangements were made. Half of the profits would go to Margaret and her squire as they would be doing the work of the estate, a fourth held back in safekeeping for any lean days to come, and a fourth would go to Isabel. The inheritance would go to Margaret's children, as Isabel's own were to be well-supplied.

While Margaret remained ever flighty, her squire was a sensible fellow and everybody had confidence in his abilities. Should he fall short or need assistance, Lord Bertridge was right down the road and Bemmy could always be called on for household matters. It was unlikely to come to that, though, as Mr. Browning held on to the steward's reins rather firm. The butler that was finally hired was a further reinforcement. Mr. Crane went by the book, and that very stern book had been written by himself.

THOUGH THE EARL of Somerdon had proclaimed he did not like change, after a suitable period of time the changes did not seem as changes anymore. It also could not be denied that he was rather fond of the expansion of his wine cellar and the new and varied dishes that were to be found on his dining table. He also discovered that he could not argue with his butler, Mr. Crane, as he never got anywhere with it. Mr. Crane had written his own book on how a house should proceed and anybody stepping out of line did so at their peril, including the earl.

Lord Somerdon never did take to speaking in full sentences though and his grandchildren made a great game of imitating him during their years in the nursery.

A nursemaid would say, "Now, get in bed this instant." The children would answer with a string of: "No? Yes? *Late*. Tired. Yes. *Nooooo*." This was, for some years, considered the height of wit in that location, though the nursemaids and nannies subjected to it may not have seen it so.

Though they imitated him mercilessly, all his grandchildren held a real fondness for the earl. They spent their summers wandering his wood and eating blueberries until their stomachs ached. As the earl never proscribed a bedtime or how many marzipans were too many, they were perennially in a state of giddy exhaustion and considered him the best grandfather alive.

LADY REDFIELD MARRIED Lord Jeffries within a year, which came as a surprise to nobody. They were, in their own way, very well suited—he was just as agreeable as she was. Their few arguments were always regarding who ought to get their way, with neither of them wishing to win the debate.

A conversation over whether they should bring strawberry jam or marmalade on a picnic went something like this: "Now, my dear, I insist we follow your judgment."

"I must disagree. You ought to have things your way."

"I would find myself downhearted were I to consider your disappointment."

"I find myself with the same view! How can I be comfortable knowing you did not get what you would prefer?"

In the end, the housekeeper very sensibly suggested that they take both jars, and so a marital contretemps was averted.

What they were to never to have a roundabout disagreement on was the idea of wearing wooden shoes to a masque. That idea was firmly *out*.

THOUGH MISS RIGHTSTONE would haunt society's ballrooms and the gentlemen in them for yet another season. She finally did marry a gentleman who was entirely oblivious to her less than sparkling intellect, her vile temper, and her penchant for using her fan as a weapon.

Lord Maynard was an elderly gentleman intent on finally getting around to producing an heir and he was no more clever than she was. The new Lady Maynard continued with her over-enthusiastic appreciation for wine, but as Lord Maynard was generally asleep by seven, he was in a constant state of befuddle-ment as to how there were so many glasses broken.

They routinely argued over whether Shakespeare was still alive or not, usually with other people, as they both agreed he must be.

AS FOR CARLSON, he settled rather comfortably into the idea that there could be no accurate prediction of the weather, as the whales and dolphins were too unpredictable. This made any prediction he came up with right, even when it was wrong, and accounted for the vagaries of English weather. He also developed a silent motto—*when in doubt, say it will rain*—that served him well over the years.

The duchess never lost her faith in Carlson's predictions, it would have been too much of a blow for her to take in. She possessed the only butler in England who could predict the weather, and she was intent on keeping it that way.

Were the sun to be out on a day that a blinding side rain with tornadic gusts and a swerving fog were predicted, well…there was no accounting for dolphins.

BEN, THE YOUNG thief who had been so hopeful of getting two pounds for the duchess' tiara, was guided with a firm hand by Harry's coachman. He learned the business of running a stable and he was good at it. Some years later, Rumson, the duchess' coachman, retired. Ben was hired to take over the position. The lady never did discover that the fellow who drove her from place to place had once made off with her emerald and gold diadem. It made Harry laugh every time he thought about it.

THE SIX LADIES who had founded *The Society of Sponsoring Ladies* would maintain their peculiar brand of friendship for the rest of their lives.

Lady Mendleton remained unrepentant in bragging about her Very Advanced Babies, the first that had arrived by no means being the last. Little Daisy, who had been so renowned for breaking porcelains in her toddlerhood, would grow into a young lady no less adept at shattering delicate items in her sphere. Fortunately, she was very charming and so her sobriquet, *Lady All-Thumbs*, did not particularly weigh against her. Very predictably, whenever something crashed to the floor, Lady Mendleton wondered who had placed the item in such a precarious position or speculated that it had never been an attractive piece anyway.

Lady Heathway was just as bad about her own Very Alert Babies of extraordinary high intelligence. Was that first grand-niece really reading books at two and a half? Or was the lady persuaded that she was because the little mite enjoyed ripping out the pages?

It was presumed that these two ladies had sons and nephews occasionally arriving to their notice, though they never mentioned them. Nor did any of the other ladies mention their own, as sons could not be dressed in silk or learn stitches or look lovely at the pianoforte or take on all the graces of being a hostess.

The duchess and Lady Easton happily gossiped about their two baby-mad friends regularly and with joyful disdain, though Lady Easton privately thought her grandniece the superior of them all.

After a good long gossip with the duchess, Lady Easton would return home and inform her lord that the duchess was *still* refusing to wear anything but brocade, though the queen had the opinion that she looked like a pair of curtains set in motion.

The duchess, for her part, would return to her duke and entertain him over Lady Easton's clock-watching. The duchess had even gone so far as to put two clocks in her drawing room, running three minutes apart, just for the hilarity of noting her friend's distress over it.

As Lady Easton *did* retain her love of precise time, Lady Redfield was sometimes late to meet her on purpose, as a mark of bold but silent protest. Lady Heathway took it a step further—she sometimes arrived early and then pointed out how early she was.

Lady Featherstone continued on as a rather bumbling sleuth, while her friends loudly sighed over it. Rather than take offense, she invented bloodcurdling crimes and told them to her friends to keep them up at night. They all still thought there was a devil roaming the streets of London named *The Forlorn Executioner*. This particular madman stole into people's houses, slit their throats, and then used their blood to write sad and dejected poems on their walls.

Lady Heathway kept her habit of denouncing white soup, while Lady Redfield sometimes had the nerve to serve it and then swear she'd forgot. This did not upset Lady Heathway as much as one might have thought, as it gave her an excellent opportunity to lecture everybody on why almonds in a soup was lunacy.

The duchess continued to name things noble, which Lady Heathway found rather *ignoble,* unless it was something to do with herself. In which case, she was perfectly satisfied. The duchess was also in the habit of proclaiming that Mr. Vance had been her idea all along, as the Duchess of Hastings was too opinionated to be borne.

The duchess, of them all, was the most athletic of the group, and the lady maintained her habit of occasionally risking her person, including swimming in Brighton in rough weather with the help of the redoubtable Mrs. Gunn or making a mad gallop down Rotten Row. Her son, Lord Blackwood, shuddered when he received a communication describing her latest adventure.

They were a competitive and often petty cabal of managing matrons. They had nothing in common beyond their wish to find themselves the mamas of charming daughters.

Considering their wildly different temperaments, the society they created should have had little chance of success.

Though, what has ever been impossible for six determined ladies who bind themselves together in pursuit of a long-held dream?

As it turns out, nothing at all.

The End

About the Author

By the time I was eleven, my Irish Nana and I had formed a book club of sorts. On a timetable only known to herself, Nana would grab her blackthorn walking stick and steam down to the local Woolworth's. There, she would buy the latest Barbara Cartland romance, hurry home to read it accompanied by viciously strong wine, (Wild Irish Rose, if you're wondering) and then pass the book on to me. Though I was not particularly interested in real boys yet, I was *very* interested in the gentlemen in those stories— daring, bold, and often enraging and unaccountable. After my Barbara Cartland phase, I went on to Georgette Heyer, Jane Austen and so many other gifted authors blessed with the ability to bring the Georgian and Regency eras to life.

I would like nothing more than to time travel back to the Regency (and time travel back to my twenties as long as we're going somewhere) to take my chances at a ball. Who would take the first? Who would escort me into supper? What sort of meaningful looks would be exchanged? I would hope, having made the trip, to encounter a gentleman who would give me a very hard time. He ought to be vexatious in the extreme, and *worth* every vexation, to make the journey worthwhile.

I most likely won't be able to work out the time travel gambit, so I will content myself with writing stories of adventure and romance in my beloved time period. There are lives to be created, marvelous gowns to wear, jewels to don, instant attractions that inevitably come with a difficulty, and hearts to break before putting them back together again. In traditional Regency fashion, my stories are clean—the action happens in a drawing room, rather than a bedroom.

As I muse over what will happen next to my H and h, and

wish I were there with them, I will occasionally remind myself that it's also nice to have a microwave, Netflix, cheese popcorn, and steaming hot showers.

Come see me on Facebook! @KateArcherAuthor